The Theory of Karma Revisited

Adventure of Consciousness

8

- Analytical Ayurveda
  Dr. K A Latheef
- Upanisads and Edith Stein: *A Dialogue on Models of The Person*
  Thomas Marottipparayil
- Tīrthaṅkarāsana: *A Work on Jaina Yoga*
  Shantilal D. Parakh
- Aparokṣānubhūti: *The essence of Self Realization*
  Mukta Walvekar
- A Critical Study in The Schism in Early Buddhist Monastic Tradition: *Dasavatthu and Pancavatthu*
  Lokananda C. Bhikkhu
- Mystical Poems of Jnaneshwar
  Ananda Mundra
- Exclusion of Sudras from Brahmajijnasa
  Jaison Vadakkan
- The Theory of Karma Revisited
  Vibha Chaturvedi

Other Published Works

- Sri Matrka Vilas: *The Interplay of Little Mothers/ Swami Jayramdas*
- Kashi Satsang/ Pt. Nar Chowbey
- Bhagavad Gita/ PK Agarwal
- Hatha Yoga/ Shanti Gowans
- Food for Life/ Shanti Gowans

The Theory of Karma Revisited

Vibha Chaturvedi

MLBD
PUBLICATIONS

The Theory of Karma Revisited/ Vibha Chaturvedi

First Edition : Delhi, 2021

ISBN : 978 81 942438 9 2

Published by

MOTILAL BANARSIDASS PUBLICATIONS
93, Shyam Lal Marg, Darya Ganj, New Delhi - 110002
Email: mlbd@mlbd.com; Website: www.mlbd.com

MLBD Cataloguing-in-Publication Data
The Theory of Karma Revisited
by Vibha Chaturvedi
ISBN : 978 81 942438 9 2
I. Preface II. Acknowledgment III. Foreword IV. Index

Dedicated to my children, Ritu and Nitin who gave a new meaning to my life and have given me three delightful grandchildren, Nikita, Dhruv and Riya.

Vibha Chaturvedi

Dr. KARAN SINGH

3, NYAYA MARG
CHANAKYAPURI
NEW DELHI 110 021

FOREWORD

Karma is one of the most fascinating concepts in Indic philosophy; Hinduism, Buddhism, Jainism and Sikhism. It can refer to any kind of action, but its deeper significance revolves around the whole adventure of birth and rebirth. Positive Karma is believed to lead us towards a better rebirth, while negative Karma would pull us down in the opposite direction. One danger of this approach is that it can lead to a fatalistic approach whereby we feel that if everything is due to our past Karma then we have to accept our present situation howsoever miserable it may be. This is totally unacceptable. In fact, Swami Vivekananda described Karma as the greater declaration of independence because it means that we can shape our destiny ourselves by the way we act and behave. Another equally unacceptable approach is the one which held that because all work entangles us in Karmic consequences, the only solution is to shun work altogether and retire into some kind of solitude. This is not a workable proposition, firstly because whatever physical solitude we are in, our mind continues to work feverishly, and also in this day and age it is simply not possible for us to get away and live permanently in seclusion and solitude.

What, therefore, is the way between these two extremes of fatalism and solitude? The answer has been given to us both in the Upanishads, which are the cross-jewels of Hindu philosophy and the Bhagwatgita.

The Ishavasaya Upanishad in its first verse teaches us to realize the all pervasiveness of the divine and, therefore, not to covet the wealth of others. The second verse exhorts us thereafter to work here in this world with that attitude for a hundred years, and assures us that we will not be entangled in Karmic consequences. The Bhagwatgita, of course, has the famous teaching that if we renounce the fruits of our Karma then the works themselves become a powerful vehicle for spiritual realization. My own approach is that we need to dedicate all our work to our chosen deity; yad-yat-karma karomi, tat-tad-akhilam shambho tava-araadhanam, "whatever action I do is an offering to Lord Shiva". In fact, Karma Yoga – the way of dedicated works, is considered to be one of the four main pathways to the divine, the other three being Gyan Yoga – the way of wisdom, Bhakti Yoga – the way of devotion and Raj Yoga – the way of psycho-spiritual practices.

In this book, Dr. Vibha Chaturvedi, who was Professor of Philosophy in Delhi University, has made a fascinating study in depth of the various theories of Karma and their application to our present human condition. Apart from various theories in Hinduism, Dr. Chaturvedi has studied the Buddhist approach to Karma as well as the social implications of individual Karma. Each one of us are not an island to ourselves, rather in the course of life we necessarily interact with a broad spectrum of people whether in the family, in work or in social activities. Our Karma, therefore, necessarily impacts other people, and any serious theory of Karma has to factor in this dimension. Also, Karma as a process of spiritual growth is a significant feature which we need to keep in mind. Dr. Chaturvedi has studied the whole concept in considerable detail, and I am sure her work will be welcomed by students of Indic Philosophy, specially Hinduism. I commend her for the intellectual energy and scholarship that this book reveals.

Karan Singh
1 Sept. 2019

TEL (011) 2611-5291 2611-1744, FAX (91-11) 2687-3171, 2462-7102
Email : karansingh@karansingh.com

Table Of Contents

Preface

I got interested in the theory of karma almost two decades back and published two research articles on the theory. My studies on this issue continued all this time, though not in a very systematic and sustained manner. The more I read, the more interested I got in this area. One issue that perplexed me was how the karma theory is related to astrology and do these together imply fatalism. I attended classes on astrology for a brief period to get some clarity in this respect. The present book is an outcome of my study and reflections on the issue of karma. There is a surfeit of discussions of the theory, which are rather general in nature and neither present the views found in the classical Indian philosophy, nor subject the theory to a rigorous philosophical analysis. However, there are a few relatively modern books that present detailed exposition of the philosophical accounts found in ancient texts and different schools of Indian philosophy. A few works offer a mix of expository and critical accounts. We also find articles in anthologies and academic journals that present a critical analysis of the claims of the theory. The vast literature on accounts of the karma theory in the classical Indian tradition, encompassing centuries, poses a serious challenge for any researcher.

In the present work I have not tried to give a detailed exposition of the various formulations of the karma theory in the Indian tradition. However, the basic features of some of the important formulations have been touched upon while explaining the karmic process and other issues like, agency and personal identity, etc. I have also tried, albeit briefly, to mention the diversity of views on the issues of karma and its consequences in the tradition and not focus solely on the strict version put forward by modern Indian scholars as the standard version of the theory. My focus is primarily on analyzing the central claims of the theory, clarifying their implications and subjecting these to a critical stance. I have tried to utilize my familiarity with the modern Western philosophy at places in my analytical endeavor, especially on issues that have not been discussed much in the Indian tradition. I hope that this cross-cultural perspective has made the discussion richer and more interesting. The brief exposition on different aspects of the theory is based primarily on well-respected secondary sources written or edited by eminent scholars, which have discussed philosophical standpoints on karma based on original sources and have quoted extensively from the original texts. The study of these helps a reader to get a clearer perspective on what the theory claims, the concepts it uses to establish those claims and the diversity of views on its scope and modality.

My discussion is divided in six chapters. The first chapter gives a brief introduction to the formulations of the theory put forward by modern Indian philosophers and the central claims of the theory. It also includes a brief discussion on the logical status of the theory, an important issue, which has not received adequate attention in philosophical literature. We find difference of opinion on this issue among philosophers and find views ranging from those which regard it as a scientific theory or at par with fundamental scientific principles, to those which regard it as a dogma. It is important to be clear about the logical nature of the theory because that clarifies what kind of supporting reasons can be plausibly advanced in its favour. The second chapter clarifies the nature of the karmic process and important concepts used in this context by different schools of Indian philosophy. I have tried to mention the differences in philosophical standpoints regarding these. A brief account of views, which differ from the strict version of the theory regarding certain central claims in it, is also included in this chapter.

My initial inquiry into the karma theory had begun with examining the plausibility of the claim that the relation between actions and their morally appropriate consequences is causal. I was skeptical about it since the conception of duties of an individual in the Hindu tradition is relative to the caste (*varṇa)* and stage of life (*āśrama*) of that individual. This led me further to examining the idea of a moral order in the world, which is supposed to ensure perfect karmic justice to every individual. The third chapter of the book is devoted to these two issues. The discussion in this chapter borrows heavily from the ideas expressed in two of my papers published earlier in JICPR and a volume of the Centre for Study of Civilizations respectively. The next chapter is devoted to the issue of the criterion of personal identity in the context of belief in rebirth. This issue is generally not given much attention in discussions of the karma theory within the Indian tradition. To analyze and clarify the various dimensions of the issue in this context, I have taken help from extensive discussions on the problem of personal identity within the Western philosophical tradition. The last two chapters carry forward the analytical and critical exercise and discuss some major objections against the theory with a view to assess whether and how far these objections can be said to be valid. The issues discussed in this chapter include implications of the theory for individual freedom, social impact of actions and fatalism among others. The discussion in the present work is aimed at clarifying the explanatory framework of the theory of karma and pointing out its strengths and limitations.

A note about the English translations of Sanskrit words is necessary here. It is widely acknowledged that this task is extremely difficult. Some concepts in Indian philosophy are impossible to capture in English language, for example, the Sanskrit term '*dharma*' which has several meanings. Similarly, the English translation of the Sanskrit word '*darśan*' as 'philosophy' is problematic. Conversely, we are unable to find a synonym for the English word 'religion' in Sanskrit or Hindi. For the sake of easier and wider accessibility of readers to the discussions in the book, it was necessary to mention English translations of the Sanskrit terms used in Indian philosophy. As far as possible, I have tried to mention the Sanskrit terms along with their English translations initially, though not subsequently. The term 'caste' for the Sanskrit word '*varṇa*' has been used following other writers. I wish to make it clear that I am using the word to refer primarily to the four-fold division of *varṇa* and do not wish to refer to the complex network of sub-divisions and groups arising out of this classification like sub- castes, mixed castes, *jatis* etc. In spite of the fact that the term 'caste' carries a historical baggage and its connotation is not exactly the same as that of the term '*varṇa*', I have used it for want of a better word. It may also be noted that diacritic marks have not been used in writing names like Shankar, Ramanuj and others.

Vibha Chaturvedi

ACKNOWLEDGEMENTS

I am deeply grateful to all those who have helped me in the preparation and finalization of the present work. I am extremely grateful to Dr. Karan Singh for writing the foreword of this book. His learned comments will greatly contribute to the scholarship on this issue. I extend my grateful thanks to Dr. Antony M. Devasia and Dr. Pragati Sahni for their help in locating textual and other relevant resources and their comments. Thanks are due to Shri Krishna Rao for helping me in formatting the manuscript. I wish to take this opportunity to express my gratitude to *JICPR* and the Center for Study of Civilizations, Delhi for publishing my articles on the theory of karma. I have used some ideas and content from those articles in the present work. I am extremely grateful to Pranav Jain and his team specially, Manju Arya at Motilal Banarsidass Publications, Delhi, for undertaking the publication of the present work. I also wish to thank my husband B.K. Chaturvedi and my family for their continuous support and encouragement.

Vibha Chaturvedi

Chapter - 1

The Teory and Its Logical Status

Schools of classical Indian Philosophy exhibit great diversity with regard to their metaphysics and epistemology but most of them accept the theory of karma in some form. Not only all orthodox (*āstika)* systems but heterodox (*nāstika*) schools like Buddhism and Jainism also subscribe to the theory. *Cārvāka* and materialists alone do not accept it. The theory of karma is widely regarded as a distinctive feature of Indian philosophical thought. Most modern scholars of the history of Indian philosophy regard the theory as one of the fundamental postulates of classical Indian philosophy. It is believed to have a deep impact on the thinking of common people, who may not be well conversant with the philosophical tradition. As a result, many people believe that an individual's present life is shaped by one's actions in past lives and the actions in the present life will impact the quality of one's future births. It is, therefore, important to analyse the conceptual dimensions of this theory and subject its implications to rigorous philosophical analysis and evaluation. The task is not easy because the views on karma accepted in different schools of classical Indian Philosophy, Epics, *Smṛtis* and *Purānas* vary in several respects. These variations have been documented in detail in some contemporary writings on the issue.[1]

Philosophical writings on the karma theory in general, however, do not always reflect this inner complexity and diversity of views on the functioning of karma and very often a reader may be misled into thinking that all schools subscribe to essentially the same or a very similar theory. Moreover, the discussions of the karma theory generally focus more on exposition rather than rigorous philosophical and critical analysis. Rajendra Prasad complains

> "it is a little surprising that in spite of the great importance accorded to the law of *karma*, it has not been given a detailed conceptual or logical analysis or scrutiny either in any classical or contemporary work. It seems we inherited it as a dignified constituent of our culture, as an article of faith, and have let it enjoy that honour undisturbed by the inconvenient probing of a non-partisan, investigative reason."[2]

Some scholarly books and articles on the karma theory in academic journals and anthologies, however, do analyse its problematic dimensions though it is true that expository accounts outnumber the critical ones. The support for the theory of karma, including rebirth, is widespread in the Indian tradition but the views on the issues are diverse. This diversity, as mentioned earlier, is not always taken into account in discussions of karma. Karl Potter comments that we do not find one theory, which may be regarded as 'the theory of karma' and the existing literature on this issue often conflates various different notions. He rightly points out that each central concept in the theory has been variously interpreted within the Indian tradition and it is important to unravel and take note of the different strands. In his view, "…

we have yet to understand fully the complexities of karma."[3]

Well respected modern scholars of Indian philosophy like S.N. Dasgupta, M. Hiryanna, S. Radhakrishnan and others present a broadly similar, law-like strict version of the theory of karma as the paradigmatic formulation. This version has come to be widely accepted as the standard version of the theory found in the classical tradition, though it does not reflect the diversity of views found therein. Rajendra Prasad also takes the same route in his hard hitting, critical analysis of the theory. The strict version reflects the widely shared basic claims regarding karma and rebirth in its various discussions in the classical tradition. The present work would discuss the strict version in detail and try to present an analytical and critical discussion of the important aspects and implications of the theory emerging from that. The aim is not a comprehensive textual exegesis of all the various views on karma found within the Indian tradition however, the diversity of views has been briefly outlined. The emphasis remains on providing a critical analysis of the central claims of the theory.

The term 'theory' rather than 'doctrine,' has been chosen partly because the latter suggests a religious association, but more importantly, because claims about karma and rebirth attempt to provide a theoretical framework to explain the inequities at birth and apparently undeserved suffering of, for example, small children and good people. The theory provides a perspective on the relationship between actions of an agent and her quality of life, which is quite different from the one found in other major religions.

By 'theory' here is meant a systematic account involving one or more hypotheses/suppositions, which together explain certain phenomena or some aspect of reality. The term is being used in a somewhat loose sense to highlight the fact that the concepts of karma and rebirth are used in the Indian tradition to provide an explanation of inequities at birth and the occurrence of suffering or happiness disproportionate to the moral quality of an individual's actions. There is wide ranging agreement among philosophers writing about the theory that it has explanatory objectives and many also think that it is successful in satisfying those objectives. The karma theory attempts to explain inequities at birth and the quality of life of a person through establishing a connection between these and the moral quality of a person's actions in past lives. Thus, while the theory attempts to explain some aspects of our experienced reality, it has a moral dimension and a moral message. Consequently, it becomes difficult to decide what type of a theory it is, as we shall see later.

While explaining the use of the term 'theory' for karma and rebirth, Karl Potter observes, "A theory, as I shall use the term, is a set of connected hypotheses, involving postulation of unobservable or uncommonsensical items, that purports to predict, postdict, or otherwise explain processes in the world."[4] Potter believes that the karma theory satisfies the conditions outlined above. It has an explanatory objective and it tries to fulfil it by bringing in suppositions of rebirth, residue of actions, ripening of fruits of actions and other such unobservable elements. It tries to explain the inequities at birth and seeming injustice in the quality of experiences people have in life by linking these to the morally appropriate consequences of past actions of that person in the current or previous births. It makes a general prediction that good actions bring good results and happiness and bad ones suffering and misfortune for people. It also asserts that people get what they deserve on the basis of their actions in the present or past lives. Sometimes, discussions on the theory go farther and make specific claims about what type of actions will lead to what type of results in future or next birth. Thus, it tries to explain events in one's life by linking them to one's past actions. Generally speaking, it seems to do *ex post facto* analysis.

Very simply put the theory of karma states the principle, 'as you sow, so shall you reap.' In other words, it states that everyone has to bear the fruits of one's actions in accordance with the moral quality of those actions, either in the present life or subsequent lives. The belief that everyone has to reap the consequences of one's actions can be found in almost all major religions of the world. In monotheistic religions like Christianity and Islam, an omnipotent and omniscient God is the ultimate judge of human actions and ensures that everyone gets the reward/punishment in accordance with the moral quality of one's actions, if not in this life then after death. It is important for people to have the faith that morally right actions will bring them success and happiness and morally wrong actions will bring them misery.

Unfortunately, this does not always happen in our lives. We often find bad people prospering and good people suffering. Religions like Christianity and Islam try to explain such injustices of life by an appeal to God as the supreme divine judge of human actions and after-life. The Christian idea of 'the Last Judgement', for example, gives the assurance that God as the divine judge ensures that everybody gets appropriately rewarded or punished for one's actions, if not in the earthly life then in life here after in heaven or hell. Islam also establishes the connection between one's actions and their deserved consequences or rewards/punishments through the ideas of resurrection of persons, Allah's judgement and conceptions of heaven and hell. Judaism, Christianity and Islam do not support the idea of rebirth and regard death as the end of a person's earthly life. The Indian tradition accounts for perfect justice of actions and their deserved consequences through the supposition of successive rebirths of a person in which the person reaps the consequences of actions performed in earlier lives.

The connection posited between actions and their deserved consequences in the Indian context has two special features. One, the process of actions leading to their appropriate rewards or punishments is generally not supposed to be dependent on the judgement and agency of God but on causal connections between actions and their appropriate consequences, which operate on their own and ensure that agents get the fruits they deserve on the basis of the moral quality of their past actions. This is the stand supported by the strict law-like formulation of the theory. Secondly, these causal chains between actions and their consequences are believed to operate through successive lives of an agent on earth. Thus, the belief in rebirth is inextricably linked to the theory of karma and provides the foundation of the moral ideal of complete justice of actions and their rewards and punishments. The quality of one's present life is determined in many respects by one's actions in one's past life/ lives and one's actions in this life, together with the residue of actions of past lives, determine the quality of one's future births and one's share of happiness and unhappiness in those. In its atheistic versions, the theory of karma thus attempts to explain the perfect justice of actions and their just deserts spread over successive lives of individuals, without bringing in the idea of a divine judge. Even in some theistic philosophical systems, God's role is believed to be only that of the supreme regulator, who ensures smooth and proper functioning of karmic processes. However, we also find views where God or the Supreme Reality is vital to the working of the karmic processes and the *Bhakti* tradition admits the possibility of divine intervention in the unfolding of karmic processes. The central message of the theory is that doing good will lead to good results for the individual, if not in this life then in later lives, through the unfolding of karmic causality. The moral dimension of the theory consists in its claim that what one gets as a result of unfolding of karmic process is what one morally deserves to get on account of one's actions. That is why the theory is sometimes referred to as the 'Law of moral causation.'

The theory states that when an agent performs an action, it gives rise to a karmic residue, trace or potentiality, which after ripening brings about some consequences for that agent through a causal mechanism and the consequences are an appropriate reward or punishment for that action. As already mentioned, we find that various schools in Indian philosophical tradition exhibit differences on the issue of unfolding of the process of karma. The theory is supposed to guard against two weaknesses, one, that the consequence of some action of an agent is lost (*kṛtapraṇāśa*) and two, that an agent reaps the consequence of an action not performed by oneself but by someone else (*akṛtabhayupgama*). Thus, the theory in its strict version claims that everyone invariably gets the consequences one deserves in the light of the moral quality of one's actions in the present or future lives. Every individual goes through a series of births and deaths (*saṃsāra*) as a result of one's past actions till one attains liberation (*mokṣa*). Liberation brings the cycle of births to an end. All orthodox, as well as unorthodox, schools like Buddhism and Jainism, except *Carvakas* and materialists, regard liberation as the ultimate aim of human life. However, within this broad framework many differences can be found within the tradition and these will unfold as the different aspects of the theory are discussed in the following pages.

Let me begin with the formulations of the theory by some well-known modern scholars of Indian Philosophy. The theory is often referred to as the doctrine or the law of karma, since the relationship between actions and their consequences is regarded as causal and necessary and the karmic process is supposed to operate without fail. This law is viewed as an extension of the Law of Causation to the moral realm.

Explaining the theory S.N. Dasgupta states, "whatever action is done by an individual leaves behind it some sort of potency which has the power to ordain for him joy or sorrow in the future, according as it is good or bad."[5]

> D.M. Datta is of the view that the function of the law "... is to equip the individual with the body and the environment which his past career entitles him to. Nature and the events of nature, good or bad, which form the common background of the people of an age or a country are just what are deserved by all of them according to their common moral worth."[6]
>
> Hiriyanna observes, "... the karma doctrine signifies not merely that the events of our life are determined by their antecedent causes, but also that there is absolute justice in the rewards and punishments that fall to our lot in life...The law of karma accordingly is not a blind mechanical law, but is essentially ethical."[7]
>
> Radhakrishnan comments, 'The law of karma is the counterpart in the moral world of the physical law of uniformity. It is the law of the conservation of moral energy .... According to the principle of karma there is nothing uncertain or capricious in the moral world. We reap what we sow. The good seed brings a harvest of good, the evil of evil."[8]

Yuvraj Krishan describes the classical formulation of theory as representing '*karma* as a law of personal responsibility, inescapable, inexorable and self-operating. It became the most serious challenge to the concept of an all-powerful, all-knowing and all pervasive Creator and Governor."[9]

The formulations quoted above are not exactly similar, however, broad similarities on basic claims can be seen among them. Each of these formulations is put forward as representing the standard formulation of the theory or the Law of Karma in the classical Indian tradition. They are in agreement that the connection between actions and their morally appropriate consequences is causal and law like and karmic processes operate on their own in a regular manner such that everyone without fail gets the consequences that one deserves in the light of the moral quality of one's actions. While Dasgupta mentions the connection between an individual's actions and her quality of life, especially pleasant or unpleasant experiences, Datta goes further and specifies that one's body and natural environment is a result of one's past actions. He also asserts that natural events, which form the common background of people in a certain place or area and affect them, are also deserved consequences of the actions of those people. This suggests that the totality of the past actions of a group of people (group karma) determines the natural events that affect their lives. This is a rather unorthodox and problematic contention.[10] The views mentioned above do not mention the difference of opinion on some central issues within the tradition.

We find that all the above mentioned philosophers emphasize the moral dimension of the theory, which is regarded as the most important aspect of it. Hiriyanna regards it as an ethical law and Radhakrishnan refers to it as the law of the conservation of moral energy. Similarly Datta and Chatterjee refer to it as the "... law of the conservation of moral values, merits and demerits of action."[11] The moral dimension refers to the claim that the consequences that an individual faces are deserved by the individual in the light of the moral quality of one's actions. Two points need to be noted here. One, the analogy between natural laws and the law of karma is quite evident. Natural laws ensure orderly functioning of nature and the law of karma is supposed to establish a moral order in the human world. Two, there is agreement on the point that good actions lead to happiness and bad ones to sorrow, which are their morally appropriate consequences or reward or punishment. This brings out the retributive nature of the theory.

Rajendra Prasad in his detailed analysis of the theory describes it as "a conjunction of three claims: (a) every action produces some pleasure or pain, (b) which and only which its doer necessarily experiences in the present or next life because, (c) he deserves, or ought, to experience them and them alone."[12] He rightly points out that the first claim is an application of the Law of Causation to human actions, the second makes a factual claim but the third makes a moral claim. Clarifying the moral dimension of the theory Prasad observes, "It is this claim of the theory about what the doer deserves, is entitled to, or what his deserts are, which makes the law of *karma* a moral law or a postulate of morality, and not merely the claim that good actions lead to happiness, etc. nor the claim that one always gets what one deserves."[13] It is to be noted that Prasad rightly regards intentional actions alone as subject to moral evaluation. Our intentional actions in most cases, lead to pleasure or pain. However, it needs to be kept in mind that our intentional actions are very often directed towards achieving certain states of affairs which are believed to give pleasure to us or enable us to avoid pain. Moreover, the theory maintains that not only acts of commission but also acts of omission lead to consequences and also, in some formulations, accepts the possibility that performance of some kinds of action does not accrue any merit to the agent. Prasad is right that the theory of karma implies that all the happiness or suffering an individual experiences in life is a result of one's own past actions and one morally deserves it. The formulations discussed so far, by and large, capture the basic principles on which there is broad agreement in the tradition.

An important aspect of the theory of karma is its focus solely on those consequences of a person's actions that accrue to oneself. The theory actually rules out that one person's actions can have consequences for others. Since the consequences can occur in the present life or a future life of the individual, rebirth becomes a necessary corollary. Rebirth of a person occurs because of that person's accumulated residue of past actions and the cycle of birth and death continues till the person achieves liberation. The theory makes a strong moral claim that all the consequences that an individual experiences are deserved by the individual. This moral claim has two aspects, one, that causal connections between actions and their consequences ensure that every individual bears the consequences of all morally relevant actions that one has performed either in the present life or past lives, and two, that the morally appropriate consequences of actions accrue to the agent and agent alone. The causal links between actions and their consequences operating through successive rebirths ensure that every individual necessarily or without fail gets what one deserves in the light of one's actions sooner or later. During this process of birth, death and rebirth of an individual the potency or residue of actions is not lost and continues to shape the circumstances at birth and the overall quality of the life of the individual. Nobody can escape the consequences of one's actions.

I will briefly mention the diversity of views on central concepts and claims of the theory and try to evaluate the broadly agreed basic tenets of the theory. Potter points out that the central concepts like 'karma', '*karmaphala*' and the causal link between action and its consequence can be interpreted differently. An action may be taken to mean a single act of an individual, the moral valence of an individual's actions to date, a single act by a group of people or some function of one or more actions of a group. Again an action may refer to an intention or a verbal or bodily behaviour; it may involve a desire or may be a detached one. Similarly, the consequence may be a physical or a mental event, an experience or affective response, a disposition to have a certain kind of affective responses, a disposition to act in certain ways, a verbal, mental or vocal act, length of life, the type of rebirth one gets or natural events. The causal link may involve a trace, a substance or a quality. Moreover additional factors may be involved like God or Fate etc.[14] It is important to understand such complexities of the theory within the tradition. Yet the various formulations of the theory seem to share some central claims. The task of a critical account of the karma theory becomes a difficult task as a result of the wide variety of views on it. Clearly the representation of the theory in many discussions primarily as a claim that good actions lead to good results and bad actions to sorrow or that one reaps what one sows is simplistic and inadequate.

THE LOGICAL STATUS OF THE THEORY

Before proceeding further, I wish to take up the question of the logical status of the theory. Theories are of various types and pertain to different domains. Scientific theories aim to explain natural phenomena and the hypotheses they use are subject to confirmation through empirical evidence. Speculative or metaphysical theories also attempt to explain the nature of the fundamental reality but these do not derive support from empirical evidence. Epistemological theories address questions of possibility and extent of our knowledge. Moral theories relate to the issue of right and wrong conduct and what ought to be. It is clear that the domain to which a theory belongs would determine the nature of evidence or reasons that can be advanced to support it. What kind of a theory is the karma theory? This question is important for conceptual clarity.

The advocates of the theory put it forward as an explanation of the inequities at birth and why good people sometimes seem to suffer and bad people prosper. Our experience shows that some people are born in prosperous families, some in dire poverty; some are born with healthy bodies, intelligent minds or great talents, while some others are born with a sickly body or dull mental faculties or little talent. It is important to note that the Indian tradition attempts to explain the morally problematic dimension of such occurrences and neither ignores it, nor subsumes it in the general problem of evil and suffering in the world. The karma theory explains these differences by referring to actions of children in their past lives. The occurrence of seemingly undeserved suffering of children and good people is also sought to be explained in a similar manner. Granting that the theory has an explanatory character, it remains a further question what sort of explanation it attempts to provide.

As mentioned earlier, some scholars suggest that the theory should be seen as being at par with scientific theories. Let us see whether there are good reasons to do so. The law of karma can be compared to a natural law in so far as it is supposed to be a causal law operating in the world like the natural laws. It is clear that the supposition of causal connections between actions and their deserved consequences cannot be said to be an empirical generalisation derived from experience. Personal experiences, one's own or of a group of people, are unable to support the central claim that the happiness and sorrow in one's life is directly proportionate to the moral quality of one's actions. The theory actually begins with this acknowledgement. In any case our experiences are limited to our present lives and actions in past lives and their causal connections, as well as, future ones are not subject to observation. The theory makes claims about one's past actions and how these determine the quality of one's present life and present experiences by positing several unobservable elements. Many of the suppositions in the theory like residue of actions and the transmigration of the residue across successive lives of individuals are in principle incapable of empirical verification. Empirical evidence seems irrelevant to the question of justification of such claims and is not offered in discussions of karma. The issue of rebirth is an exception to some extent. Evidence derived from psychic research, especially of people who appear to have memories of their past lives, is sometimes cited to support the idea of rebirth. First of all, the number of such reported cases is very small and secondly, it remains an open question whether such cases are best described as examples of memories of past lives or through other kinds of psychic phenomena like clairvoyance, telepathy etc. Clearly we cannot claim that there are strong scientific grounds to support the belief in rebirth or the belief is held on the ground of evidence in its favour. I will have more to say on this issue later in chapter four. It is clear that scientific theories are subject to requirements of verifiability and falsifiability by empirical evidence. A scientific theory is in principle open to the possibility of modification or even rejection in the light of new evidence. Then there are requirements of repeatable experiments under controlled conditions, predictability of results and more. These features do not seem applicable to the theory of karma. It is thus not tenable to regard the theory of karma as a scientific theory or its claims as scientific principles.

R. Puligandla, however, argues that non-verifiability or non-falsifiability of a principle cannot be a decisive objection against taking it as fundamental to a scientific understanding of the world. He maintains that theoretical terms referring to presumptive objects, events or attributes that cannot be observed directly, are indispensable to scientific enterprise. He regards the law of karma as the universal law of causes and effects, which states that every event, be it thought, speech or action, produces effects and these in turn cause other effects. According to him, the insight behind the law of karma is Leibniz's Principle of Sufficient Reason. It explains why things are what they are. Whether the Law of Causation and the Principle of Sufficient Reason can be said to be the same is debatable but let us ignore this issue here. Puligandla states that the law of karma serves the rational purpose of making the world intelligible to us. He does not find it problematic that the karma theory involves unobservable theoretical entities and argues that scientific laws also involve theoretical entities that cannot be directly observed by us. 'Theoretical terms,' which refer to such entities, are in his view, necessary for a scientific understanding of the world. Puligandla compares the law of karma to the Principle of Conservation of Energy and says,

> ".. to give up the karma theory on grounds that it is not potentially falsifiable is to give up the view that things do not happen arbitrarily but there are reasons for their happening or not happening. Just as the principle of conservation of energy, although not potentially falsifiable, guides our rational inquiry, so also the principle of karma, although not potentially falsifiable, guides our attempt to rationally comprehend the world, including ourselves."[15]

Puligandla's argument is that if scientific principles, which are not verifiable or falsifiable, can be acceptable then so is the law of karma. This comparison with fundamental scientific principles is misplaced and questionable. Science has its own methodology and its basic principles are pretty well defined. Fundamental principles like those of causation and conservation of energy may not be conclusively verifiable or falsifiable but these principles are part of a coherent system of principles and theories and the system as a whole is ultimately open to empirical verification/falsification through its predictions and conclusions. It is not relevant here to go into debates in philosophy of science about the nature and status of scientific theories. It would suffice to say that the theory of karma is not comparable to scientific principles in important respects. Surprisingly Puligandla adds that the theory of karma, though not falsifiable, is nonetheless partially verifiable in one's present life. He draws support from Eliot Deutsch's view that the karma theory implies that 'as one acts so one becomes' and says that this is demonstrable in one's present life since "… one can see the belief that one's actions do reverberate back into one's nature and condition one's personality."[16] This, for him, constitutes verification of the belief that one's condition in life is determined by one's actions. This position is clearly unacceptable; Deutsch represents one view of the consequences of karma but there are other views which elaborate consequences differently. Secondly, it is clear that our experiences do not support the conclusion that our present life is solely determined by our own actions. His idea of verification is obviously different from its understanding in science.

The law of karma, according to Puligandla, is a synthetic apriori principle, which is fundamental to the very possibility of a systematic rational knowledge of the world.[17] Puligandla is making three major claims here. One, the law of karma is comparable to a fundamental scientific law, two, it is synthetic apriori and three, it is necessary for a rational understanding of the world. He seems to come close to Kant's view that some fundamental principles of natural sciences are synthetic apriori.[18] Kant's notion of synthetic apriori propositions was based on a certain complex epistemological perspective, which maintains that certain synthetic apriori principles constitute the necessary conditions of the possibility of knowledge of objects. Many aspects of his epistemology are controversial. The idea of synthetic apriori propositions has been critiqued extensively and rejected by the empiricists. It is not necessary to discuss important aspects of Kant's epistemology and its difficulties here. It would suffice to say that the law of karma is not situated in the classical tradition in an epistemological perspective like that of Kant. Moreover, a synthetic apriori proposition, as conceived by Kant, is not subject to empirical verification. His suggestion that the law of karma is verifiable in experience is baffling, given that it is held to be apriori.

Puligandla argues that the law of karma is essential for a rational understanding of the world; its rejection makes the world unintelligible for us. As mentioned earlier, several philosophical writings on the theory of karma emphasize its explanatory value. It provides a certain perspective of the world and life but we know that there are other perspectives as well. It is debatable whether the perspective provided by the theory of karma can be said to be essential to a rational understanding of the world or even rationally superior to other perspectives. We will be in a better position to judge the adequacy of the explanation provided by the theory after we have discussed its various aspects and their implications.

Karl Potter also supports the view that the theories of karma and rebirth should be regarded as scientific theories. According to him, classical Indian philosophy treats these as scientific theories. Potter gives a detailed analysis of the domain of the theory and its theoretical postulates. He employs three criteria of accuracy, adequacy and explanatory power to evaluate the theory and concludes that it is more successful than other alternative theories in explaining its domain, namely birth and time of death of a person and quality of experiences during the person's lifetime.

> "... karma and rebirth are treated in Indian thought in the manner of scientific theories. Just as one does not prove a rich scientific theory by one or two key arguments, but rather by spelling out in detail its systematic interconnections and thus indicating how it explains the domain overall, so karma and rebirth are developed, especially by those systems in India which are not superskeptical, in systematic terms, their details fitting with experience constituting their demonstration. For those systems karma and rebirth are fundamental features of any world view which it is felt fits experience more closely than any alternative account."[19]

Three major points emerge from the account mentioned above, one, that the theory of karma is a scientific theory or comparable to it, two, it is applicable to our experiences and explains some of those and three, that it does the explaining much more adequately than any other alternative theory. Let us take up these points one by one.

As explained earlier, the theory cannot be called a scientific theory because of its in-principle unverifiable and unfalsifiable nature. One of the important features of a scientific theory is its ability to make predictions about future events, which are verifiable through observations. The theory of karma is unable to do so because most of the time its formulations do not tell us that such specific actions will give rise to such consequences at such and such time but only make a general claim that good actions will lead to good consequences and bad ones to bad. Moreover, the time of the actualization of consequences remains uncertain and a mystery. This will be clear when we discuss different formulations of the theory later. In some versions, however, an attempt is made to link specific kind of actions with specific kind of results in the person's next birth. Such predictions are in principle unverifiable and unfalsifiable. Potter and Puligandla do not find the unfalsifiable character of the karma theory a problem but it raises a serious difficulty in this context. Some western empiricists have gone to the extent of saying that a putative assertion, which is not in principle falsifiable by empirical evidence, actually does not assert anything.[20] This view may be open to difficulties but the point is that a scientific theory is in principle revisable in the light of future evidence. If the theory of karma is a scientific theory, it must be shown to satisfy the requirements of verifiability and falsifiability through empirical evidence. Following later Wittgenstein one may argue that Puligandla and Potter's approaches are examples of a failure to understand the logical grammar of a metaphysical or religious assertion.[21] As for the claim of superiority over other explanations, it is best postponed till the various aspects of the theory have been clarified.

We had discussed earlier that the theory of karma posits a connection between actions and their deserved or morally appropriate consequences. This dimension of the theory is its central emphasis. It lays down a necessary connection between a person's actions and their morally appropriate and deserved reward or punishment for that person. Hiriyanna regards the law of karma not merely as a mechanical principle but as an essentially ethical principle. The Law is sometimes referred to as the law of moral causation. Keeping in view the moral dimension of the theory, can we regard it as an ethical one? If so, we need to know which ethical issue it pertains to. The theory is not about the criterion of right actions, it is not about the distinction between morally right and wrong actions, it is not a meta-ethical theory about the meaning of ethical terms or the nature of ethical language. In short it is not about the issues that are generally the subject matter of ethical theories. Normative Ethics relates to the issue 'what ought to be done'. The theory of karma envisages a morally desirable state of affairs; a world where right actions bring for the agent morally appropriate good consequences and bad ones bring morally appropriate bad consequences. It asserts that an ideal situation is actualized in the world through a causal mechanism linking actions to their morally appropriate rewards or punishments. However, a causal law operates mechanically, so the law of karma will also be operating mechanically. Moreover, it tells us how certain actions lead to certain consequences. To this extent it cannot be said to be like an ethical or moral law.[22] The law claims that the consequences of a person's actions constitute morally appropriate rewards or punishments of those actions and yet the law is supposed to operate mechanically. This makes it difficult to accept that the law is a moral or ethical one. Rajendra Prasad rightly points out that the extension of the causal law to the moral domain does not change its causal non-normative character.

> "It is clear then, that the (causal) law of *karma*, by being extended to the moral domain, does not become a moral law. By describing it as a law of causation operative in the moral sphere, or even as a law of moral causation, we do not gain anything. A law of moral causation is a law of the causation of moral things and not a moral law (of causation). Rather a moral law is not, or cannot be, a causal law, not even a law of moral causation."[23]

It would be pertinent at this point to mention Immanuel Kant's view, which provides an interesting insight in this context.[24] He argued that our idea of the highest good demands that people should get happiness in proportion to the moral quality of their actions. This state of affairs can be realized, only if, we accept the existence of God and immortality of the soul. Belief in God as the divine judge is required to ensure that everyone gets happiness and unhappiness in accordance with the moral quality of one's actions. Belief in immortality of the soul is required to ensure that those persons who have not experienced the appropriate rewards and punishments of their actions during their earthly life can experience these after death. Therefore,

Kant regarded the existence of God and immortality of the soul as necessary presuppositions of morality. It is to be noted that Kant's epistemology implies that neither God nor eternal soul were objects of knowledge and he gave the above mentioned moral argument to prove their existence. Kant seems correct when he says that our highest moral ideal demands complete justice of rewards and punishments in accordance with the moral quality of our actions such that good actions should bring happiness for the doer. He takes God and immortality of soul as presuppositions of the possibility of such justice. Indian philosophy seeks to realize this ideal through the theory of karma and rebirth. We have here a different theoretical framework to create the possibility of complete justice of happiness or unhappiness experienced by an agent in the light of the moral quality of one's actions with the difference that the rewards or punishments are experienced by the agents during their successive earthly lives. However, it remains a big question whether the gap between 'what ought to be' and 'what is' can be bridged thus and whether the theory of karma is a coherent and plausible way to do so.

In the light of the preceding discussion what can we say about the logical status of the karma theory? It is definitely intended to explain certain phenomena in our lives but to do so it employs suppositions like karmic residue, transmigration of the soul and rebirth that are not verifiable or falsifiable through empirical evidence even in principle. It cannot, therefore, be regarded as a scientific theory. It is not plausible to regard it as a moral theory either. In my view the karma theory is a metaphysical theory, which is inspired by our hope that good actions will bring us good results and happiness and bad ones will bring us bad results and sorrow. The theory has an explanatory dimension as also a moral dimension and both are equally important. No wonder then that Rama Rao Pappu calls the law of karma a 'naturalistic principle', which is both "descriptive and prescriptive, naturalistic and normative."[25] It is this multifaceted nature of the claims in the theory, which makes it difficult to categorize it. Sometimes it is claimed that the theory is being accepted on the authority of scriptures or seers. If so, it becomes a dogma and an article of faith. The disadvantage is that this claim puts it beyond the scope of rational scrutiny.

To conclude, we find difference of opinion among philosophers on the issue of the logical status of the karma theory. It has been characterized as a scientific theory, as a synthetic apriori or transcendental principle, a moral law and a dogma. The attempts to show the theory to be a scientific one are misplaced. It makes a metaphysical claim and how tenable that claim is remains open to question. Subsequent chapters will aim to clarify the conceptual dimensions of the theory and their implications.

An outline of the theory of karma and its central claims has been given above. The issue of the logical character of the theory has also been briefly discussed. Different aspects of the theory will be analysed and critically evaluated in subsequent chapters. The karmic process would be outlined on the basis of discussions found in the classical tradition with a view to achieve greater clarity regarding the concepts of agent, action, karmic residue and consequences. In this context an attempt will also be made to briefly mention those views, which differ from the strict theory regarding its central claims. These reflect the diversity of views on karma within the Indian tradition. The detailed examination of karmic causality will try to show why it is not tenable to regard the relation between actions and their consequences as causal and will also discuss the problematic dimensions of the idea of a karmic moral order in the world. The supposition of rebirth raises issues regarding personal identity and moral responsibility of individuals for their past actions. Since the issue of the criterion of personal identity has not been discussed much in the Indian tradition, the discussions on this issue in Western philosophy have been used to clarify the problems that arise in this context. The last two chapters are devoted to discussing some important objections against the karma theory and its limitations and difficulties. In this context it has been briefly mentioned how modern scholars have responded to the central claims of the theory.

Notes and References

1. Two such works are Wendy Doniger O'Flaherty, (ed.) *Karma and Rebirth in Classical Indian Traditions,* first published by California University Press, 1980, Indian edition by Motilal Banarsidass, Delhi, Patna, Varanasi, 1983, and Yuvraj Krishan, *The Doctrine of Karma, Motilal Banarsidas Publishers, Delhi, 1997*

2. Rajendra Prasad, *Karma, Causation And Retributive Morality,* Indian Council of Philosophical Research, New Delhi in association with Munshiram, Manoharlal Publishers Pvt. Ltd., New Delhi, 1989, chapter 13, p. 210.

3. Karl Potter, 'How Many Karma Theories are there?', *Journal of Indian Philosophy,* 29, 2001, p. 239, (pp.231-239). Potter tries to provide a classification of various types of views on karma.

4. Karl H. Potter, 'The Karma Theory and Its Interpretation in Some Indian Philosophical Systems', in Wendy Doniger O' Flaherty, (ed.), *Karma And Rebirth In Classical Indian Traditions,* p. 241.

5. S.N. Dasgupta, *A History of Indian Philosophy,* vol. 1, Cambridge University Press, Cambridge, 1922, p.71

6. D.M. Datta, *Philosophical Perspectives: A Selection of Essays,* Bharati Bhawan, Patna, 1971, p.93

7. M. Hiriyanna, *Essentials of Indian Philosophy,* George Allen and Unwin, Great Britain, 1949, p. 48

8. S. Radhakrishnan, *Indian Philosophy,* vol. 1, H. D. Lewis, (ed.), Muirhead Library of Philosophy, George Allen and Unwin Publication, 1929, p. 244

9. Yuvraj Krishan, *The Doctrine of Karma,* Preface, p. xi

10. The issues related to the relationship between karmic causality and natural causality will be discussed later.

11. S.C. Chatterjee and D. M. Datta, *An Introduction to Indian Philosophy,* University of Calcutta, Calcutta, 1939, p.18

12. Rajendra Prasad, *Karma Causation And Retributive Morality,* p. 221

13. Ibid, p. 215

14. Potter, 'How Many Karma Theories are there?' p.239

15. R. Puligandla, 'Karma, Operational Definitions and Freedom', S.S. Rama Rao Pappu, (ed.), *The Dimensions of Karma,* Chanakya Publications, Delhi, 1987, pp. 128-29

16. Eliot Deutsch, *Advaita Vedanta: A Philosophical Reconstruction,* East West Press, Honolulu, 1969, p.71, Puligandla, op cit. p. 130

17. Puligandla, op cit, p. 137

18. Immanuel Kant introduced the notion of a synthetic apriori proposition. He defines it as a proposition whose denial is not self-contradictory and yet the proposition is universal and necessarily true. For Kant synthetic apriori propositions were necessary because these give the necessary presuppositions of the very possibility of knowledge of objects. According to him, such propositions are found in Mathematics and also among the foundational principles of Natural sciences. It is to be noted that Kant's epistemology implies that something that is not given in sensation cannot be an object of knowledge. He, therefore, denied that there is knowledge of God, Soul or the World. The unobservable entities referred to within the theory of karma cannot be objects of knowledge in his scheme. Immanuel Kant, *Critique of Pure Reason,* Norman Kemp Smith, (tr.), The Macmillan Press ltd., London and Basingstoke, 1978.

19. Karl H. Potter, 'Karma and Rebirth: Traditional Indian Arguments' in Rama Rao Pappu, (ed) *The Dimensions of Karma,* p.162

20. Antony Flew, R.M. Hare and B. Mitchell, 'Theology and Falsification', Basil Mitchell, ed., *The Philosophy of Religion,* OUP, Oxford, 1971. Many western empiricists have argued that a cognitively meaningful statement must be verifiable by observation statements. They conclude that metaphysical sentences or putative assertions about

God, Soul etc. are pseudo statements and not genuine assertions. They ascribe non-cognitive significance to such sentences. Flew came to the same conclusion on the basis of unfalsifiability of such sentences.

21. Cyrill Barrett, (ed.), *Ludwig. Wittgenstein, Lectures and Conversations on Aesthetics, Psychology and Religious Belief,* Basil Blackwell, Oxford, 1966. Wittgenstein in his analysis of religious belief in his later works emphasizes that the logic of religious discourse is different from that of scientific or empirical discourse. He argues that believing in religious contexts is primarily a matter of having affective attitudes and regulating one's life on the basis of one's beliefs. He says that treating the belief in Last Judgement, for example, as a scientific belief turns it into superstition. Other philosophers like Norman Malcolm and D.Z. Phillips have also emphasized the distinct nature of religious discourse.

22. The assumption that the law of karma operates mechanically is open to serious difficulties, which will be discussed later in the context of karmic causality.

23. Rajendra Prasad, *Karma Causation And Retributive Morality,* p. 231

24. Immanuel Kant, *Critique of Practical Reason,* Mary J. Gregory, (ed.) Cambridge University Press, Cambridge,1997

25. Rama Rao Pappu, (ed.) *The Dimensions of Karma,* Introduction, p.3

Chapter - 2

THE KARMIC PROCESS

The formulation of the karma theory has been briefly outlined in the first chapter. This chapter would elaborate the process through which actions are supposed to bring about their consequences as discussed in different schools of thought. The process is as follows:

An agent performs an action, the action leaves some residue or traces, these traces are preserved and at some later point of time in future mature and bring about their consequences for the agent. All the traces of actions of an agent do not bring consequences to the agent in the present life; the traces of present and past actions that do not fructify in the present life of an agent are carried over to the next life/lives of the person and after maturation bring about their morally appropriate consequences for the agent. Except in some theistic versions of the theory, the actions are believed to bring about their consequences on their own through causal connections. The karma theory emphasizes that an individual cannot escape the consequences of one's actions, if these are not experienced in the present life, they will be experienced in subsequent lives.

The important terms employed in the context of the karmic process are, agent (*kartā*), action (karma), residue/potentiality or traces of an action, ripening or maturation (*vipāka*) of the residue, and the consequences of an action (*karma-phala*). The term 'karma' is used in more than one sense in the literature on the theory. It is used to refer to actions and often to refer to the residue of past actions as well. For the sake of clarity, I will restrict the use of the term 'karma' to actions performed by human beings. The potency or residue left by the actions may be referred in a general way as '*karmāvaśeṣa*.' Different terms have been used by philosophical systems to refer to the residue of actions and these will be mentioned later. The residue of an individual's actions need not yield consequences immediately but only after a time-gap and even in the next birth of the individual. This time-gap is accounted for by the concept of maturation of the residue. Let us now discuss the above mentioned terms briefly:

THE AGENT (*KARTĀ*)

By an 'agent' we ordinarily mean a human being who is conscious and has desires and intentions etc. Sometimes the concept of agency is used in the context of companies and organizations also, even for inanimate objects like chemical substances. But this is a derivative sense of 'agent' and the primary sense remains as used in the context of human beings. Ordinarily, one does not apply the concept of agency to non-living things, not even to living things like plants, insects and animals. Its primary application is in the context of human persons. The crucial requirement for ascription of agency to a being is possession of sufficiently developed consciousness. Human beings satisfy this requirement. They are conscious and have desires, motives and intentions. They perform actions in accordance with their intentions.

However, we find that mythology sometimes ascribes agency to animals and non-human beings also. Opinions differ on the question whether agency can be meaningfully ascribed to some higher animals also, specially those who possess relatively advanced level of consciousness, though not as developed as in human beings. For a long time in the Western philosophical tradition, animals were regarded almost like machines. Now it is widely accepted across the world that animals are conscious and can feel pleasure and pain. In case of some higher animals it seems as if they have some emotions and are capable of intentional actions in a limited way. Researches in biology have shown that there is no sharp dividing line between humans and other animals; it is more plausible to see the animal world as a continuum with varying degrees of conscious activities with human beings situated at the highest stage. India has a long tradition of depicting animals as agents in mythology, educative stories and even religious systems. The *Panctantra* teaches state craft through stories woven around the actions of animals like rabbits, monkeys, elephants and lions. Buddhist *Jātaka* tales maintain that before his birth as a human being, Gautam Buddha was born in animal form in his previous lives. The Hindu pantheon of gods includes Hanumana, who is depicted as a monkey-god. Moreover, reincarnations (*avatārs*) of God Vishnu include animals like fish (*matsya)*, tortoise (*kaśyapa*) and boar (*vārāhā*) besides beings whose body is partly of an animal and partly human like *Narsimha.*

Hindu mythology also mentions agency of non-human beings and beings who are somewhat like human beings, for example, *rākṣasa* and *daitya*. It is to be noted that the theory of karma admits that a human being may be reborn as an animal in the light of past bad actions and can also move from a birth as an animal to birth as a human being by performing good actions. However, I will confine the discussion to human agents.

As already mentioned, we ordinarily understand 'agent' to refer to a person or a human being. The concept of a human being and that of a person are, however, not identical; nor are they co-extensive. There can be non-human persons like angels and fairies and not all human beings may be regarded as persons, for example, severely retarded ones or those in a vegetative state. Still, a human being is a paradigm example of a person and an agent. A person is a being who has a body and is also capable of conscious or mental activities of fairly sophisticated kind. These include perception, thinking, believing, reasoning, having desires, emotions, memories, hopes and expectations and intentions. Human beings are capable of performing intentional, purposive actions and have a developed moral sense. Mind- body dualism regards a person as a combination of a body and a soul.[1] It can be said that dualism has been the dominant view both in the Indian and the Western philosophical tradition, though there are also views which differ from it in significant ways. Let us start with a brief outline of the conception of a person in the Western tradition and mention a few contemporary developments before moving on to the concept of an agent in the Indian tradition.

Descartes presents a classical formulation of the mind-body dualism in modern Western philosophy.[2] He states that the soul is a spiritual substance with the essential attribute of consciousness and body is a material substance with the essential attribute of extension. The two substances are distinct and logically independent of each other. The soul is independent of the body and though it is conjoined with a body in case of a human being, it does not depend for its existence on that body. The soul is the seat of all conscious activities. His dualistic view left a deep influence on the subsequent thinkers and has an impressive list of supporters. Though the concept of a person in its primary sense represents an embodied being, however, dualists like Descartes believe that the person is essentially a soul, which is contingently related to a body. They do not think that having a body is an essential aspect of being a person. In other words, having a human form or having any physical form is not essential to being a person for dualists but having a soul with capacity for conscious activities like thinking and reasoning is. The dualists attribute all conscious states of a person to the soul and all physical properties to the body. Mind- body dualism allows the possibility of survival of a soul after death and hence of a person. Monotheistic religious traditions like Judaism, Christianity and Islam accept immortality of the soul, however they believe in resurrection of a person and not in rebirth. A person's soul survives after death, carries the moral responsibility for one's actions performed during the embodied state and will bear the rewards or punishments for those actions in accordance with the divine judgement after resurrection.

Two major challenges to Cartesian dualism are posed by the empiricists and the materialists. The empiricists like David Hume, William James, Bertrand Russell, A.J. Ayer and J.J.C. Smart, among others, denied the existence of a substantive soul on the ground that it is not given in experience. David Hume challenged the claim that we are every moment aware of our self as the subject of our experiences. He analysed self as a series of independent perceptions and asserted that, strictly speaking, it neither has unity nor identity over time.[3] Empiricists do not necessarily deny the distinction between physical and mental states of a person but they do deny a unitary, permanent spiritual substance as the subject of experiences. Their denial of a subject of experiences and their reductive analysis of self in terms of a complex or series of experiences is open to several difficulties and these have been debated at length. Materialists try to explain consciousness in terms of material or physical phenomena and do not think that a spiritual or immaterial substance over and above material phenomena is needed to explain mental phenomena. Some twentieth century philosophers tried to reduce mental states to events in the brain and nervous system. This approach draws support from the modern scientific outlook, especially Neuro-science. Contemporary researches on functions of the brain and central nervous system show strong correlations between these and mental activities of people.

An interesting view on the concept of a person was put forward by P.F. Strawson, who rejected both Cartesian dualism and the serial view supported by empiricists.[4] He designates the latter as an example of 'no-ownership theory.' He advocates that our concept of a person is not of a complex of two substances-body and mind but is the concept of a subject to which corporeal characteristics (M-predicates) and predicates presupposing consciousness (P-predicates) can both be applied. Thus in his view both physical qualities like weight and height and psychological states like thinking and memory are ascribed to the same subject, namely, a person. The concept of a person is thus of a unique kind of subject to whom both kinds of qualities can be ascribed. This view is often referred to as the 'dual aspect theory' of a person. Strawson argues that a person can neither be identified with a soul, nor with a series of experiences devoid of a unitary subject, nor to a complex of a body and a soul. The concept of a person is logically 'primitive' and it is not reducible to the concept of a soul or the concept of a body, nor can it be analysed as a complex of a body and a soul. Its distinctive character consists in the fact that it is the concept of a subject to which both kinds of predicates are equally ascribable.

> "What I mean by the concept of a person is the concept of a type of entity such that both predicates ascribing states of consciousness and predicates ascribing corporeal characteristics, a physical situation, etc. are equally applicable to a single individual of that single type."[5]

Supporting a similar view Antony Flew observes:

> "... person words refer to men and women like you and me and the other fellow...They do not refer to anything invisible and elusive, to any mysterious incorporeal substances...But that is not to say that they refer merely or at all to bodies. 'Person' is no synonym for body...Person words do not mean either bodies or souls nor yet any combination of the two."[6]

In place of a distinction between two kinds of substances, Strawson puts forward a distinction between two kinds of characteristics. M-predicates ascribe physical qualities and P-predicates either ascribe states of consciousness or imply possession of consciousness by the subject to which these are ascribed. He admits that the distinction does not reflect two mutually exclusive classes of predicates; some predicates do not clearly fall into either category, for example, 'going for a walk', and 'is smiling.' His critics point out that Strawson fails to provide a clear criterion of P-predicates and it is debatable whether the distinction between P-predicates and M-predicates can be clarified without some degree of circularity. Bernard Williams defines 'person' primarily in terms of a body. He argues that the concept of a person is not primitive because we can define 'person' as a 'material body which thinks.' For him the basic distinction to be made should be between 'material bodies which cannot think' and 'material bodies which can.'[7]

The standpoints of both Strawson and Williams result in making the concept of a person underdetermined since animals also fulfil the conditions laid out by them.

If the animal world presents a continuum, then it is not surprising. It seems that as far as conscious activities are concerned the difference between human beings and other animals is a matter of degree rather than kind. However, it is extremely difficult to clearly outline the list of conscious activities, which provide a necessary and sufficient condition of being a person.[8] It seems that such lists end up making the concept of a person either too narrow or too wide and in both circumstances we face unacceptable consequences. It is not necessary to discuss in detail the strengths and weaknesses of the theories provided by Strawson and Williams. It would suffice to say that our ordinary concept of a person represents a subject who possesses physical properties and also advanced mental and linguistic capabilities, etc.

In my view the dual aspect theory, though not free from difficulties, captures our ordinary notion of a person, exemplified in a paradigm way by human beings, much more adequately than dualism or the serial theory. Persons' agency is executed through their bodies but the conscious activities of thinking, judging and intending are indispensable to human agency. The dualists believe that these have their seat in the soul and, therefore, the soul becomes the real subject and indispensable for human agency. The body, though an instrument of carrying out actions, is not considered to be essential for being a person. As mentioned earlier, many religions support the distinction between the soul and the body and accept the possibility of survival of the soul after death. If one's body is regarded as essential to being a person, then the possibility of a person's survival after death gets ruled out.

We find that rationality figures prominently in the analysis of the concept of a person in the Western tradition. Aristotle defines 'man' as a rational animal but gives predominance to rationality over animality. John Locke, the British empiricist, defines a person as "... a thinking intelligent being that has reason and reflection and can consider itself as itself, the same thinking thing in different times and places...."[9] He thus includes a sense of one's identity over time in his definition of 'person' alongside possession of consciousness and rationality. Philosophers have often regarded rationality as both a necessary and a sufficient condition of being a person. Locke said that a rational parrot can be regarded as a person but a human being devoid of rationality does not qualify to be a person. Aristotle did not regard all human beings as persons and this was based on the claim that they did not possess rationality, for example, slaves. Moreover, he regarded women and children as inferior because in his opinion rationality was not adequately developed in them.[10] While other aspects of consciousness like emotions, feelings and desires are also supposed to be important in characterizing persons, rationality is generally taken as their defining quality. This predominance given to rationality has often been used to justify exploitation and subjugation of women in human history.

In a general sense 'rationality' means the capacity to think coherently, to reason on the basis of arguments, to draw conclusions from premises, etc. Sometimes its paradigmatic sense is taken to consist in the capacity to form moral judgments, at others in the capacity to find the best means to the goals one has. It is clear that rationality is an extremely important component of the concept of a person along with other capacities, like emotions, feelings and linguistic capabilities etc. Having a developed moral sense is also a distinguishing property of human beings. Personhood provides the basis of citizenship and civil and political rights of people. Thus, denial of personhood, we find, has been made a ground for denial of such rights to certain sections of human beings. The predominance given to rationality in defining a person has invited sharp criticism from feminists who argue that it has been used to support the idea of subjugation of women and has led to undervaluation of qualities and attitudes regarded as feminine.

Let us now briefly outline some of the conceptions of the individual and agency in Indian philosophical systems. We can find points of similarity between the Indian views on persons and the dualistic view discussed earlier, even though these are separated by several centuries. But there are also many significant points of departure in the Indian tradition from the Western dualistic picture of a human agent. Indian conceptions of an agent have to be seen in the context of the complex metaphysics where these belong. The metaphysical contexts bring in their own complexities and problems. Generally speaking, the embodied individual (*jīva*), who has thoughts, desires and intentions and performs actions, represents an agent. However, there is disagreement regarding the nature of the individual among different schools and also on the question as to whom agency is to be ascribed. The dualistic conception of a person can be said to be the dominant one in the tradition, which regards human beings as a complex of a body and a soul or self. However, mind (*manas*) is regarded as a sense organ and distinct from the soul in the Indian tradition.

The materialist school *Cārvāka* does not accept the existence of a soul over and above the material body. For it the body characterized by states of consciousness constitutes the individual. They also deny the possibility of survival of a person after death. Most of the orthodox systems, however, support the view that an embodied being has a unitary substantive self or soul (*ātman*) over and above the body consisting of various sense organs and mind. However, not all of them accept that consciousness is a necessary attribute of the soul. *Nyāya-Vaiśeṣika* regard self as a unitary substance, which is eternal. The self is the basis of the psychological life of a person and desire, aversion, cognition, experience of pain and pleasure and volition are its characteristics. Hiriyanna observes that *Nyāya* does not regard self as intrinsically or essentially conscious; rather consciousness is accidental to it. The self has cognition and experiences when it is associated with a mind (*manas),* which is not spiritual in nature. Thus the conjunction of the self with the mind seems to be a necessary condition of the possibility of experiences of a person. *Nyāya* maintains that every individual has a unitary, eternal soul, which has its separate mind and that remains with it till the soul is liberated.[11] In this conception a soul together with its own mind seems to provide the seat of a person's psychological functions, including intentions.

Clearly this view is different from the classical Western dualism discussed earlier. *Nyāya* accepts the possibility of the survival of the soul after the destruction of the body or death. Not only the soul but the mind conjoined with it also survives after the death of a person. Both then can be said to be independent of the body with which they are associated during life, since their existence is not logically dependent upon the body. The soul along with the mind gets a new body at the time of rebirth. It seems that mind is indispensable to the possibility of agency of a person here. However, it cannot be said to be the agent. Dasti observes that agency consists in the capacity of an individual to initiate action and it requires capacities for cognition, desire and volition and *Nyāya* regards the self (*ātman*) as the bearer of these. Even though a self requires a body and a mind to be able to have cognitions, emotions and feelings, and perform actions, it is the self which is the agent. The body and the mind provide the conditions for the self to actualize its potential for agency.[12] Dasti emphasizes that volition and agency are to be ascribed to the self and not to the mind or the intellect. He adds that the *Nyāya* conceptions of karma, individual moral responsibility and liberation cannot be understood unless the self is regarded as the direct bearer of the properties that are synthesized in agency.[13] The *Pūrva-Mīmāṃsā* view of self is quite similar to that of *Nyāya*. It also accepts the existence of many selves. However, it has significant differences with the *Nyāya* view on questions of knowledge of the self.

Sāṁkya-yoga also accepts many individual souls. They accept two basic ontological categories-material and spiritual. The material principle (*prakṛti*) is one while spirits or conscious selves (*puruṣa*) are many. Unlike *Nyāya, Sāṁkhya* regards consciousness as the essential attribute of the self. However, this self in its essential nature is neither a subject of experiences (*bhoktā*) nor an agent (*kartā*), but only an observer (*dṛṣṭā*). In individual human beings the self is associated with a body, which consists of evolutes of the material principle. Due to ignorance the soul does not realize its distinction from the body and identifies with the body and the sense organs and mistakenly ascribes experiences and actions to itself. In its essential nature it remains distinct from the body, which belongs to the material principle. Thus in an ultimate sense the self can neither be regarded as a subject of experiences nor an agent.

Bryant observes that agency presupposes the ability to make choices and discriminative faculty to select one option from among many. However, the self being eternal is unchangeable and, therefore, cannot be an agent. According to him, agency is to be ascribed either to intellect (*buddhi*) or to the ego-sense (*ahaṃkāra*). Being an agent implies activity and undergoing change, and since the self is unchanging, it can "do nothing other than be aware or be proximate to the source of action". Because of conjunction with the body the self, which is the indifferent one appears as if it is the agent.[14] The self in its embodied, empirical state fails to discriminate between itself and the material principle and, therefore, mistakenly identifies with experiences and actions associated with its body.

The *Bhagvad Gītā* also supports a similar view. Taking the unconscious material principle (*prakṛti)* and the conscious self (*puruṣa)*, as the two basic categories, it denies that the self is really an agent. Upadhyaya observes that on this view the self in its true nature is inactive (*akartā*), indifferent, pure witness (*udāseen sākṣī*), beyond qualities (*guṇātīta*) and unique (*kevala*). However, because of its delusion arising out of its association with ego-sense (*ahaṃkāra*), the self mistakenly takes itself to be an agent or doer. In the ultimate sense, all activity belongs only to the material principle and the self cannot be said to be an agent.[15] *Sāṁkhya* and *The Bhagvad Gītā* regard the soul as independent of the body and accept that it continues to exist even after the destruction of the body.

The perspective mentioned above is dualistic but does not ascribe knowledge and action to the self. As a result, it becomes difficult to explain the idea of individuals' moral responsibility for their actions. It is important to distinguish between what seems as real at the empirical level and what is ultimately real as regards the nature of the self. The conscious self cannot be ascribed moral responsibility for the actions performed by an individual, since ultimately it is not an agent. The self mistakenly regards itself as knower and doer due to ignorance. But it does not seem plausible to ascribe moral responsibility to the unconscious intellect or to the ego-sense. *Sāṁkhya* faces serious difficulties in explaining the association between the self and the body, rebirth and liberation. However, it is not within the purview of this study to discuss these problematic dimensions of its metaphysics. The question of karmic causality is relevant only at the empirical level or till the self is not liberated. In the embodied state the self ascribes to itself the actions performed by the individual even though 'regarding itself as an agent' is a manifestation of its ignorance. Therefore, it seems reasonable to take the self as an agent in this context.

Shankar's *Advaita Vedānta* regards the entire reality to be of the nature of consciousness. It advocates non-dualism and maintains that *Brahman* alone is ultimately real, who is real (*sat*), consciousness (*cit*) and bliss (*ānanda*). This philosophy is famous for its view that the world of multiplicity is an illusion and not real (*mithyā*). It distinguishes three levels of reality. Dreams and what we commonly regard as illusions belong to the level of *prātibhāsika sat*. Such experiences are negated by subsequent experiences. For example, dreams are negated by experiences of the waking life. The ordinary world belongs to the category of conditional reality (*vyavahārika sat*); it is neither ultimately real, nor totally unreal and will be superseded or sublated by the ultimate truth once a being attains true knowledge. Only *Brahman* is ultimately real (*pāramārthika sat*).

At the level of conditional reality, we distinguish between different objects and different individual selves. Each person regards oneself as separate and distinct from other persons. From the ultimate point of view there is no such distinction. Ultimately all individual selves are identical with *Brahman* and each self's thinking of itself as distinct from other selves constitutes ignorance. A liberated self becomes identical with the ultimate reality and all distinctions and multiplicity is destroyed. A question arises, who is the agent in the context of the worldly existence of individuals where distinction between body and self and between one self and another are maintained due to ignorance? It is to be noted that the idea of karma and its consequences is applicable only at the worldly level and at this level there appear to be many individual conscious selves, each with its own experiences and actions. The concept of a subject of experiences and an agent also has its application only at the worldly level or the level of the conditional reality. Therefore, at this level it would be legitimate to talk of many souls; each is essentially conscious, has several experiences and performs several actions in its embodied state. Every individual bears moral responsibility for her actions and has to face the consequences of those actions. Shankar accepts rebirth and says that an individual cannot escape the consequences of those residue of past actions which have matured. A person goes through a series of births and continues to bear moral responsibility for her actions and must face their consequences. The cycle of rebirths ceases only when liberation is attained. From the point of view of the ultimate reality there is no agency and no action. However, from the point of view of empirical reality there are agents. it seems reasonable to say that, as far as, the worldly level is concerned, agency is to be ascribed to the individual soul. However, it is evident that Shankar's philosophical standpoint makes the issue of agency and moral responsibility very complex.

It is clear that the ontological commitments of a school or thinker provide the context in which the issues of actions and moral responsibility are taken up and answered. Unlike Shankar, Ramanuj accepts the reality of many individual selves whose essential nature consists in consciousness and ascribes knowledge and agency to them. Ramanuj regards the Supreme Self as the ultimate reality, which is the cause of all other things and maintains that the embodied individual self is a real agent. Ganeri observes that the agency in his system is to be ascribed to the embodied individual as a whole, not to the self alone. He adds that agency is a product of a complex causal process in which not only the individual finite self and the material body associated with it are involved but also the Supreme self as its inner controller. However, Ramanuj maintains that actions of an individual self are not determined by the agency of the Supreme Self.[16] Ganeri points out that Ramanuj believes that an individual self as a conscious subject exercises real and free agency. But at the same time he emphasizes its dependence on the Supreme Self and maintains that without the agency of the Supreme Self, the individual's liberation cannot take place. He thus maintains, "... a form of compatibilism that can be found in other classical theistic traditions."[17] It is open to question whether agency can be explained in Ramanuj's philosophy without giving rise to a conflict between the individual self and the Supreme Self. I will have more to say on the issue of free will in the last chapter.

Let us now very briefly take up the issue of agency in two major heterodox systems, Jainism and Buddhism. Jainism accepts two basic categories-animate or living beings (*jīva*) and inanimate or non-living things (*ajīva*). It accepts the existence of many souls and regards sentience (*cetanā*) as the essential attribute of spirit. The self in its true nature is pure, perfect, simple, immaterial and formless. In its embodied state it is characterized by life force (*prāṇa*) and is limited within the confines of the body with which it is associated. The spirit pervades the body it occupies (*deha-mātra*). Its contact with the external world gives rise to various kinds of actions and these give rise to karmic particles. These particles defile the pure nature of the self and it becomes subject to the cycle of rebirths or transmigration. The veil of karmas obstructs the inherent capacity of the spirit for self-realization. The spirit in its true nature is omniscient but during the embodied state its knowledge is limited. The particles of karma form a karmic body (*karma-śarīra*), which remains attached to the soul till it gets emancipated by either expelling or removing the karmas by following the prescribed ethical rules. The souls belong to higher or lower classes depending upon the number of sense organs possessed by the being. Lowest are plants and highest are human beings. They possess five sense- organs and also *manas* and are rational.[18] Jainism puts great emphasis on non-violence or not taking life and not doing harm to others as a way to purify oneself. It believes that each individual is free and totally responsible for her actions and must bear the consequences of those actions. Nobody can intervene or alter these consequences. Jainism has no place for the divine will or the idea of curse or boon by higher souls. Each individual has to decide for oneself whether to follow the path which leads to accumulation of karmas and bondage or the one that leads to purification and liberation.

Buddhism, however, denies the existence of a substantive permanent soul (*anātmavāda/ anatta*). In keeping with its notion of dependent origination, it analyses a person as a continuous series of psycho-physical elements (*skandhas*) in which each momentary stage in the series causally gives rise to another and so on. At the time of death one series comes to an end but it causally gives rise to another. This accounts for rebirth and the karmic process is implemented in successive rebirths. The process of rebirths comes to an end only after an individual attains liberation. The denial of a permanent soul in Buddhism is a corollary of its theory of momentariness (*kṣaṇabhaṅgavāda*), which maintains that things are impermanent. What we commonly regard as one thing is a flux of momentary states. Thus, Buddhist view denies that a person as a subject remains unitary and identical throughout one's life. A person is a series of impermanent elements/ stages. The similarity of perspective between the Buddhist view of self and the serial view of self-supported by modern Western empiricists like Hume and others is striking, though the two differ significantly with respect to details. While Buddhism denies the existence of unitary and permanent souls, it accepts rebirth. An individual is morally responsible for her actions and is reborn in accordance with the consequences of those actions. From the ultimate perspective only a flow of impermanent elements exists but from the perspective of conventional truth persons exist. The conflict between these two perspectives is not resolved satisfactorily. Thus, strictly speaking, actions cannot be ascribed to agents in Buddhism. Yet it accepts both the karma theory and the theory of rebirth.

The Buddhist theory faces serious difficulties in explaining mental phenomena like memory and recognition. It maintains that each momentary state leaves its mark behind and the subsequent state is informed by it. However, this explanation raises more questions than gives answers. A denial of a unitary subject of experiences is extremely problematic and makes it very difficult to explain the features of our mental life revealed in our introspective experiences. It is difficult to understand how rebirth can be explained on this view. The issue of moral responsibility of persons for their actions also becomes highly problematic, since the Buddhist view seems to imply denial of personal identity in a strict sense. (I will have more to say on this issue later). Given the absence of a unitary, permanent subject, agency is either to be ascribed to each momentary state in the series that constitutes a self or to the series as a whole. Both the views are open to serious difficulties. These difficulties and Buddhist responses to them have been a matter of detailed debates in the Indian philosophical tradition. I do not propose to outline these debates here. However, it would suffice to mention that the Buddhist view is open to additional difficulties in the context of the theory of karma and rebirth because of its denial of a permanent soul.

It would be pertinent to recapitulate some important points that emerge from the above discussion. It is the embodied person who performs actions and is the agent. While the actions in most cases cannot be performed without the body, the dualistic perspective ascribes desires, motives and intentions to do something to the conscious soul. Therefore, the soul seems to be the real agent, though it performs actions through the body with which it is associated. The moral responsibility for actions is also believed to rest with the soul since the body gets destroyed at the time of death and what remains common between the agent now and the agent after rebirth is the soul and the karmic residue. It may be said that the soul is the agent and like a pilot drives the body to do something. This seems to be applicable in case of the standpoints of *Nyāya*, Ramanuj and Jainism, despite their diverse metaphysical systems. Rebirth and karmic responsibility is accounted for on the basis of the continued existence of a unitary soul.

Sāṁkhya accepts the existence of conscious souls but holds that in its essential nature the self is neither an agent nor a subject of experiences. However, as argued earlier, as far as the theory of karma is concerned, the empirical self or the embodied individual alone is primarily relevant. It is not plausible to ascribe agency to the material body and, therefore, it has to be ascribed to the self. It is a further matter that the ascription of agency is a result of ignorance on the part of the self. It is not possible to give a plausible account of an individual's moral responsibility for actions across rebirths without accepting that the soul is an agent and it performs actions and experiences their consequences as an embodied being in successive births. Shankar also maintains that from the ultimate point of view neither agency nor multiple souls are real. However, it seems karmic causality belongs to the empirical level and at that level agency is to be ascribed to the conscious individual soul. In case of Buddhism, souls cannot be regarded as agents since it denies the existence of permanent souls. It is not clear how agency, moral responsibility for actions and rebirth are to be explained in this perspective in a cogent manner.

We find that both the classical Indian philosophy and modern Western philosophy generally assign lesser importance to the body of a person than the soul or the conscious principle in the context of personhood and agency. The dualistic perspective on the concept of a person takes the soul as the seat of consciousness and the body as an important adjunct or instrument but not indispensable for the existence or the identity of a person. This picture finds favour with most of the major religions of the world because it allows for the possibility of survival after death of a person and disembodied existence of the soul. We do find some conceptions of a person, which give adequate importance to the body but the dualistic picture remains the dominant one. It is undeniable that our paradigm of a human person is an embodied being with developed consciousness, rationality and a moral sense. It also seems undeniable that agency of individuals in large majority of cases cannot be explained without bringing in the body of the agent. However, while a person's body is regarded as relevant, perhaps even necessary, it is generally not taken as essential to being a person or the sense one has of oneself. A classic expression of this attitude is found in the saying in *Bhagvad Gītā* that a body is like a set of worn out clothes, which one discards at the time of death and acquires a new one.(I will have more to say on this issue later when I discuss the issue of personal identity). However, this undervaluing of the body does not seem correct. A person's self-awareness at any point of time does include awareness of one's physical features as much as one's mental states, so also one's awareness of one's identity over time. Imaginary thought experiments or mythological stories of change of body where a person's soul is said to enter the body of some animal or another human being and continues to perform its thinking in much the same way as earlier, are highly problematic. Imagine a male's soul to enter into a female body or a good looking person's soul to enter into an ugly body or a wrestler's soul to enter the body of a weak sickly person and it becomes clear that the supposition of a change of body is extremely complicated and far from understandable or tenable. Discussions of change of body in Sanskrit literature show awareness of such difficulties.

The above discussion shows that it is problematic to regard a person as essentially a soul. Being embodied is an important aspect of being a person. It seems that the perspective that Strawson's dual aspect theory presents is closest to the concept of a person as reflected in ordinary language. However, it has significant consequences for the possibility of a person's survival after death. The karma theory maintains that an agent's moral responsibility for the actions performed in one life continues through successive lives of that person. For this to be plausible, it is necessary to define the agent as essentially a soul. If we include embodiment in the definition of a person, we cannot admit disembodied existence of a person; even if a soul is supposed to continue to exist in a disembodied state after the destruction of the body, it cannot be regarded as a person in a full-fledged sense of the word. Moreover, identity of the body becomes an important consideration in the context of identity of persons. It seems that in order to account for individuals' karmic responsibility across several births, it becomes important to regard individual souls as the locus of agency and moral responsibility. The difficulties in the Buddhist account of rebirth and personal identity without accepting a permanent soul seem to support the above contention.

ACTION (KARMA)

Persons perform actions of various kinds. The actions that are relevant here are those which fall within the purview of moral evaluation, to which moral terms 'right' and 'wrong' can be ascribed. Actions are distinguished from events, which happen because of natural causes. Actions do not just happen but are deliberate and are prompted by desires or decisions of human beings. Intention is essential to defining an action. In a weak sense, bodily activities like breathing, sneezing, blinking the eyes, etc., are also bodily actions but these are not actions in the full-fledged sense of the term. Such activities are not within the control of a person and the person cannot choose to do or not to do these. An action is prompted by the desire or motivation of the agent and is a goal directed activity. It is performed by a self-conscious agent to fulfil some purpose. It is this element of intentionality and purposiveness that distinguishes an action from something that just happens. For example, if a person suddenly trips while walking because of some obstruction on the road, it is not an intentional action, but if a person deliberately trips, it is an action. The bodily movements in accidental tripping and deliberate tripping are the same; it is the presence of intention, which makes all the difference. Actions cannot be reduced to bodily movements, since the same bodily movement can be part of different actions. Raising one's hand can be for greeting another person, for hitting another person, or for drawing attention to oneself. Actions are goal directed activities but it is possible that an action may end up achieving something different from the intended goal or may achieve something else besides the intended goal. Each of us performs various actions daily and they fulfil different needs and purposes in our lives. Generally speaking, intentional actions performed by an agent are subject to moral evaluation. An action, which is an appropriate object of moral evaluation, makes its agent entitled to approbation or blame, reward or punishment. A paradigmatic example of a morally relevant action is one performed by an agent intentionally to fulfil a certain purpose. The concepts of intention and goal-directed activity give rise to several philosophical issues which are not pertinent here.

The reasons behind the performance of an action explain it. One's intentions give us the reasons behind one's actions. Reasons are to be distinguished from causes of an action. A causal connection between 'x' and 'y' requires a regular connection between the two, 'x' precedes 'y' and 'y' follows 'x'. In a way such a general connection can be found between a person's intentions and her actions. An action of a person is preceded by the intention to do so and a person would normally try to execute her intentions. We find that people having similar intentions are likely to perform similar actions. However, we need to take note of the possibility that a person may intend to do something but may not do so and the expected action therefore may not follow the relevant intention. It is also possible that the intended goal may not be achieved by the action prompted by it. Intention to do 'x' on the part of an agent is thus a necessary condition of her performing that action but not its sufficient condition. It is important to recognize that an explanation in terms of reasons behind an action is logically different from a usual causal explanation. Reasons behind actions usually mention purposes and these purposes can be judged as good or bad. We are morally responsible and accountable for our intentional actions. There is general agreement among philosophers that intentional actions alone are morally relevant and can be judged as right or wrong. However, some intentional actions are not appropriate objects of moral evaluation, for example, actions relating to daily ablutions, personal hygiene like bathing, eating a meal, etc.

We find examples in Indian mythology, which are deeply problematic from the point of view of ascription of moral responsibility to concerned agents. Let us consider a few such examples. It is said that Shakuntala was one day so absorbed in the thoughts of king Dushyant that she did not notice the arrival of sage Durvasa. The sage got very annoyed at her lack of courtesy and placed a curse on her. As a result, she had to undergo a lot of humiliation and suffering later on. Ahalya was seduced by Indra, who came in the disguise of her husband, the sage Gautama. According to one version, Ahalya had no intention of being unfaithful to her husband but was duped by Indra's appearance. Yet Gautama blamed her for sexual transgression and turned her into a stone. In Shakuntala's case her omission to notice the sage was unintentional. In Ahalya's case her action was intentional but she was duped. It is open to question whether the punishment meted out to them can be said to be justified. We also find examples where the intention of an agent was good but it had unintended and unforeseen bad consequences. King Dasharath, while on a hunting trip, shot an arrow from a distance to kill, what he thought was a deer drinking water from the river, but it hit the old father of Shravan Kumar. As a result, Dasharath was placed under a curse to bear separation from his son. Complexities of the kind mentioned above are very important from the point of view of moral evaluation of actions and judgements of appropriate reward or punishment for them. I will have more to say on this issue later. It would suffice to say here that in general only intentional actions are morally relevant and an agent bears the moral responsibility for the intention behind an action and the action resulting from that intention.

However, in the context of moral responsibility not only acts of commission but acts of omission are also relevant. Not doing something, which is one's duty or is morally obligatory makes one entitled to blame and sometimes even punishment. For example, it is the responsibility of parents to look after their young children to the best of their ability and failing to do so will bring not only criticism but very often legal punishment also. Not keeping one's promise is morally undesirable and liable for punishment. But it is not the case that if doing something is good, not doing it is necessarily bad. Donating money for charity is good but not doing so need not constitute a wrong action. An act of omission also needs to be a result of the intention of an agent in order to be morally relevant. While both the acts of commission and acts of omission are morally relevant, I will generally be focussing on the former in my discussion of karmic justice for the sake of simplicity.

We find differences among various schools of Indian philosophy on the issue of moral relevance of actions and their implications for karmic causality. Metaphysical issues like whether karma is material or not are not significant here and, therefore, it is not important to touch upon them. A good way to clarify the conception of action would be to clarify the ways in which actions have been classified by philosophical systems. A distinction is generally made between mental, vocal and bodily actions. Calculating mentally, planning, constructing arguments are examples of intentional mental actions, giving a speech, telling a lie, abusing or praising someone constitute vocal actions and hitting, killing, distributing food or money to others, etc., are bodily actions. Early *Upaniṣads* distinguish between good actions (*śubha karma*), which bring good results and bad ones (*aśubha karma*), which bring bad results. *Vedic* thought gives prominence to sacrificial rituals (*yajña karma*) and these, if performed correctly, are supposed to necessarily bring desired results. *Purva-Mīmāṁsā* classifies actions in four categories-obligatory (*nitya*), which must be performed, actions for special occasions (*naimittika*), optional actions, which may or may not be performed (*kāmya*), and prohibited actions (*niṣiddha*). Performance of obligatory actions does not bring any merit but their non-performance brings bad results. Prohibited actions obviously are immoral and their performance leads to bad results. In case of actions aimed at fulfilling some desired goals, the moral value of the action will be dependent on factors like the moral value of the goal in question. Thus, we find that, generally speaking, 'karma' covers both intentional actions in general and religious and ritualistic actions. *Purva-mīmāṁsā* emphasizes performance of actions in accordance with *vedic* injunctions.

Sāṁkhya and *Yoga* hold broadly similar views regarding actions. Yuvraj Krishan elaborates that *Sāṁkhya* classifies actions on three grounds.[19] Firstly, on the basis of the bodily mechanism for performance of actions, a distinction is made between mental actions (*manas karma*) and external actions (*bāhya karma*), which include actions of speech (*vācana*) and of body (*śarira*). Secondly, on the basis of the time for ripening of actions, a distinction is made between karma, which are bound to fructify (*niyata vipāka*) and those whose maturation and fructification in future is uncertain (*aniyata vipāka*); it remains possible that the latter may not give rise to consequences. Veda Vyāsa, in his commentary on *Yoga Sūtra*, further divides the former class of actions in two categories, those which will generate consequences in the present life of the agent (*dṛṣṭa janma vedanīya*) and those which will definitely bring their consequences at some time in future (*adṛṣṭa janma vedanīya*), though the time remains uncertain. The third criterion for classification of actions is their moral quality and distinguishes between good and righteous actions (*dharma)*, and evil, wrong actions (*adharma*). Veda Vyāsa classifies actions as black or evil (*kṛṣṇa*), white or pure (*śukla*), good and bad (*śukla kṛṣṇa*) and neither good nor bad (*aśukla akṛṣṇa*). The last are morally irrelevant or non-moral. All actions for *Sāṁkhya* are a result of ignorance (*avidyā*), i.e., the inability of the self to distinguish itself from the material principle. It becomes problematic in this system to explain why actions take place and who the agent is. In the ultimate analysis agency, actions and experiencing of their results are to be ascribed to the unconscious material principle. However, as already mentioned earlier, agency in its primary sense can only be ascribed to a conscious being and not to a material entity. The retributive justice, which is an essential part of the karma theory, also makes sense only in the context of conscious rational agents.

The Bhagvad Gītā introduces the important concept of 'disinterested action' (*anāsakta karma*), which is central to its conception of *Karma-yoga.* Yuvraj Krishan explains that it recognizes three kinds of actions, detached or enlightened actions (*sāttvika karma*), actions born of desire or passion (*rājasika karma*) and actions born of ignorance (*tāmasika karma*). The first are pure (*nirmala*), free from deficiency (*anamya*), and possess the light of knowledge (*prakāśa*) and produce happiness (*sukha*). The second kind of actions lead to people getting attached to worldly activities. The third are born of indolence and lack of discrimination (*pramāda*). All the three kinds of action are binding. The similarities between the *Sāṁkhya* standpoint and the view of *Gītā* are evident. *Gītā* also believes that all actions belong to the material principle (*Prakṛti*) and are binding. Actions have their appropriate consequences. However, detached actions, where the agent performs one's duty without attachment to its consequences, do not bring results.[20] *Gītā* defines one's duty in terms of *varṇaśrama dharma*. Human beings cannot give up actions but if they perform their duties ordained by the sacred texts in a detached manner, they can get rid of the binding force of actions. *Gītā* teaches that one has a right to action but the action should not be prompted by the expected fruit of one's actions (*karmaṇye-vādhikāraste mā phaleṣu kadācana, B.G. 2.47*). Such detached action constitutes the path of actions (*karma-yoga*), which alongside the path of knowledge (*jñana-yoga*) and the path of devotion (*bhakti-yoga*) enables one to get liberation. Actions, according to *Gīta,* are by their very nature binding, but it shows a way by which the binding nature of actions can be overcome and their performance can become a path to liberation.

Shankar's *Advaita Vedāntā* advocates a monism, which states that *Brahman* alone is ultimately real and the plurality in the world belongs to the domain of empirical or conditional reality. In the ultimate sense then the empirical individual self as an agent and all its actions also belong to this domain. Ignorance (*avidyā*) is at the root of the perception of the individual self as distinct from the ultimate reality and as an agent. The concept of action is only applicable when there is plurality of agents and their motives. The conception of levels of reality and the denial of plurality from the ultimate point of view introduce problematic metaphysical dimensions in the theory of karma. For example, the plurality of empirical agents is not real from the ultimate point of view and actions which presuppose plurality in the world also have only conditional reality. The significance of actions, therefore, gets diminished. As far as the empirical world is concerned, karmic causality is operative and binding. But actions are not the means to liberation, only knowledge is. One point to be noted is that Shankar takes desire (*kāma*) to be the cause of actions. This implies that the actions under consideration are intentional ones.

The metaphysics of both *Sāṁkhya* and *Advait Vedānta* introduce complexities with regard to their understanding of the concepts of agent and actions and are open to various difficulties. However, these need not concern us here. Yuvraj Krishan points out that Ramanuj in his *Viśiṣṭādvaita* equates actions with evil; their influence constitutes bondage. He regards the Supreme Soul to be the source of the moral distinction between good and evil actions. The Supreme Being lays down which actions are good and which are bad and provides individual souls with bodies and sense organs with the help of which they can perform actions. The individual souls choose which actions to perform and have to face their appropriate consequences. Ramanuj is thus concerned with intentional actions of persons. An individual who performs good actions wins the grace of the Ultimate Divine Being or the Lord.[21]

Buddhism and Jainism, specially the latter, provide detailed discussions of the nature and kinds of action. Buddha ascribes the inequality of human beings and their suffering to their past actions. The causative function of actions is regarded as having a moral dimension. According to Buddhism, the cause of actions is craving (*tṛṣṇā*) and actions arising thus give rise to consequences. However, once an agent has achieved suppression of desire (*tṛṣṇā nirodha*), her actions are detached and these do not produce consequences. Buddha also maintains that the roots of actions lie in ignorance (*avidyā, ajñāna*). Buddhism distinguishes three kinds of actions on the basis of the organs through which actions are performed, namely, actions of body (*kāya kamma*), those of speech (*vāci kamma*) and actions of mind (*mano kamma*). Yuvraj Krishan mentions that we also find a classification made on the basis of the quality of actions in *Majjhimanikāya.* Here actions are divided in four categories, dark actions with dark results, bright actions with bright results, actions, which are both dark and bright and produce both bright and dark results and actions, which are neither dark nor bright. A different classification is offered by Harivarman who divides actions into three categories, good (*kuśala)*, bad (*akuśala*) and indeterminate (*avyakṛta*). Good actions give happiness to others while bad ones cause pain to others.[22] Buddha gives primacy to intention for determining the moral quality of actions. 'The Buddha for the first time propounded that moral *karma* is essentially mental in its nature, that *puṇya* (merit) and *pāpa* (demerit) depend on the intent of the doer and not on an act devoid of intent, good or evil.'[23]

Jainism, as mentioned earlier, regards karma as material, which clings to the soul of the agent and defiles its nature. Jainism also classifies actions in three categories, mental (*manas*), physical (*kāyā*) and of speech (*vāca*). Moreover, as Kalghatgi points out, Jainism puts forward an eightfold division of karma, (a) those which obscure right knowledge (*jñānāvaraṇīya*), (b) those which obscure right intuition (*darśanāvaraṇīya*), (c) those which give rise to feelings and emotions, (*vedanīya*), (d) those which delude (*mohanīya*), (e) those which determine the age of the individual (*āyukarma*), (f) those which make up individual existence (*nāmakarma*) and determine the family and social standing (*gotrakarma*) and (g) those which obstruct the energy of the soul and prevent performance of good actions (*antarāya karma*). It may be noted that many categories mentioned above distinguish actions on the basis of their consequences and seem to indicate the residue or potentiality of actions. Each type of karma has sub classes and each kind has a time limit within which it gets exhausted. Jainism also classifies karma as auspicious (*śubha*) and inauspicious (*aśubha*) on the basis of whether it leads to pleasure or suffering.[24]

We find general agreement on the classification of

actions as mental, verbal and bodily and on the twofold classification as good or bad actions. Apart from these broad categories, actions are classified in different ways in various systems of Indian philosophy. A brief outline of these has been given above. It is proposed now to focus on the implications of actions for the quality of life of individuals.

RESIDUE *(KARMĀVAŚEṢA)* AND CONSEQUENCES *(KARMAPHALA)* OF ACTIONS

The theory of karma states that our actions lead to their appropriate consequences for the agent at some point in this life or future lives of the individual. The process through which this is ensured is causal and according to the dominant strict version of the theory, it operates on its own. The actions of an agent leave some potency or residue (*avaśeṣa*), this residue accumulates, and, transmigrates along with the soul and the subtle body (*liṅga śarīra*), matures later at some point of time and then brings about its consequences for the individual in her present or subsequent lives. Different terms are used by philosophical systems to refer to the residue of actions. The theory makes two significant suppositions in this context. One, every action leaves a residue, and two the residue brings about its consequences after maturation (*vipāka*). The latter supposition explains why there may be a time-gap between actions and experience of their consequences by the agent. There is broad agreement that the residue is of three kinds, those which are being accumulated in the present life (*sancīyamāna/āgāmī karma*), those which have been accumulated but have not matured (*sañcita karma*) and those accumulated residue, which have matured (*prārabdha karma*). Thus, some of the accumulated residue of actions may lie in a state of potency and not bring about its consequences in the present or even the next life of the individual but even later. However, the residue, which has matured, is bound to bring about its consequences in the current life of the individual and the individual cannot escape the consequences of these. It is clear that the supposition of rebirth and the above mentioned classification are intimately connected. An agent invariably experiences the consequences of matured residue of one's actions in her current life, irrespective of the moral quality of actions in that life. Therefore, even if a person's actions are predominantly good in her present life, she may still suffer pain and unhappiness due to the matured residue of her past actions and an evil person may get happiness due to such residue of past good actions. The consequences of actions, whose residue has not matured, get cancelled once a person attains liberation and actions performed by the individual thereafter do not accumulate any residue. *Sāṁkhya school* and Shankar maintain that even a person who has attained liberation during life (*jīvanmukta*) continues to live till the consequences of one's matured residue of actions have been exhausted.

Different terms are used by philosophical systems to refer to the residue of actions. *Sāṁkhya* maintains that actions produce merit (*dharma*) and demerit (*adharma*), which form a collection (*karmāśaya)*. After death the individual's soul transmigrates with the subtle body and the collection of the residue of actions and the individual experiences the consequences of those past actions after rebirth. *Yoga* school regards the form of existence (yoni*)*, life-span, (*āyuh*), caste (*jāti*) and happy and painful experiences of a person as consequences of one's past actions. Potter observes that when an individual is reborn:

> "The karmic residues operate within this new body to determine three things: the kind of body it is (its "birth" *[jāti]*, cat or human); the length of its life (*āyus*) under normal circumstances; and the affective tone of experiences (*bhoga*) the person will have, whether his experiences will be pleasurable or painful."[25]

Yoga school also believes that the residue, which does not fructify in the next life of an individual, continues to persist in the form of latent deposits or dispositions (*vāsanā* or *saṃskāra*) and fructifies in subsequent lives of the individual. However, *Yoga* philosophy does admit the possibility that some residue and dispositions can be made ineffective through yogic practices and self-mortification (*tapas*). *Sāṁkhya* and *Yoga* regard the operation of the law of karma to be inexorable such that an individual has to invariably bear the consequences of one's actions. However the possibility that one may be able to burn or exhaust some through yogic practices, etc is allowed.[26]

Purva-Mīmāṃsā refers to the potency left by actions as *apūrva*, something which did not exist earlier. This system, as discussed earlier, emphasizes performance of actions enjoined by Vedas. *Nyāya* uses a different term '*adṛṣṭa*' to refer to the residue of actions, which means something invisible or unseen. The residue resides in the soul of the agent and transmigrates after death and after maturation determines the circumstances at birth and the experiences of happiness or sorrow in the next birth. The nature of the subsequent births of the individual and the quality of experiences in these are thus determined by this subtle causative force. The cycle of birth and rebirth is terminated when the residue of past actions (*adṛṣṭa*) is exhausted. We find a broad agreement among the philosophical systems in India on the point that ordinarily an individual cannot escape the consequences of one's past actions. As mentioned earlier, a few ways of mitigating or exhausting residue of actions are allowed such as meditation, devotion, etc. In *Sāṁkhya* an individual has to invariably bear the consequences of one's past actions.

Shankar maintains that the individual soul transmigrates with the subtle body and the residue of its past actions. According to him, this residue is the cause of the body in the next birth and it determines "the locality, caste, family, shape, length of life, property, pleasure, etc., which a soul has to enjoy ..."[27] He also regards the operation of the law of karma as inexorable and maintains that even when one attains liberation while still alive, one continues to live till the matured residue of past actions is exhausted. Ramanuj maintains that the caste of an individual and the pain or pleasure the individual experiences in life is a consequence of one's past actions. "In short animate and inanimate creation, inequality and suffering therein are the fruits of *karma* of different souls and that these diversities disappear when the *karma* is destroyed."[28]

The brief discussion above shows that, generally speaking, three things are believed to be the consequences of an individual's past actions, (a) the length of an individual's life, (b) the caste and circumstances at birth of an individual and (c) happiness and pain or sorrow one experiences in life. Some other factors are also categorized as consequences of actions; for example, there seems to be a broad agreement among thinkers that the family one is born into and one's capabilities at birth are consequences of one's past actions. Good actions are believed to lead to birth in a higher caste, a longer life-span and happiness during the life. Bad actions, on the other hand, are believed to lead to birth in a lower caste, a shorter life and unhappiness or suffering. It is clear that the quality of life of an individual is substantially determined by the potency or residue of past actions. Most of the time the connections between specific actions and specific consequences are not laid out in expositions of the karma theory, only a general connection between good actions and good consequences and bad actions and bad consequences is stated. *Vedic* sacrificial actions, however, do mention specific consequences of each sacrifice and discussions in *Dharmaśāstras* sometimes mention specific connections between certain kinds of action and certain kinds of result. For example, Manu mentions several specific connections between actions and their future consequences. He says that thinking of undesirable things and adhering to false doctrines lead to rebirth in a low caste, telling lies and abusing others leads to rebirth as a bird or beast and committing adultery with another person's wife leads to rebirth as something inanimate etc.[29]

It is clear that there is wide agreement among philosophical systems on the point that the individual's caste, length of life and happiness or suffering experienced during life constitute consequences of past actions. Linking one's caste to past actions shows the powerful grip of the caste system on Indian thinking. The general assumption is that birth in a higher caste and well-placed family, a longer life, and happy experiences are good consequences and birth in a lower caste, a shorter life and experience of pain or suffering are bad consequences. However, this supposition is debatable. While one would find a general agreement that happiness is good and suffering bad, the other two assumptions about caste and length of life are open to question. Is a longer life afflicted with disease or deprivation or unhappiness better than a shorter but healthier and happier life? Similarly, birth in a higher caste by itself is not a guarantee of longevity or greater success and happiness in life. It cannot be assumed that birth in a higher caste or a longer life necessarily leads to greater happiness in life. The point is that many different factors can be said to be determinants of a good life and people may have different opinions about the relative importance of these factors. Most discussions of karma single out a greater share of happiness in one's life as the most important factor in the context of good consequences. This is problematic. For example, a life consisting of great achievement or accomplishment, though not very happy on the whole may be regarded by some as more valuable than a happier but less accomplished life. Similarly, a person born in a lower caste may lead a more worthwhile life than one born in a higher caste. In other words, the assumption that there would always be a positive correlation among three factors, birth in a higher caste, longevity and happiness, is debatable. Our experience tells us that many things like good health, longevity, good family, accomplishments and wealth, knowledge and power etc are sources of happiness for people in life, they value and prioritize these differently and the more of the valued ones individuals possess, greater the chances of their being happy.

It is important to note in this context that the karma theory stipulates that actions bring consequences for the agents of those actions alone. As mentioned earlier, the possibility that one person may bear the consequence of an action performed by another person is not admitted in the theory because this idea is regarded as morally problematic. The karma theory emphasizes that each individual gets the consequences of only those actions which the individual himself has performed. Since the consequence of an action is viewed as a morally appropriate reward or punishment for the action in question deserved by the agent, it follows that the consequences of actions performed by other people cannot be said to be morally deserved by the agent. Clearly the possibility of an individual's actions affecting other persons is not being acknowledged here. Our experience, however, shows that our actions can have beneficial or harmful consequences for others. This aspect of our agency constitutes a very problematic issue for the theory of karma.

Since the theory does not accept that the actions of one person can have consequences for others, it is often criticized for making people oblivious of their social responsibility. Some of our important social obligations like not stealing from others, not telling a lie, not killing others, helping others, etc. are included in the list of duties prescribed for people and are taken care of by the exhortation that we should follow the right path. The theory says clearly that performance of bad actions would bring bad consequences for the individual and this may be a way to discourage people from doing what is harmful for others and encouraging them to do what is beneficial for others. However, it remains true that the karma theory only focuses on consequences of one's actions for oneself and not for others. It is an integral part of the karma theory that the basic quality of an individual's life is impacted by one's own past actions alone and that implies that one cannot put the onus for one's suffering or happiness on others; one has to take total responsibility for it. This aspect of the theory is open to serious difficulties. I will have more to say on this issue in subsequent chapters.

The moral dimension of the theory consists in its assertion that the consequences of one's past actions are deserved by the agent in the light of the moral quality of those actions. Thus one's caste, family circumstances, length of life and share of happiness and suffering are regarded as just rewards or punishments for one's past actions. However, this claim becomes seriously problematic given the supposition that karmic causality functions independently like a law to ensure that everyone necessarily gets what one deserves.

Consequences of an action cannot be said to be deserved ones without referring to a process of moral evaluation of the action in question. It is problematic, therefore, to treat the law of karma as a causal law and also claim that the causal consequence of an action is a deserved reward or punishment of some past action of the agent in question. This and other related issues will be taken up in greater detail later while discussing the causal character of the law in chapter three. It must be noted however, that both the causal and the moral dimension of the theory are its integral aspects. A consequence of an action here is not merely the causal effect of that action but also the morally deserved reward or punishment for that action.

INTERNAL DIVERSITY OF THE KARMA THEORY

It is important to mention here that the Indian tradition exhibits diverse views on karma and the modalities of the karmic process and we find that some important claims made by the strict version of the theory discussed above are qualified in significant ways. As discussed earlier, strict formulations of the theory maintain that the karmic process unfolds on its own. Some theistic versions of the theory, however, take the role of the ultimate divine reality as indispensable to the unfolding of the karmic causality and differ from the strict version supported by modern writers like Radhakrishnan and others. *Nyāya and Vaiśeṣika,* for example, maintain that the residue of actions (*adṛṣṭa*) is unintelligent and cannot lead to its maturation and consequences on its own. It is God, an intelligent being, who brings about the maturation of the residue of actions and confers rewards or punishments on the individual agent in accordance with the nature of this residue. Thus God here is regarded as the administrator of the karmic process. Shankar shares the view that unintelligent principles like matter and karma cannot work on their own to ensure that an individual gets appropriate consequences of one's actions. According to him, *Brahman* is the catalyst for deeds of each individual to culminate in appropriate good and bad results. Actions, therefore, have results via *Brahman*.[30] Ramanuj supports a theistic version of the theory. He maintains that the Supreme Self, the Lord, determines which actions are good or bad. The Lord confers good or bad consequences on the individuals in accordance with the quality of their actions. In his formulation the Lord is the divine judge of the moral quality of actions performed by individuals and also ensures that individuals are appropriately rewarded or punished.

> "The Lord, then recognising him who performs good actions as one who obeys His commands, blesses him with piety, riches, worldly pleasures, and final release; while him who transgresses his commands he causes to experience the opposites of all these."[31]

As discussed earlier, the dominant strict version of the karma theory claims that every individual has to necessarily bear the consequences of past actions. However, we find difference of opinion on the issue whether an individual can escape the consequences of actions. *Purāṇas* admit that a person can attain release from the consequences of one's actions through various means like meditation, renunciation, glorification of shrines and pilgrimage to holy places. These enable individuals to overcome or escape bad consequences of their past actions. *Yoga* school, as mentioned earlier, also admits the possibility that an agent can exhaust the residue of past actions through performance of self-mortification (*tapas*) and yogic practices.[32] Bhakti tradition in general accepts that a devotee may be able to purge one's sins by winning the grace of God through devotion. Once a devotee dedicates his actions to God, surrenders himself totally to the Supreme Divine Being, subsequent actions performed by the devotee are neither good nor bad and do not lead to further consequences. Jainism, an atheistic philosophy, also allows the possibility of partial exhaustion of past actions. It maintains that austerities enable an agent to purge residue of past actions.[33] Bhakti tradition puts emphasis on devotion to God and accepts that a devotee may be able to avoid the bad consequences of one's past actions and win beneficial results through divine intervention. We find many examples in Bhakti literature and mythology in which God intervenes to save a devotee from imminent danger or suffering caused by the devotee's bad past actions. We also find concepts of boon (*varadāna*) and curse (*śrāpa*) in mythology. These show that an agent may get a reward as a result of a boon granted by a deity or a sage or suffer due to a curse given by a deity or a seer. In many such stories the boon is given to a person by a deity after a long and hard process of tapas by the devotee or because of the intensity of the person's devotion to the deity. Similarly, a curse is placed on a person because of some wrongdoing by the person. In some stories a person is punished for not performing a required devotional ritual in part or as a whole. Such examples are not consistent with the assertion that an individual gets a deserved consequence of one's own actions alone as a result of independent functioning of karmic causality. These stories claim that a true devotee can win God's grace and be able to mitigate or avoid the bad consequences of one's past actions and also win favours, which may not be consistent with the moral value of the devotee's past actions.

It was mentioned earlier that all intentional actions are not always supposed to give rise to karmic residue. *Purva-Mīmāṁsā* believes that performance of obligatory actions does not give rise to merit but their non-performance gives rise to demerit. *Bhagvad Gītā* states that performance of unattached action does not accrue consequences for the agent. All philosophical systems believe that the actions of a liberated person do not give rise to any consequences for that person and are not binding. These are exceptions to the claim that our intentional actions always give rise to inescapable consequences. So long as a person is not liberated, however, an individual's actions are said to invariably lead to consequences for that individual. Moreover, we also find that exceptions are allowed to the claim that a person necessarily faces the consequences of one's own actions alone. We can find the concept of transfer of merit in *vedic* literature and *Purāṇas*. Possibility of transfer of merit from husband to wife and vice versa is accepted. Such transfer "indicates the process by which one living creature willingly or accidentally gives to another a non-physical quality of his own, such as a virtue, credit for a religious achievement, a talent or a power-often in exchange for a negative quality given by the recipient."[34] The concept of *śrāddha* seems to enshrine a belief in transfer of merit from children to parents and ancestors. Flaherty maintains that the institution of *prasāda* in later Hinduism also reflects a belief in transfer of merit. A gift of food is made to a deity, through which the devotion of the devotee is transferred to the deity and then through the mediation of the priest this gift is returned to the devotee with added merit upon it because it transfers the deity's grace to the devotee.[35] Sometimes it is suggested in the *Purāṇas* that the birth of a child is affected by the actions of the parents.[36] Dayakrishna has argued that the notion of sacrifice (*yajña*) shows a contradiction in the doctrine of karṁa. It implies transfer of merit; the merit resulting from performance of an action accrues to a person other than the one who performs it. A sacrifice is a collective action done by a group of persons (*Ṛtviks*) for someone (*yajamāna*) who has engaged them for performing that action by paying the prescribed fee. However, the action is not regarded as the action of that group of priests and the fruit of this action does not accrue to these persons. It accrues to the person who has paid the fee. Thus, the fruit of the action does not accrue to those who actually perform the action, but to the person who has paid them to do so. This implies that one can reap the fruit of an action performed by someone else, a possibility not allowed by the karma theory.[37]

Some discussions of the karma theory do not explain the quality of life of individuals through consequences of their own actions alone but through multiple causes. The strict version of the theory maintains that an individual's circumstances at birth, length of life and quality of experiences are dependent solely upon the consequences of that individual's own actions. However, we find that sometimes other factors like fate (*daiva*) or time (*kāla*) are also accepted as causes of what one has to go through in life. These sometimes appear to be agencies different from residue of past actions or karma. The question whether fate can be overcome by an individual's efforts (*puraṣakāra or puruṣārtha*) is also discussed in the tradition. Flaherty quotes many examples from pauranic *texts* to show that sometimes it is argued that God controls fate, while sometimes gods themselves are said to be controlled by fate. Many texts hold that individuals cannot fight against the inexorable forces of fate and God, however, some argue that fate can be reversed by actions.[38] Similarly the issue whether fate or destiny is more powerful or human effort, is debated in the *Mahābhārata*. We find that sometimes destiny is regarded as a force different from consequences of past actions and the interplay of the two causative factors is debated. Sometimes it is argued that destiny cannot achieve anything without the assistance of human effort and at others that destiny is shaped by human effort.[39] We also find arguments in the Epic in which it is claimed that an individual's ultimate destiny and what happens in one's life are predetermined by a divine being. In a dialogue between Draupadī and Yudhishthir, Draupadī argues that human beings are subject to the will of God who ordains all the sorrow and happiness of creatures in accordance with their karma, even before they are born. She compares God to a puppeteer who manipulates human beings like puppets. Yudhishthir, however defends God and dharma and argues that how good or bad consequences of actions reach fruition and unfold is a mystery.[40]

Clearly we can find varied opinions in the Epic on the issue how far human actions shape an individual's life and how far it is dependent upon other agencies. The Epic sometimes regards God alone as responsible for whatever happens in the world, but sometimes fate, time or *Prakṛti* are also said to be responsible for what happens in the world. Bruce Long, in his discussion of karma and rebirth in the *Mahābhārata,* states that the Epic recognizes several different causal factors as determinants of human destinies in different parts of the Epic. These are providential acts of God (*divya-kriyā*), divine ordinances (*divya-vidhi*), divine power or fate proper (*daiva, diṣṭa, niyati, bhāgya*), time (kāla), death (*mṛtyu, kṛtāntā, antaka*), nature (*prakṛti*) and human action (*karma*).[41] He adds,

> "The fact that various spokesmen in the MBH designate first one then another factor as the cause of events would seem to indicate that they did not feel that the total complexity of forces at work in the world could be accounted for by reference to a single principle or agent. There is a variety of causal elements: human action, divine influence, hereditary traits, extenuating circumstances, and even potent actions of extraordinary personages such as sages, seers, magicians and soothsayers."[42]

If fate and time are regarded as different from karmic causality, then it follows that an individual's lot in life is dependent upon several factors and there are multiple causes of happiness or suffering a person experiences in life. This would also imply that the quality of life of an individual is dependent upon factors that are separate from and independent of that individual's past or present actions. However, we also find observations which suggest that other causal agencies like fate, time, etc. are ultimately identical with karma. The story of Gautamī's son in the Epic illustrates this point. Gautami's son died as a result of a snake bite. When Gautami blamed the snake for the death of her son, he passed on the responsibility to another agency. In this way death, time and other causative factors are mentioned one by one and each negates his own culpability and passes on the moral responsibility for this action to some other factor. Finaly Gautami comes to the conclusion that the son's own actions were ultimately the cause of his death.[43]

It was mentioned above how Draupadī says that God decides the lot of human beings in accordance with their actions. He brings about the maturation of the residue of people's actions and distributes the fruits according to the law of karma. Yuvraj Krishan quotes Draupadi's statement, along with some other comments, to support the view that the Epic rejects the idea of multiple causes of human condition and the multiple causes mentioned at various places in the Epic are identified with karma.[44] The dominant interpretation of the Epic holds that causes like time and fate, which appear to be different from the impact of past actions, are actually reducible to or identified with karma.

It is beyond the purview of this work to examine at length whether the Indian tradition accepts multiple causes of human condition or explains it solely in terms of individuals' past actions. The brief discussion above shows that we find a variety of views on the issue of karma including the view that the quality of life of a person is dependent upon many causes apart from one's own actions. The debates on the role of fate, time, God and self-effort express an acknowledgement that the life of a person is affected by factors that are different from the person's own actions and beyond her control. However, there is also a strong tendency in the tradition to reduce this multiplicity to one force alone, namely past actions and their consequences. Commenting on classical and later traditions of Indian philosophy and religion, Halbfass notes that apart from materialists and fatalists, hardly any thinkers in the Indian tradition have questioned the basic tenets of the karma theory. He observes;

> "The doctrine of karma and *saṃsāra* is projected into the most ancient texts, including the Vedic hymns; it is always taken as their indispensable background and presupposition. Concept and theories which were initially used independently of and without reference to the karma theory, and which, in its earlier phases, appear side by side with it and as its possible rivals, are reinterpreted in the light of the karma theory, are accommodated to or identified with it. *Daiva, niyati* and so forth, no longer represent an impersonal cosmic "fate", but are constituted by one's own past actions; *kāla,* "time", is no longer seen as an independent ordaining principle, but becomes a function of karma. Karma explains the causes of our present fate by means of what has been regarded as "one underlying fundamental intuition."[45]

We find that all discussions of karma do not subscribe to exactly similar claims, rather some of the important claims of the strict version of the theory are sometimes modified within the tradition. Thus human action alone is not always taken to be the sole causative force determining the quality of people's lives. The strict version of the theory of karma, however, maintains that family, caste, longevity and all the happiness or suffering an individual gets in life are determined solely by the residue of past actions of that individual. Possibility of transfer of merit, supposition of a divine being executing or directing the operation of karmic causality, and admission of ways of mitigating or avoiding bad consequences of past actions do not conform to the conception of an independently functioning karmic process delivering karmic justice flawlessly. It is important to keep such variations in mind while discussing the karma theory. Most of the modern critical discussions of the theory, however, focus on its strict version alone. The strict version has come to be seen as the dominant view in the Indian tradition and is regarded as a distinctive feature of classical Indian philosophy and the Hindu view of life.

Notes and References

1. In Indian philosophical systems mind (manas) is regarded as distinct from the soul (ātman). In modern Western philosophy, however, mind and soul are regarded as identical and refer to the same unitary conscious substance or subject.

2. Rene Descartes, *Meditations on First Philosophy*, E.S. Haldane and G.T.R. Ross, ed., *The Philosophical Works of Descartes*, Cambridge Univ. Press, Cambridge, 1911

3. David Hume, *A Treatise of Human Nature*, A. D. Lindsay, ed., J. E. M. Dent and sons Ltd., London, 1956
4. P.F. Strawson, *Individuals*, Methuen, London, 1959, ch. 3.
5. ibid p.102
6. Antony Flew, 'Can a Man Witness his own Funeral?', W.T. Blackstone, ed., *Meaning and Existence*, Holt, Rinehart and Winston, New York, 1971, pp.614-15
7. Bernard Williams, *Problems of the Self*, Cambridge University Press, Canbridge,1973
8. Vibha Chaturvedi, 'Indeterminateness of the Concept of a Person', *Indian Philosophical Quarterly*, Vol. XIX, No.2, April 1992, pp.115-124
9. John Locke, *An Essay Concerning Human Understanding*, A.C. Fraser, ed., Clarendon Press, Oxford, 1984, vol.1, Book II, chapter XXVIII, p. 448
10. Aristotle, *Politics*, Carnes Lord (tr.), Chicago University Press, Chicago, 1984
11. M. Hiriyanna, *Essentials of Indian Philosophy*, Unwin Paperbacks, London, 1978, pp .90-91
12. Matthew R. Dasti, 'Nyāya's Self as Agent and Knower', Matthew R. Dasti and Edwin F. Bryant, (eds), *Free Will, Agency and Selfhood in Indian Philosophy*, Oxford University Press, Oxford, New York, 2014, p.120
13. Ibid, p. 134
14. Edwin F. Bryant, 'Agency in Sāṃkhya and Yoga-The Unchangeability of the Eternal', Dasti and Bryant (eds), *Free Will, Agency and Selfhood in Indian Philosophy*, p.22
15. K.N. Upadhyaya, 'Karma in Hindu Thought-II: The *Bhagavad Gitā*', Rama Rao Pappu (ed.) *Dimensions of Karma*, Chanakya Publications, Delhi, 1987, p. 47
16. Martin Ganeri, 'Free Will, Agency, and Selfhood in Rāmānuja', Dasti and Bryant (eds), *Free Will, Agency and Selfhood in Indian Philosophy*, pp. 240-41
17. Ibid, p. 253

18. T.G. Kalghatgi, 'Karma in Jain Thought', Rama Rao Pappu (ed.) *The Dimensions of Karma,* pp. 95-97. Also, Hiryanna, *Essentials of Indian Philosophy,* George Allen and Unwin, Great Britain, 1949, pp.61-62
19. Yuvraj Krishan, *The Doctrine of Karma,* Motilal Banarasidass Publishers Private Limited, Delhi, 1997, chapter 11, pp. 141-142
20. Ibid, pp. 109-111
21. Ibid, pp. 155-156
22. Ibid, pp.59-62
23. Ibid, p. 62
24. T.G. Kalghatgi, 'Karma in Jain Thought', Rama Rao Pappu, (ed.), *The Dimensions of Karma,* p.100, 102
25. Karl H. Potter, 'Karma Theory In Some Indian Philosophical Systems', Wendy Doniger O'Flaherty, (ed.) *Karma And Rebirth In Classical Indian Traditions,* first published by University of California Press, 1980, Indian edition by Motilal Banarasidass, Delhi, Patna, Varanasi, 1983, p. 244
26. Yuvraj Krishan, *The Doctrine of Karma,* p. 146, p.154
27. Ibid, p. 154
28. Ibid, p.156
29. Ludo Rocher, 'Karma And Rebirth In The Dharmasastras' in Flaherty, ed., *Karma And Rebirth In Classical Indian Traditions,* p. 64
30. Francis X Clooney, 'Evil, Divine Omnipotence and Human Freedom: Vedānta's Theology of Karma', *The Journal of Religion,* vol.69, 1989, (530-548), pp. 531-32
31. Yuvraj Krishan, *The Doctrine of Karma,* p.156
32. Ibid, p. 145
33. G. Thibaut, SBE, vol. XXXVIIII, part II, p. 488, quoted by Yuvraj Krishan, *The Doctrine of Karma,* p. 156
34. Wendy Doniger O'Flaherty, 'Karma and Rebirth in the Vedas and Purāṇas', Flaherty (ed.) *Karma and Rebirth in Classical Indian Traditions,* p.3. Flaherty mentions several examples suggesting

transfer of merit from one person to another found in the Vedas and Purāṇas.

35. Ibid p.12

36. Ibid pp 22-23.

37. Daya Krishna, 'Yajña and the Doctrine of Karma', in *Indian Philosophy, A Counter Perspective,* Sri Satguru Publications, Delhi, 2006, ch.9, pp.225-226

38. Flaherty, (ed.) *Karma And Rebirth In Indian Classical Traditions,* pp 25-27

39. Yuvyaj Krishan, op cit pp.103-4

40. The dialogue between Draupadi and Yudhishthira occurs in the 'Vana Parva', part 1, ('Arayanyaka Parva', MBH, 3.31.21-39). V. Sukhantara (tr. and ed.), *The Mahābhārata,* Bhandarkar Oriental Research Institute, Poona, 1933, 1969 J. Bruce Long mentions this dialogue and other passages to show how Fate, Time and God are referred to as causes of human condition. 'The Concepts of Human Action and Rebirth in the Mahābhārata', in Flaherty, (ed.) *Karma And Rebirth In Classical Indian Traditions,* pp.46-47

41. Ibid, p.40

42. Ibid, p.47

43. MBH, 13.1.67, quoted by Yuvraj Krishan, 'Karma in the Epics- the *Ramāyana and* the *Mahābhārata', The Doctrine of Karma,* p. 97. Long also mentions it, op cit, p. 43

44. MBH, 3.33.20. quoted by Yuvraj Krishan, p.104. Krishan discusses the role of individual effort and fate and how multiple causes of human destiny are reduced to karma in the Epic, ch. 8, pp.102-105.

45. Wilhelm Halbfass, 'Karma, *Apūrva* and Natural Causes' Flaherty, (ed.) *Karma And Rebirth In Classical Indian Traditions,* p. 271

Chapter 3

KARMIC JUSTICE AND CAUSALITY

The theory of karma regards the relation between past actions and their morally appropriate consequences as causal. As mentioned earlier, the law of karma is an extension of the causal law to the moral domain. The strict version of the theory holds that karmic causal processes operate by themselves and bring about their consequences without the intervention of a divine being. Exceptions to this supposition can be found within the tradition, especially in those theistic versions in which the divine being is central to the working of karmic causality. However, the dominant interpretation of the theory regards the karmic process to work independently. This chapter would address the question whether it is plausible to hold that the relation between actions and their just rewards or punishments is causal. It would try to clarify the problematic aspects of the idea of karmic causality and its implications for the conception of Nature. I have argued that, given the concept of *dharma* in Hinduism, the idea of a causal connection between an action and its morally appropriate consequence is not tenable. Secondly, the idea of a moral order in Nature implied by the notion of karmic causality is very problematic.[1] Surprisingly the implications of the theory of karma for operation of natural laws have not been given adequate attention in scholarly studies on the theory.[2] It seems that it has generally been taken for granted that karmic justice can be subjected to causal laws without giving rise to serious philosophical difficulties. In my view this optimism is misplaced.

All of us understand the meaning of 'causality' in a way but it is not easy to define it. Philosophers have defined causality in different ways. A detailed comprehensive discussion of the notion of causation or causal connection is not within the purview of the present work. However, an attempt is made to briefly outline how we commonly understand a causal connection. In this context one conception from the Indian tradition and one from modern Western philosophy will be mentioned, which are pretty similar and express a widely accepted view of causal relation. It may be noted that some of the metaphysical debates in Indian philosophy with respect to causation are not directly relevant to the issues of karmic causality. For example, questions like 'what is the relation of the material cause to its effect', 'does the material cause impart an essence to the effect or is it completely external to the cause', 'is the effect a new production or is it present in the cause from before in a potential form' and 'does the material cause actually turn into its effect or only presents an illusory appearance.' These metaphysical debates would not be discussed.

The *Nyāya* school offers a definition of 'cause', which is close to the regular sequence view of causation, widely accepted in modern times. *Nyāya-Vārttikam* defines cause of something as a necessary and sufficient condition of that thing, such that in its presence the effect is produced and in its absence the effect is not produced. (*kāraṇam hi tadbhavati yasmin sati yadbhavati, yasminscasati yanna bhavati).*[3] In a similar vein, *Tarka-Bhāṣā* defines 'cause' as an invariable antecedent, which is necessary for the occurrence of the effect (*yasya kāryātpūrvabhāvo niyatonānyathāsiddhaścatat*).[4] Several other adherents of *Nyāya* school support this definition. Sometimes the condition of spatio-temporal contiguity between the cause and the effect is also added in the definition, which requires that the cause must be an immediate antecedent of the effect.[5]

David Hume provides a definition of 'cause', which comes close to the *Nyāya* conception mentioned above. He argues that a proposition about a causal relation is not analytic and logically necessary; its denial is not self-contradictory. It is an empirical proposition and its truth depends upon verification by experience. It is experience, which tells us that a certain object is causally related with a certain other object. He defines the causal relation as 'constant conjunction' of events of one kind with events of another kind or 'regular sequence' between two kinds of events. Two events 'x' and 'y' are causally connected, if 'x' regularly precedes 'y' and 'y' regularly succeeds 'x', and all events similar to 'x' and 'y' are related in a similar way. It follows that a causal relation is a relation between two kinds or types of events such that one kind invariably succeeds another kind.[6] Several other Western philosophers, especially the empiricists, have defined 'cause' in a similar vein. J. S. Mill, for example, defines cause of a phenomenon as the antecedent or the concurrence of antecedents on which it is invariably and unconditionally consequent.[7] Two important points that emerge from Hume's analysis are, one, the causal relation holds between two kinds of events and two, the truth of propositions about causal relations can be established only through observation. In other words, propositions about causal relations are subject to verification by empirical evidence.

It would be pertinent to mention two major difficulties that arise with respect to definitions of causation in terms of regular sequence. One, we can find cases where the required regular sequence is present but we cannot assert a causal relation. For example, night follows day and day precedes night but day cannot be said to be the cause of night. Some philosophers argue that this example does not show the inadequacy of the definition. Day is a period of light and night a period of darkness. All periods of light and all periods of darkness do not show a regular sequence. The definition requires that not only two individual events but all events similar to those two should have relations of precedence and succession. The example of day and night, therefore, is not a counter example to the definition of cause. This way of answering the objection, however, gives rise to a further problem. The issue of relevant similarities between certain events becomes crucial. What degree of similarity between concerned events and in which respects is to be taken as sufficient? A very narrow conception of similarity may lead to the conclusion that no two events can be said to be similar, while a very broad conception may lead to conclusions, which are in conflict with our considered judgements of causal connection. The second difficulty with the definition mentioned above is that it is possible to give examples in which a causal connection seems to hold but the required regular sequence is not present. Suppose a person is shot with a gun and dies as a result of the gun-shot. Here one would say that the gun-shot caused the death of that person. However, in many cases a gun-shot may not lead to the death of the person who is shot. This objection, however, can be answered by saying that a gun-shot exactly similar to the one in the example and in conditions exactly similar to the one in the example would most probably lead to the death of the victim. The crucial issue here is the degree of similarity between two events and that, as already mentioned, is a problematic issue. In general, however, we can say that a causal relation between two kinds of events means regular sequence between these.[8]

After Hume, it is generally accepted that a causal relation cannot be regarded as a logically necessary relation such that its denial is self-contradictory. Two important features of a causal relation are universality and uniformity. When one asserts a causal relation between 'x' and 'y', it is implied that all events similar to 'x' will be causally related to events similar to 'y'. Uniformity implies that similar causes will have similar effects. These features of a causal relation enable us to predict future events and manipulate causes to bring about desired effects. Causal relations among events give us the conception of a law governed universe. The supposition that every event has a cause is a fundamental assumption in scientific inquiries. Philosophers make an exception to the law of causation in the context of human free will. The following discussion of karmic causality, would be in the light of the notion outlined above, that a causal relation is a universal and uniform relation of regular sequence between two kinds of events.

We can explain the causal relation further through the ideas of necessary and sufficient cause; 'x' is the necessary cause of 'y', if 'y' cannot occur unless 'x' occurs, and 'x' is the sufficient cause of 'y', if when 'x' occurs 'y' follows. How a cause brings about its effect, whether an effect is potentially there in its cause before coming into existence, whether a cause has some power or energy through which it gives rise to its effect are questions which can be ignored in the present discussion. Since we take a cause to be an invariable antecedent of its effect, clearly the causal relation holds between two kinds or types of events and yields a general law. A statement about a well established causal connection is universal in the sense that it holds in all cases of a type, and necessary in the sense that its denial has very little, or negligible probability. We need to include the concepts of 'mediate cause' and 'causal chain' also in our discussion here. Suppose 'x' invariably precedes 'y' and 'y' invariably precedes 'z.' Here 'x' is the cause of 'y' and 'y' is the cause of 'z' but 'x' is not an immediate cause of 'z', it is a mediate cause of 'z.' The relationship between actions and their consequences cannot be explained without bringing in mediate causes. The theory of karma, as mentioned earlier, posits intermediaries between actions and their consequences. Actions are said to bring about their results through their residue after a time-gap. Moreover, sometimes a natural event becomes the instrument of an individual experiencing the consequences of past actions, sometimes actions of other people. Henceforth this general notion of causality would be relied upon in the discussion of karmic causality. Different views on the unfolding of the karmic process have already been discussed in the earlier chapter. The discussion here will be focussed mainly on the strict version of the theory and its implications.[9]

The discussion will be confined to intentional actions, which include both the acts of commission and omission of various types. As already mentioned, all actions, barring a few exceptions, are supposed to be subject to karmic causality. The causal chain outlined in the theory of karma can be summarized as follows:

(a) Every intentional purposive action by an agent (except unattached actions or actions of a liberated person, etc.) leads to some consequences for the agent.

(b) The action is the necessary cause of these consequences.

(c) The action leaves a karmic residue, which upon maturation brings about the consequences. The maturation of the residue thus is the sufficient cause of the consequence.

(d) Every purposive, intentional action is either morally right or morally wrong.

(e) Every right action under normal circumstances is the cause of some good consequences and every wrong action of some bad consequences.

(f) A good consequence brings happiness to the agent, a bad one suffering and pain.

(g) Happiness is the just reward of good actions and suffering the just punishment for bad actions.

A right action is supposed to lead to consequences like birth in a high caste, long life and happiness and a wrong one to birth in a lower caste, short life, disease and suffering, etc. for the agent. Every individual, under normal circumstances, invariably has to bear the deserved reward or punishment of one's past actions. The theory maintains that all the happiness or suffering an individual gets in life is due to one's own actions and constitutes the just reward or punishment of those actions in accordance with their moral quality. The quality of life of an individual is a reflection of the deserved consequences of her past actions. The causal process admits the possibility of deferment of consequences of one's actions. An individual may not get the consequences immediately after performance of an action but only after a considerable gap of time in the present or the next life. It is important to note that the theory implies that all the happiness or suffering one gets in life is a morally deserved reward or punishment for one's own past actions. Even when one's happiness or suffering appears to be due to natural events or another person's actions, in reality it is a consequence of one's own actions alone. K W. Morgan comments that the law of karma is conceived to reflect the operation of the law of causation in the moral realm. The law is a moral law corresponding to the physical law of causation. Just as the law of cause and effect works in the physical world, the law of karma works in the moral world.[10]

It is clear that the idea of karmic causality is very different from the ordinary idea of causality. As mentioned earlier, specific connections between particular kinds of actions and particular kinds of consequences are hardly ever mentioned in the Indian tradition. We also find disagreement among scholars about what is to be included in the class of consequences. However, there is broad agreement upon three things constituting consequences, an individual's caste, span of life and happiness or sorrow. It is not clear though whether high caste and longevity are good in themselves or these are good because they lead to happiness. If the latter is true, then happiness is good as an end and other things are good as means to happiness. Many things can be said to be instrumental to happiness of people and high caste and longevity need not always be positively correlated with happiness. Moreover, the theory posits a general connection between good actions and personal happiness. We are not told, however, which actions lead to which results. It remains unclear whether a certain consequence like birth in a higher caste is a result of some specific kind of good actions or of any kind of good actions. Even when Manu, for example, mentions some specific connections between actions and circumstances of rebirth as their consequences, (chapter 2) we find that more than one kind of action is supposed to lead to the same kind of birth.

In many writings on karma, only happiness and sorrow are mentioned as consequences of past actions. It seems that various kinds of good actions are claimed to lead to happiness and various kinds of bad actions to sorrow in general, without specifying a one to one connection between some actions and some consequences. The theory, thus, establishes only a general connection between good actions and happiness and bad actions and sorrow. Specific causal connections between actions and their consequences of the kind established for example by *vedic* sacrifices are not found in discussions of karmic causality. Sometimes, it is claimed that the theory of karma has great motivational effect on people and it enables us to know, control and manipulate the law of karma to provide guidance for better conduct and better future life. However, this can be possible only when connections between specific actions and their specific consequences are mentioned. In the absence of clear understanding of such connections, it seems one would not be able to relate events in one's present life to one's past actions and would not know how to modify one's conduct in the right direction.

It is evident that the causal connections between actions and their consequences cannot be established on the basis of empirical evidence. Since the events in an individual's present life are traced to actions performed in the past life of the individual and consequences of actions performed in the present life occur in future lives, it is in principle impossible to justify such connections on empirical grounds. Moreover, the modalities of the operation of karmic causality have not been clearly defined. The theory does not clearly state how actions lead to their consequences, sometimes natural events are mentioned in this context as instrumentalities (*nimitta*), sometimes other persons' actions are mentioned as intermediaries and sometimes no intermediaries are mentioned. In short, it remains unclear which occurrences in an individual's present life are consequences of which past actions. As mentioned earlier, even when somewhat specific connections are mentioned as, for example, by Manu, neither the actions nor the consequences mentioned are absolutely specific and determinate but only suggest a range of possibilities. In most discussions of karma even such broad connections are not provided. In the absence of connections between specific kinds of actions and specific kinds of results, one may even question whether the supposed relation between actions and consequences can be said to be causal at all. It is debatable whether the general claim that good actions lead to happiness and evil actions to suffering can be said to represent a causal relation in the ordinary sense of the term 'causal.'

The notion of consequence here is also different from the ordinary notion of a causal consequence. It is defined primarily in terms of the effect some event has on an individual, more specifically whether the event makes the individual happy or sad. All happiness or sorrow an individual feels is taken as a consequence of past actions without it being clear which past actions have resulted in those experiences. The theory lays down that the consequences of actions are for the agent alone and these are deserved reward or punishment of the agent's past actions. If a person's action brings about some changes in natural phenomena or affects other persons, these changes and effects themselves are not considered important, rather how these affect the agent in question becomes important. The connection between actions and consequences in the karma theory definitely has a moral dimension but causality as we understand it does not involve ethical considerations. The idea of karmic causality, therefore, appears very different from the ordinary notion of causality. One may justifiably question whether the relation between actions and their morally appropriate consequences in karma theory can be called causal.[11]

When we talk of actions and their just rewards or punishments, a process of moral evaluation is implicit in it. Such evaluation requires norms or standards of evaluation and somebody who judges on the basis of those norms. Firstly, the moral value of an action has to be judged and secondly, what constitutes a just reward or punishment for that action needs to be evaluated. Even if there is a causal connection between a wrong action and some specific kind of suffering, for example, the suffering cannot be taken as a just punishment for that action unless someone judges it to be so in accordance with some ethical norms. Rajendra Prasad rightly observes that the concepts of a causal consequence and that of reward or punishment are not of the same logical type; the latter is not causal or empirical but normative and evaluative. The concept of the causal consequence of an event is based on a temporal relation between the two, but the concept of reward or punishment of an action is a normative and evaluative one based on judging in accordance with a moral norm or criteria.[12] This conceptual distinction should not be ignored, ".. unless the karmic process involves some judging, evaluating or decision making, it will not be a process of apportionment of rewards and punishments and, therefore, of moral rewards and punishments."[13]

It follows that unless proponents of the karma theory

can show the possibility of moral evaluation of actions and their appropriate rewards or punishments within karmic process it cannot be claimed that such processes deliver morally just consequences of actions. Clearly the concept of morally appropriate reward or punishment for an action is distinct from the concept of causal consequence of that action. Suppose a person 'A' assaults another person 'B' and injures him badly. The physical injury of 'B' is the causal consequence of action by 'A'. Suppose that 'A' is arrested and sentenced to a jail term for two years. This may be regarded as the morally appropriate punishment for his action. Suppose further that 'A' seems to be happy after assaulting 'B' despite the jail sentence and its hardships because of his vindictive nature, it is not clear how to characterize it. His happiness and sense of satisfaction certainly cannot be regarded as a morally appropriate reward for his action. Therefore, it is clear that causal consequences of actions do not automatically become their just rewards or punishments. Prasad argues that the necessity of moral evaluation of actions and their just rewards or punishments provides a ground against the karma theory. According to him, we can call some 'x' a reward deserved by an agent 'a' for having done something 'y', if and only if, following conditions are satisfied:[14]

(a) There is a norm or standard 'N' which 'y' fulfils or satisfies;

(b) Someone has the authority to evaluate 'y' in relation to 'N' and decide that 'x' is its appropriate reward and grant the reward to 'a'

(c) The reward is given to the same person as the one who did 'y'.

Prasad concludes that since the law of karma "... is an autonomous, causal law regulating the behaviour of nature, what a doer gets on account of his actions; i.e., as their consequences, cannot be called in a straight forward sense, rewards or punishments..."[15]

From the above discussion it becomes clear that the theory of karma must provide for a process of moral evaluation of actions and their just rewards or punishments. An unintelligent Nature functioning mechanically, cannot be assigned the role of making moral judgements. Nature, as we know it, is incapable of judging the moral quality of actions and their appropriate rewards or punishments. Some theistic versions of the theory maintain that God or the Supreme Being is the divine judge who judges our actions, decides the appropriate rewards or punishments of our actions and ensures that we get what we deserve. However, this form of karma theory is not as widely accepted as the atheistic strict version, which is regarded as a distinctive feature of the Indian tradition. If karmic causality is supposed to function independently, then there is no place in it for God as a judge and we do not have an agency which can make the required moral evaluations. If we argue that Nature can judge the moral quality of actions and their just rewards or punishments, then it seems that Nature is being converted into a rational being capable of making such evaluations and instituting appropriate causal processes which can deliver the just rewards or punishments. Such a conception of Nature is extremely controversial. Prasad is of the view that even such a conception of Nature would not solve the problem since this supposition amounts to 'destroying the identity of the concept of consequence by reducing it to that of reward or punishment.'[16] Prasad is right that a conceptual distinction between a causal consequence of an action and its morally appropriate reward or punishment needs to be made. One may argue that the case of karmic causality is special in the sense that in this context the causal consequence of an action is always the same as its just reward or punishment though the two are conceptually distinct. However, this implies that the assumption that the causal consequence of an action must always be its morally appropriate reward or punishment remains unsubstantiated. Prasad's comments show that the supposition of a causal relation between actions and their morally appropriate rewards and punishments raises serious conceptual issues.

It is necessary for the strict theory of karma to show how moral evaluation of actions and their just rewards is possible within an independently functioning causal process. As mentioned above, the capacity to do moral evaluation cannot be ascribed to Nature. We also cannot ascribe this capacity to the karmic causality itself because that results in elevating the process to the status of a divine person or a deity. Herman comments that the law of karma seems to be more like a 'super Person' than a universal natural law. He mentions four features ascribed to the law of karma to support this conclusion.[17]

(a) The law is regarded as just. Everyone gets what one deserves on the basis of own actions and everyone deserves whatever he gets. This implies that the law has the capacity to discriminate and gives rewards or punishments to people which fit their good or evil actions.

(b) The law is regarded as having the capacity to hold back and defer the reward or punishment a person deserves for long periods, even a life time. However, the rationale and exact mechanism of this deferment is not clarified and remains a mystery.

(c) To be effective, the law must be supposed to be 'all knowing' and have the ability to know all actions of all the individuals performed at various points of their worldly lives.

(d) The law must be supposed to be 'all powerful', since the law is supposed to deliver perfect justice to people with regard to appropriate consequences of their actions. The law ensures that the deserved reward or punishment is delivered to the concerned agent at the appropriate time, though the mechanism of this perfect delivery remains a mystery.

Herman concludes that given these features, the best model for explaining the law of karma is not natural laws but a non-empirical metaphysical one of a divine person.[18] It should not be compared with an inexorable empirical law but a super divine being or a personal deity (karma deity). However, we find that the strict version of the karma theory envisages karmic causality to function independently and its delivery of karmic justice is not regarded as dependent on any divine power. Herman's objection is that the conception of perfect karmic justice can be plausible, only if, karmic causality is regarded as an all-knowing, all powerful personal power. However, the Indian tradition certainly does not seem to suggest such a conclusion. Herman's view supports the point made earlier. If the law of karma is like a natural law, then the function of moral evaluation of actions and their just consequences has to be ascribed to an agency other than karmic causality. If this function is ascribed to karmic causality itself, then its operation cannot be compared to the functioning of a natural law. I have earlier discussed in chapter one some reasons why the law of karma cannot be compared with natural laws.

Let us move to a different point. The moral codes prescribed in other religions like Buddhism, Jainism and Sikhism are different from each other, also from Hindu code of ethics, though many overlapping similarities can be found among them. It is difficult to understand how these differences can be accommodated within the notion of karmic causality as outlined in the theory of karma. Are we to suppose that karmic causal laws would vary in accordance with different moral codes of these systems? In other words, the presence of a plurality of moral codes, different from each other, poses a challenge to the supposition of universal and uniform karmic causal laws. However, I wish to proceed to a different question, namely whether the idea of causal laws linking actions and their morally appropriate consequences is plausible in the context of Hindu conception of right action? It does not appear to be so since the concept of right action there is relative to particular features of agent in question and the context of the action. Let us first take note of a few general points about the issue of evaluation of moral value of actions. An action may be judged right or wrong either on the basis of the intention behind it or on the basis of its consequences or both. A norm to judge actions may be regarded as universal and binding for all, such that an action is right or wrong irrespective of the specificities of the circumstances of an agent. However, most of the time a norm is universal in a more restricted sense, namely that a certain action is right for everyone under certain circumstances. A norm may also have a restricted domain with respect to agents stating that an action is right only when done by a certain kind of agent. In Hindu philosophy we find both kinds of restrictions operating on the notion of duty or moral obligation (*dharma*).[19] The tradition makes a distinction between universal duties and specific duties of people, the latter are relative to the caste and stage of life of an agent. A large number of right actions prescribed for people fall in the second category. A generally accepted categorization of duties is as follows:

(a) Universal duties (*sāmānya, sādhāraṇa or nitya dharma*): These are duties valid for all persons, for example, truth, non-violence, control over senses, forgiveness, regard for parents and preceptor, looking after the guests etc.

(b) Specific duties (*viśiṣṭa dharma* or *varṇāśrama dharma*): these are duties appropriate to the caste (*varṇa*) and the stage of life (*āśrama*) of a person.[20]

Specific duties also include duties or codes of conduct prescribed for certain kinds of agents and situations. For example, we find mention of duties of a king (*rāja-dharma*), right actions appropriate to an era (*yuga-dharma*), traditions of a family (*kula-dharma)*, code of conduct for a specific gender (*stree-dharma*) etc. At times right conduct is outlined for times of extreme adversity (*āpad-dharma*) also and it is acknowledged that normal duties can be suspended or superseded at such times. Interestingly, the circumstances constituting times of extreme adversity and what a person allowed to do at such times to ensure one's survival are often fairly comprehensively elaborated, as for example in the *Mahābhārata* and *Manusmṛti*. Though not mentioned specifically in the classifications of duties, we find that gender is an important category in this context and it cuts across castes and stages of life of individuals. Duties for a woman at the householder stage (*gṛhastha āśrama*) are different from those of a man at that stage. Moreover, basic duties and rules for conduct remain more or less the same for women, whichever caste or stage of life they may belong to. Specific duties outlined for different castes are applicable mostly to men only. For example, women belonging to the warrior class are not ordinarily supposed to engage in warfare and those belonging to the trading classes are not supposed to undertake business activities and all women are expected to conform to some broadly similar norms, though some different norms can be found which apply to certain class of women only like women belonging to royal families, etc.

The concept of the specific code of conduct prescribed for a person within the *varṇāśrama scheme,* namely one's own duties (*svadharma)* is important in this context. Individuals are supposed to always follow the specific norms prescribed for them. Any attempt on the part of an individual to switch to conduct prescribed for a different caste is generally disapproved of. Even in cases of conflict between universal duties and specific duties, an agent is encouraged to follow one's own caste duties. The *Bhagvad Gītā* maintains that one should follow one's own *svadharma,* even if it is faulty, rather than *dharma* of others which may be better outlined and death while following one's own caste duties is better than following duties prescribed for other castes. Manu expresses similar sentiments and observes that it is better for a person to discharge his own duties imperfectly than to follow others' duties perfectly.[21] The tradition thus lays emphasis on maintaining the status quo of social order. Like right actions, wrong actions or sins have also been classified in the tradition, sometimes on the basis of the degree of their wickedness, for example, deadly sins, big sins and minor sins, sometimes on the basis of the kind of action involved, for example, mental, bodily and verbal sins. Actions that violate the universal code of conduct can be said to be wrong for everyone. Violation of specific duties would fall in the category of wrong actions for the specific group for whom those duties are prescribed. Therefore, in this case what is right or wrong for one person may not be so for others.

The classification of duties within the Hindu tradition presents an interesting combination of rigidity and flexibility. On the one hand, the code of conduct varies with an individual's station in life, profession, circumstances, gender and the age one is living in, on the other, the code within each category is often fairly rigid and further differences necessitated by specific, particular nature and situation of an agent are not always accommodated. We find that in the case of specific duties, the question of the moral value of an action is relative to an agent's particular category. Therefore, a judgement of the moral value of a certain action done by a certain individual becomes more complex. The same action 'a' when done by one kind of agent may be right but when done by another may be wrong and, therefore, its consequences would have to be different in the two cases. In the context of a large number of actions, the karmic causal laws would be required to relate an action with its consequences in the light of the agent's caste and stage of life, profession, etc. It follows that the same action, when performed by one person would lead to good consequences because it is considered right for that agent but to bad consequences when performed by another agent for whom it does not constitute right action or to less severe bad consequences in case of one person but more severe ones in case of another. We find examples where killing a Brahmin is said to be much more evil than killing a non-Brahmin, extramarital relations in case of women constitute serious wrongdoing but not so in case of men and many things that are supposed to be good for higher castes, are forbidden for lower castes like reading scriptures. In short, a similar action may be right when done by certain kinds of agents and wrong when done by another kind. It follows that, as far as specific duties are concerned, there cannot be universal causal laws relating some actions and some consequences applicable to all kinds of agents. Universal laws would arguably be possible in case of actions prescribed or forbidden for all but this also become problematic since an agent is advised to prioritize one's caste duties over universal duties in a situation where the two clash. Karmic causality would be required to adjust to this moral preference also.

Moreover, if a separate code of conduct is recognized for times of distress, which supersedes moral commandments for normal times, a separate set of causal laws would be needed to accommodate its prescriptions. Causality, as we understand it, is not agent relative. A causal process works in the same way irrespective of the specific social position of the agent starting the process or being affected by it. But here we require a causal connection between an action and its appropriate reward or punishment, which allows that the result of an action would vary with the caste, specific age, profession and gender of the agent in question. Clearly the notion of causality here is different from the commonly understood one discussed earlier. It, therefore, becomes debatable whether such a relation can be called 'causal' at all.

The idea of consequences of actions as constituting reward or punishment to agents for their actions ensures retributive justice. The idea of a consequence as a deserved reward or punishment implies a moral judgement about the appropriate consequence of an action. Ordinarily, a judgement about punishment to be given to a person for some wrongdoing is dependent upon several factors. One of these is whether the action is a deliberate and calculated one done with the intention to harm somebody. It is also relevant whether the wrong doer has a history of such misdemeanours. The degree of evilness of an action is determined on the basis of such considerations. Take the example of someone killing another person. Killing a person with a deliberate intention with the sole purpose of undue gain to oneself is definitely more evil than killing someone accidentally or in a fit of passion or under severe provocation. One's intention behind the act of killing is morally important so are the circumstances surrounding the act. Under certain conditions killing another person is not considered wrong, as for example killing the other in self-defence or killing enemy soldiers in order to defend one's country or killing a dreaded terrorist to save the lives of innocent people. Any system of justice delivery would have to take note of such factors while deciding the appropriate punishment for an act of killing a person. Moreover, thinking about killing another and planning it but not actually doing it cannot be said to be as evil as actually executing one's intention to kill. In short, the punishment for an act of killing another person would vary from case to case and would depend on the specificities of that case. A decision about an appropriate reward for an action also has to take into account the intention of the agent and other relevant factors like personal risk taken to fulfil one's duty, etc.

Apart from the agent's intentions, the impact of an action on property and people also constitutes a very important consideration in deciding an appropriate reward or punishment for that action. For example, if several people are killed or seriously injured during a bank robbery, then the punishment is likely to be much harsher for the robbers than if only one or two persons are injured. Sometimes, consequences of an action may not matter at all, for example, if a person jumps in the river to save another, but does not succeed because of the strong current, even then the good deed deserves a reward. Similarly, if unpleasant consequences occur while one is doing one's duty, the agent may not deserve punishment. Krishna's exhortation to Arjuna in the *Bhagvad Gītā* to fight against Kauravas, even if it implies killing his relatives and dear ones, is a case in point. Undoubtedly, one is faced with a difficult choice when one can foresee the unpleasant consequences of one's action, even if the action is in the line of duty. In the context of wrong actions, consequences matter enormously; the degree of wickedness of the action may depend on these and a judgement of appropriate punishment will have to take into account the consequences. It is clear thus that a judgement of an appropriate reward or punishment for an action is a complex affair and is dependent upon several factors.

It seems that not only the intended consequences of an action, but the unintended and unforeseen ones also may be important for a judgement of appropriate reward or punishment for that action. Suppose a caretaker's negligence leads to a serious fire in a multi-storey building and that causes not only massive damage to property but also loss of several lives, the ascription of guilt to the caretaker would be much more than it would have been, if the fire was minor and lives were not lost. How a person has to bear the burden of even those consequences of one's actions, which are unintentionally produced, is beautifully depicted in the story of Dasharath, mentioned earlier, who had to suffer separation from his son Rama due to an unintended, accidental killing. What has been said about punishment applies to judgements of reward also. It becomes clear that the agent-relative and context-dependent nature of duties in Hinduism introduces a very high degree of complexity in judgements of moral value of actions and their morally appropriate rewards or punishments. Each action would have to be judged individually for determining its moral quality and its appropriate reward or punishment. Therefore, causal laws, stating universal and uniform connections between a certain class of actions and a certain kind of reward or punishment, do not seem possible.

The theory of karma asserts a causal connection between good deeds and happiness for the agent and bad deeds and suffering for the agent. This claim is also problematic. What gives happiness to one varies from person to person. It depends a great deal on a person's likes, inclinations, desires, aspirations, situation and goals, etc. While one person may derive happiness from material prosperity, another may derive it from increase in knowledge and yet another may derive it from selfless service of society. Even if we grant that more or less similar things give happiness to people generally speaking, difficulty remains. Happiness is a matter of degree and the same gain or result may give a lot of happiness to one, moderate happiness to another and leave the third dissatisfied. Which gain makes one happy and in what degree depends a great deal on the goals and ambitions of a person. Age also affects the source of happiness for people. While things like good health, wealth, knowledge, success in career and well-being of children, etc. are source of happiness for most people, the prioritization of various means of happiness may vary from person to person. This is important because a positive correlation between good deeds and happiness needs to include a correlation between the moral worth of an action and the degree of happiness or sorrow experienced by the agent in question. It is not plausible to suppose that the same things make everybody happy at all times and in the same degree. One student may be very happy at securing 55% marks in school examination, while the other may feel miserable with such scores, depending on their hard-work, expectations and goals. Things that make people happy in young age may lose their charm when they are old. What has been said about happiness also applies to unhappiness; we cannot assume that same things make everybody equally unhappy. Therefore, general causal connections between certain kinds of gains or losses and happiness or sorrow seem questionable.

From the above discussion it follows that the idea of karmic causality is extremely complex and highly problematic. One, it involves judgement of ethical merit of actions, which in Hindu thought is relative to the specific situation and caste of an agent. Two, it requires judgements of appropriate and just rewards or punishments for actions, which are subject to several conditions, including some that are agent-relative. Three, it requires a positive correlation between a just reward and happiness and just punishment and suffering for the agent in question, which again is agent-relative and subject to conditions. Our ordinary concept of causality does not allow for agent-relativity in the working of a causal process. Therefore, the idea of karmic causality is open to serious question. Buddhism and Jainism, etc. do not accept the *varṇāśrama* scheme and, therefore, do not face the first problem mentioned above. But the rest apply to these systems also.

The strict theory of karma implies that all the happiness or suffering a person experiences in life is the just reward or punishment of one's own actions; it is deserved by the person in the light of the moral worth of one's past actions. Everybody reaps the consequences of one's own actions alone. Our experience tells us that a person's happiness or sorrow can be due to three kinds of sources, one's own actions, natural processes and actions of other persons. Conversely one's action may have an impact not only on oneself but also on the natural environment around one and other persons. Since the theory asserts that the quality of life of a person is a consequence of one's own actions alone, the apparent impact of natural processes and others' actions on a person's quality of life makes it necessary to explain these somehow in terms of that person's own past actions. A few examples would be useful to illustrate the difficulties mentioned above.

Example 1: We find that natural phenomena and events like beautiful natural objects, hot or cold weather, rains, etc. cause pleasant or unpleasant experiences in people. Natural events like floods, intense heat or cold, excessive rain and natural phenomena like poisonous plants or animals can cause suffering to people. When a natural calamity occurs, it affects a large number of people. Whether it be the effect of a natural event on an individual or a group of people, it is not clear how it is to be explained within the framework of the karma theory. It becomes especially problematic while dealing with huge destruction of property and loss of a large number of human lives resulting from a natural calamity. It is extremely counter-intuitive to say that all the people adversely affected by such calamities are being punished for their own past wrong doing. It is equally difficult to explain the gains resulting from good soil or good rains in terms of good past deeds of affected people. More will be said on this point later. Interestingly environmentalists do argue that our collective actions over a long period may affect the environment adversely, which may cause serious problems for us. However, this explanation is very different from the karmic explanation.

Example 2: Suppose Rakesh burns the dried plants and grass in his yard. The sparks from that fire fall on the house of his neighbour Mohan and cause substantial damage to his house and the trees in his compound. The huge financial loss as a result of the fire causes hardships in Mohan's business and leads to unhappiness. Here the effect of Rakesh's action in the form of a natural event becomes the cause of the suffering of Mohan. If Rakesh suffers some fine or punishment for his omission to take adequate precautions, then his sorrow and hardship can be explained in terms of his own action. Ordinarily, one would also take Rakesh's action as the cause of the damage to the property of Mohan and his unhappiness. However, the karma theory will make it necessary to trace the cause of Mohan's sorrow to his own past actions. It is not clear how this kind of example can be reconciled in a plausible manner with the claim that all the happiness or suffering of a person is due to her own actions.

Example 3: Suppose Rakesh shoots Mohan with a gun, injuring and incapacitating him seriously. As a result, Mohan has to incur huge expenses in medical treatment and is not able to earn his livelihood for two years. Mohan suffers a great deal of pain and his wife, children and parents also face severe hardships and suffer a great deal. Rakesh is sentenced to three years' imprisonment for his crime and as a result his own family members also suffer. Ordinarily the suffering of all the individuals in this example will be said to be caused by Rakesh's action. However, according to the theory of karma, each person's suffering will have to be traced back to that person's own actions. Again it is not clear how this can be done in a plausible manner.

Does bringing in the concept of 'instrumentality' help us to provide a satisfactory solution to the difficulties mentioned above? One may argue that in the first example, natural events are the instrumentality of executing karmic consequences. In the second example, the suffering of Rakesh is due to his own action, brought about through the instrumentality of fire. The suffering of Mohan and his family members appears to be caused by Rakesh's negligent action, but in accordance with the karma theory it will also have to be regarded as caused by their own past deeds; fire being the instrumentality to fructify the consequences of those actions. This line of argument leads to a very convoluted explanation of an ordinary event and its plausibility is seriously suspect. It is to be noted that in example two, a natural event becomes the instrumentality of implementing karmic consequences but that event is initiated by a person's action; in example three, however, another person's action itself is the instrumentality of implementing consequences of someone's past actions. According to the karma theory the suffering of each person is due to that person's own past actions but one may argue that another person's action may be the means through which consequences of one's actions are realized. Thus, through the act of Rakesh's shooting Mohan, karmic causality ensures that everybody concerned faces the deserved consequences of their own actions. Such examples are more problematic since these involve the impact of another person's actions on the victim which is not admitted by the karma theory.

There are two possible explanations that can be offered in the context of above mentioned examples. One, it may be said that the instrumentality (a natural event, another person's action, etc.) through which a person gets the reward or punishment of one's own actions is pre-determined by the karmic causality, or two, that karmic causality only determines that a person gets one's deserved share of happiness or suffering, but the instrumentality of implementation of the relevant experiences remains indeterminate. Let us take the first option. It implies that the karmic causality predetermines that a certain natural event would occur at a certain time and place or a certain person would perform a certain action at a specific time and place, which would implement the specific appropriate consequences of affected people's own actions. It follows that consequences of a person's past actions are capable of determining not only Natural events, but also people's actions in some cases at least. The story of Gautami's son dying due to a snake-bite in the *Mahābhārata,* mentioned earlier, provides a good illustration in this context. Multiple agents are mentioned in the story like time, death, fate and beginning with the snake, each one pleads helplessness and blames someone else for the death. Ultimately, Gautami comes to the conclusion that her son's and her own past actions have brought about this result.[22] This approach raises serious questions about individual freedom and people's moral responsibility for their actions. These issues would be discussed later in some detail.

Conversely one may argue in line with the second option that the karmic causality does determine that a person surely gets the deserved happiness or suffering, but it does not determine the means through which this is brought about. This implies that the causal connection is between the residue of a person's actions, on the one hand, and happiness or suffering on the other, while the source of the happiness or suffering remains indeterminate and open. In the example mentioned above, Mohan suffers due to a gun-shot injury inflicted by Rakesh but his suffering might have resulted due to some other kind of injury inflicted by some other source. On this interpretation, karmic causality would need to ensure a perfect match between the deserved consequences of a person's actions and natural events and/ or other people's actions. Moreover, it would have to ensure that right kind of people, by virtue of deserved consequences of their actions, are placed appropriately in the world so that consequences of their actions can be realized. It is far from plausible to suppose that such perfect matching can be done by causal processes operating on their own or by unintelligent Nature.

Both the options mentioned above are fraught with serious difficulties. If the karmic causality is supposed to determine the particular natural event, which will be the instrumentality of delivering the deserved consequences, then it follows that natural events are subordinate to karmic causality. If we suppose that the natural event which would implement karmic consequences is not predetermined, it would imply that karmic causality brings about a perfect match between considerations of karmic justice and natural events. Both the suppositions are highly problematic. It is even more problematic to argue in examples where people's actions appear to be the cause of happiness or sorrow of others, that karmic causality governs such actions. Yet it seems clear that natural events and actions of others affect people's happiness or sorrow greatly.

A question arises whether natural causality and karmic causality are to be regarded as distinct or identical. If these are distinct then the relationship between the two and their interaction needs to be clarified. It is by no means obvious that natural processes or events work to ensure karmic retributive justice. Therefore, strong supporting reasons are required and these reasons must be independent of the suppositions or interpretations parasitical upon the theory of karma. If we suppose that the two causalities are identical, then it implies that nature is morally ordered in the sense that its processes are subordinate to requirements of karmic justice and work to fulfil those. The idea of a moral order in the universe would be discussed a little later but it would be usefull to first summarize some of the important points that emerge from the above discussion:

(a) If karmic causality is claimed to operate without the intervention of a divine being, then the possibility of moral evaluation of actions and their appropriate reward or punishment has to be established within Nature itself and that is highly problematic.

(b) If it is argued that Nature is capable of making moral judgements then Nature seems to be turned into an intelligent, powerful personal existence. This idea of Nature requires justification.

(c) The existence of different moral codes raises questions about the coherence of the idea of universal and uniform causal connections between actions and their morally appropriate consequences.

(d) Within the framework of '*varṇāśrama dharma*' universal causal connections between certain kind of actions and certain kind of consequences are not tenable because the moral value of actions becomes agent-relative. This problem gets more complex in the light of additional classifications of *dharma* on the basis of profession, gender, family, era, etc.

(e) It is not clear how causal connections between actions and happiness or suffering are possible since what makes a person happy or sad and in what degree varies from person to person.

(f) Natural events cause happiness or suffering to people. The issue of delivery of karmic justice through natural events has not been cogently explained. We find that a person's happiness quotient is affected by other people's actions also. This is contrary to the supposition in the karma theory that all the happiness or suffering one gets is due to one's own actions alone.

(g) The notion of causality in the theory of karma is significantly different from the scientific or ordinary notion of causality. This notion needs to be clearly defined. The connection between actions and their just consequences cannot be said to be causal in its ordinary sense.

THE IDEA OF A MORAL ORDER IN THE UNIVERSE

Many scholars writing on the karma theory assume that natural events unfold in a manner that karmic consequences can be implemented. As mentioned earlier, the theory claims that the physical and mental capabilities of a person at birth and longevity of a person are determined by an individual's past actions. D.M. Datta says clearly that Nature equips an individual with a body appropriate to one's past actions and natural events that form the common background of people are what they deserve.[23] Rama Rao Pappu also endorses the idea that the universe is governed by the law of karma. He thinks that the law is a naturalistic principle.[24] Jhingran asserts in a similar vein that "... the moral quality of our deeds, thoughts and desires not only conditions our future character, but also manipulates the natural world order, so that we are thrown into external circumstances that are most suited to materialize or effect the kind of rewards and punishments, which our moral character deserves.[25] Experience tells us that often natural events cause happiness or sorrow to people. The karma theory argues that these natural events are the instrumentality of implementing the deserved consequences of people's actions. Rajendra Prasad points out that the theory's claim that 'individuals unfailingly bear the consequences of their actions' is not a factual or empirical claim backed by evidence. Rather the theory assumes that the character of the natural world is such that its functioning ensures that all individuals naturally get what they are entitled to get in the light of their actions.[26] This gives us a "moral conception of Nature".[27] Does this mean that all natural processes are governed by considerations of karmic justice? If so, it follows that Nature does not work in a purely mechanical way but represents a moral order. If it is claimed that some natural events work in a way that ensures karmic justice, it implies that Nature partially works according to a moral order.

The idea of a moral order in Nature or the universe is available in the Indian tradition from very early times. The idea of a cosmic order (*ṛta)* is found in the early *vedic* tradition, which is not merely a physical force. According to Eliade, it signifies,

> "an impersonal and powerful force upon which the ethical and physical worlds are based, through which they are inextricably united, and by which they are maintained...Thus *ṛta* signifies the cosmic law that allows the universe to run smoothly, the dynamic structure in which every object and all actions have their proper place and in which all parts support and strengthen the whole in a flowing symbiosis."[28]

It follows that the cosmic order represents a natural, as well as, a moral order. It signifies the order in Nature and also the moral order, which governs the conduct of human beings. According to Eliade the *vedic* seers consider the world as a system in which natural forces and human beings are in harmony and both function in an orderly manner. However, they also admit the possibility of disorder (*anṛta*) and acknowledge that human beings can break the order and that is evil. Eliade observes that thinkers in early *vedic* times believed that *vedic* sacrifices, when performed correctly, would bring rewards for individuals who performed these sacrifices and ensure their well-being. Sacrifices, thus, express a connection between certain kind of actions and good results. The cosmic order was believed to be ruled by gods and human beings could obtain favours from them through performance of sacrifices. Eliade maintains that this belief was later modified and the ritual of sacrifice itself came to be emphasized and it was believed that when a sacrificial ritual is performed correctly by a priest or priests, it would make the gods give the desired results to the sacrificer. It was also believed that cosmic processes could be manipulated by ascetic practices *(tapas)*, chanting of mantras, etc.

Radhakrishnan seems to hold similar views about the cosmic order. According to him "*Ṛta* literally means 'the course of things'. It stands for law in general and the immanence of justice".[29] He adds that in the beginning the concept of *ṛta* referred to the natural order but later it developed into the concept of a moral order, in other words, was believed to be the path of morality or righteousness. This law of righteousness matches the order of Nature. Therefore 'As sure as the sun rises tomorrow virtue will triumph. *Ṛta* can be trusted.' Radhakrishnan maintains that the concept of a moral order in the world lies at the root of the karma theory developed later. However, the theory shifts the emphasis to a person's own actions and these came to be regarded as the source of a person's prosperity and happiness or otherwise. Thus human agency rather than the favours granted by gods became the source of a person's quality of life.

If the world is believed to have a moral order immanent in it in addition to the natural order, then we get a conception very different from the scientific conception of a mechanistic Nature. This conception is an interesting but highly problematic idea and its plausibility is open to question. A moral order represents what ought to be, while the natural order represents how things are. There is a categorial distinction between the two. A moral order involves norms about right and wrong and these can only be ascribed to conscious beings with a developed moral sense. It is not plausible to ascribe these to a material impersonal force. It is also not plausible to say that the moral order is immanent in Nature in the same way as the natural order. The natural order does not exhibit a moral dimension and Nature certainly does not seem to function in a way, which expresses a moral order. The karma theory, however, seems to support the idea of a moral order in the world in so far as it implies that natural events work in accordance with the demands of karmic justice. It was mentioned earlier that the relation between natural causality and karmic causality is a problematic issue for the theory of karma. Most of the writings on the theory give little or no attention to this issue. As already stated many scholars maintain that the world is actually governed by the law of karma and natural causality works to implement demands of karmic justice but provide no justification for this supposition. It is assumed that the law of karma governs the world and natural events are subordinate to this law and work in accordance with it. However, the law of karma cannot plausibly be equated with a natural law and even if it is supposed to operate in the world through independent causal processes, it cannot be regarded as a naturalistic principle.

Even if karmic causality is accepted for argument's sake, it cannot be identified with natural causality. It is necessary to explain the interplay of karmic processes and natural processes. Wilhelm Halbfass discusses the question of the relation between natural processes and karmic causality in the context of *Nyāya-Vaiśeṣika* and *Mīmāṃsā* schools and admits that the tradition does not always take it for granted that karmic considerations govern the functioning of Nature. According to him, there are questions, ambiguities and 'grey zones', regarding the 'scope and limits' of karmic causality. He states,

> "It is by no means simply taken for granted that the whole world is just a stage for ethically committed or soteriologically meaningful events, or that natural processes are necessarily governed by or subordinate to retributive causality. The realm of cosmology and even that of biology is not *eo ipso* coextensive with the realm of *saṃsāra*, that is, of retribution and of possible soteriological progression."[30]

Halbfass discusses at some length the problems that arise from the 'encounter and juxtaposition' of karma and other contexts of causation.' He observes that though the theory of karma aims at a 'single all-comprehensive world-view, we cannot disregard the concrete historical varieties and deep-rooted tensions and ambiguities which remain with the theory even in its fully developed "classical versions.'[31]

It has been mentioned earlier that we can find diverse views on the issue of the modalities of karmic causality and these challenge some of the claims made in the widely accepted strict law like version of the theory. The writings on the theory of karma, most of the time, do not devote adequate attention to the problematic dimensions of the interaction between natural processes and karmic processes. This, therefore, remains a deeply problematic issue for the theory. The supposition that natural processes are subordinate to karmic causality is not supported by our common experience, which shows that natural processes run their course. It is a separate matter how these affect different people. Excessive heat or cold, for example, adversely affect people irrespective of the fact whether they are good or bad persons. When natural calamities like floods, storms and earthquakes occur, these affect people on a large scale. It would be counter-intuitive and morally unacceptable to assert that only bad people suffer due to these. The operations of natural causality do not distinguish between good and bad people. Therefore, we need to make a distinction between natural laws and karmic considerations. If the theory of karma claims that sometimes natural events are means of implementing karmic justice, it is imperative to justify that it is so and clarify how this is brought about.

The theory claims that whether a new born is healthy or sickly, strong or weak and intelligent or dull, has a long life or short is determined by the past actions of the child. Natural events like disease, disability are also sometimes taken to be consequences of one's actions. It is clear that natural events are being traced to karmic considerations. However, writings on the karma theory, most of the time, assume that this is so rather than justify their claims on the basis of cogent reasons. It is obvious that the quality of life of human beings is affected by natural events. The karma theory introduces a special type of causality, which has an ethical dimension, to explain the quality of life of individuals. It is not plausible to say that human beings are governed solely by karmic causality, nor is it plausible to say that natural causality and karmic causality run parallel to each other and work in harmony. If it is claimed that human beings are subject to both kinds of causality, then it becomes necessary for the karma theory to explain how this works out. We cannot say that natural laws by their very nature work in a way that karmic justice is ensured. We also cannot say that nature continuously adapts to karmic causality and ensures that the impact of natural events on people is what they deserve. Both these views violate our sense of reality. Moreover, most of the time, a natural event leaves an impact on many people. People live and work in a social environment, so what happens to one due to a natural event may affect many others also. A natural disaster affects a large number of people, causing huge loss of life and property. To invoke karmic considerations to explain such events is hugely problematic.

It is clear that the idea, of causal connection between actions and their morally appropriate consequences, has several problematic dimensions and these have not been addressed adequately in writings on the karma theory. The interplay of natural laws and karmic causality has not been explained cogently. Philosophers have often assumed that natural processes work to implement karmic consequences without subjecting this assumption to rigorous philosophical examination. The view that the universe is morally ordered is not tenable. Discussions of karma theory also do not give adequate attention to the impact of a person's actions on others' lives. The karma theory does not admit that a person's quality of experiences is affected by actions of others. But our experience shows that this happens. An attempt to explain these by regarding them as means to implement karmic consequences of one's own actions gives rise to serious difficulties with regard to individual freedom among others. Modern Indian philosophers have recognised this gap in the formulations of the theory and tried to acknowledge the social impact of people's actions. This issue will be taken up later. The idea of a morally ordered universe, where people's quality of life and experiences is determined solely by the inescapable consequences of their own actions alone, is open to serious questions. The quality of an individual's life and experiences at any point of time depends upon the complex interplay of that individual's own actions, impact of natural processes and others' actions. An attempt to provide a single unified explanation and reduce these to the consequences of an individual's own actions is fraught with serious difficulties. It seems more cogent to accept the impact of natural events and actions of other persons on an individual's quality of life and experiences rather than ascribe everything to individual's own past actions. This becomes clearer when we reflect over the impact of natural calamities on people or acts of terrible atrocities perpetrated by th e powerful on the weak and defenceless in the history of mankind. One would feel revolted if, for example, it is claimed that the Jews who suffered at the hands of Hitler or Nazi regime deserved this fate in the light of their own past actions. Attempts to explain natural disasters in terms of collective responsibility of a group of people would be discussed later. It would suffice to say here that our sense of reality around us suggests that we cannot deny that our lives are affected by natural events and other persons' actions. What one actually gets in life depends on a complex interplay of several factors, including one's own actions. The view that everything regarding the quality of life and experiences of a person can be explained in terms of consequences of that person's past actions alone may appear metaphysically more satisfactory but its plausibility remains an open question.

Notes and References

1. The discussion in this chapter borrows heavily from two of my papers published earlier: 'Causality of Karmic Justice', *JICPR,* vol. XVIII, Number3, July-Sept. 2001, pp.129-156 and 'The Idea of a Morally Ordered Universe', *Self-Society and Science: Theoretical and Historical Perspectives,* History of Science, Philosophy and Culture in Indian Civilization, vol. XI, Part 2, Centre For Studies In Civilization, 2004.

2. For example, Wendy Doniger o' Flaherty (ed.) *Karma and Rebirth in Classical Indian Traditions,* Motilal Banarsidass, Delhi, 1983 and S. S. Rama Rao Pappu (ed.), *The Dimensions of Karma,* Chanakya Publications, Delhi, 1987 are two works that include many scholarly articles on formulations of the law of karma in different schools of Indian Philosophy and different aspects of the law. Yet only one paper in Flaherty's book 'Karma, *Apūrva,* and "Natural" Causes: Observations on the Growth, and Limits of the Theory of *Saṃsāra*' by Wilhelm Halbfass takes up briefly the question of relationship between natural laws and karmic causality.

3. *Nyāya Vārttikam, a* commentary on *Gautam Sūtra* by Ūddyotakaracāryā 1.24, Calcutta 1882, cited in Bhimacārya Jhalakikar, (ed), *Nyāya Koṣa,* Bhandarkar Oriental Research institute, 1978, p.224

4. Keśava Misra, Tarka-Bhāṣā, Banarasa, 1704, p.2, cited in *Nyāya Koṣa,* op cit, p.224

5. These definitions and their difficulties have been discussed at length in *Nyāya* texts.

6. David Hume, *A Treatise of Human Nature,* L. A. Selby Biggs, (ed), OUP, Oxford, 1958, p.170

7. J.S. Mill, *System of Logic,* London, 1893, Book III, ch. V, art. 6

8. Hume also raised an interesting issue with regard to the law of causation in the *Treatise.* He distinguishes the proposition

'Everything that begins to exist must have a cause of its existence' from the proposition 'Every effect must have a cause'. He says that the latter is logically necessary but the former is not and its denial is not self-contradictory. Hume could not provide a satisfactory explanation as to why we regard the law of causation as necessary. The difficulty is that this law cannot be said to be based on empirical evidence; it is not conclusively verifiable by experience. While the law is not logically necessary, we continue to search for the cause of an event even after failure to find it. Philosophers differ on the issue how the necessity we ascribe to the law of causation is to be understood.

9. Karl H. Potter argues that defining a cause in terms of regular sequence makes the causal relation too weak and reduces it to a merely empirical relation. Potter says that this kind of definition of causation leads to scepticism, since the relation between cause and effect here is not "strong enough to guarantee results". Potter, 'The Logical Character of the Causal Relation in Indian Philosophy', in Ramji Singh, (ed), *World Perspectives in Philosophy, Religion and Culture,* Bharti Bhavan, Patna, p. 280. It is important to distinguish a causal relation from a mere correlation but statements about the relation are empirical. A true causal statement is not logically necessary; it can be denied without self-contradiction. It is subject to confirmation by empirical evidence and the possibility of it being falsified by future evidence remains open. However, the probability of the denial of a well-established causal statement is almost negligible.

10. K.W. Morgan 'The Nature and History of Hinduism', in Morgan (ed), *The Religion of Hindus,* New York, Ronald Press, 1953, p.22

11. Bruce R. Reichenbach discusses the problematic dimensions of comparing the law of karma with the law of causation in his paper 'The Law of Karma and the Principle of Causation', *Philosophy East and West,* vol.38, No.4, (Oct.1988), pp. 399-410.

12. Rajendra Prasad, *Karma, Causation and Retributive Morality,* ICPR in association with Munshiram Manoharlal Publishers Pvt. Ltd.,New Delhi 1989, p.227

13. Ibid, p. 228

14. Ibid, p. 228

15. Ibid, p. 231

16. Ibid, p. 229

17. A.L. Herman, 'Karmadicy: Karma and Evil in Indian Thought ', Rama Rao Pappu (ed.), *The Dimensions of Karma,* p.232

18. Ibid, p. 229

19. 'Dharma' is a term, which admits of many senses. Here I am using it to refer only to duties, obligations and rights of people.

20. See John Mackenzie, *Hindu Ethics,* OUP, London, 1922, 1971 and Manorama Jauhari, *Politics and Ethics in Ancient India,* Bharatiya Vidya Prakashana, Varanasi, India ,1968.

21. *The Bhagvad Gītā* observes that it is better to die while performing one's own duty (svadharma) than to follow another's (ch.iii,sloka 35). śreyānsvadharmo viguṇaḥ paradharmātsvanuṣṭhitāt,svadharme nidhanam śreyah paradharmo bhayāvaḥa'. Sri Aurobindo translates it as "Better is one's own law of works, swadharma, though in itself faulty, than an alien law well-wrought out: death in one's own law is better, perilous is it to follow an alien law." Sri Aurobindo, *Essays on Gītā,* Anil Baran Roy, ed., Sri Aurobindo Ashram, Pondicherry 1954, p.63. Manu echoes the same idea, 'varam svadharmo viguno na pārakyaḥsvanuṣṭhitāḥ, paradharmeṇa jīvanhi sadyah, patati jātitaḥ'. *Manusmṛiti,* ch.10, sloka 97, Motilal Banarsidass,Delhi, 1990, first published in 1983. Buhler translates it as 'It is better (to discharge) one's own (appointed) duty incompletely than to perform completely that of another: for he who lives according to the law of another (caste) is instantly excluded from his own'. G. Buhler, tr., *The Laws of Manu, Sacred Books of the East,* vol. XXV, OUP, Oxford, 1886, reprint, Delhi, Motilal Banarsidass, 1979, p.423]

22. Bruce Long, 'Human Action and Rebirth in the Mahābhārata', Flaherty (ed.), *Karma and Rebirth in Classical Indian Traditions* p. 43. Long points out that this is one of the few instances where it is

claimed that an individual's karma influences his own and also his close relation's future.

23. D.M. Datta, *Philosophical Perspectives: A Selection of Essays*, Bharati Bhawan, Patna 1971, p.93

24. Rama Rao Pappu, *The Dimensions of Karma*, p3

25. Saral Jhingran, *Aspects of Hindu Morality*, Motilal Banarsidass, Delhi, 1989, p.34

26. Rajendra Prasad, *Karma, Causation and Retributive Morality*, pp. 222-23

27. Ibid, p. 226

28. Mircea Eliade, *The Encyclopedia of Religion*, vol. 12, Macmillan Publishing Company, New York, p.480

29. S. Radhakrishnan, *Indian Philosophy*, vol.2, George Allen and Unwin Publication, Blackie & Son Publishers Pvt. Ltd., New Delhi, 1929, pp. 78-80

30. Wilhelm Halbfass, 'Karma, *Apūrva*, and Natural Causes' in Flaherty (ed.), *Karma and Rebirth in Classical Indian Traditions*, p.272.

31. Ibid p.272

Chapter 4

Rebirth, Personal Identity and Accountability

Belief in rebirth is a necessary corollary of the theory of karma in the Indian tradition. The cycle of death and rebirth (*saṃsāra*) continues because of karmic consequences that have not been realized in an individual's present life and these are experienced by the individual in the next birth. Rebirth thus is a presupposition of the possibility of absolute karmic justice in the world. It may be noted that Plato accepted rebirth but did not subscribe to the theory of karma and religions like Christianity and Islam accept the idea of a person's moral responsibility for one's actions even after death but do not accept rebirth. However, the idea of rebirth and the theory of karma are inextricably linked in the Indian tradition. Consequences of one's actions that have not matured and fructified during the present life of an individual lead to rebirth and determine the circumstances of the individual's birth and the quality of that person's experiences in life. Rebirth of a person makes it possible for karmic causality to unfold and ensure that nobody escapes the morally appropriate consequences of one's actions. The quality of an individual's present life and experiences is determined by the individual's own past actions and so long as accumulated karmic residue remains, the cycle of death and rebirth continues. It ceases only after an individual achieves liberation.

The theory of rebirth is accepted by almost all schools of Indian philosophy; only *Cārvāka* and other materialists do not accept it. Potter maintains that the theory of rebirth along with the theory of karma is viewed in the classical tradition in the spirit of scientific theories.[1] However, we find that most of the time, arguments to prove rebirth are not provided in the tradition. It is possible that since the belief in rebirth has wide support in the tradition, it is most of the time assumed rather than accepted on the basis of rational arguments. Sometimes the theory of rebirth is accepted on the basis of scriptural sayings and is treated as a dogma. It is important to note that the idea of rebirth involves suppositions that are in principle unverifiable by empirical evidence. Most frequently invoked evidence in favour of rebirth is drawn from cases where a person seems to remember experiences that belong to a dead person's life-history. Psychic researches cite such examples and research in this area is being conducted. Philosophical literature in the Indian tradition sometimes tries to provide evidence based on instinctive behaviour of a new-born child. Potter points out that Gautam in *Nyāyasūtra* argues that soon after birth a baby recognizes the mother's breast as a source of food and suckles at it. This and other instances of such instinctive behaviour in the baby are taken by him as evidence of recollections of experiences from one's past life and alternative explanations suggested by his contemporaries are rejected as unsatisfactory.[2]

The above mentioned philosophical arguments, as well as claims of psychic research are open to question and cannot be said to establish the truth of the belief in rebirth conclusively. Generally speaking, the Indian tradition does not discuss the issue of empirical verifiability or grounds for the theory of rebirth. It is clear that many suppositions in the theory, like continued existence of the self after death or soul of the departed person acquiring a new body, are by their very nature not capable of empirical verification. Attempts to support the theory by citing cases where a person apparently remembers events from a dead person's life seem to be based on a failure to recognize the logical nature of the theory. The theory is not derived from empirical data, nor is it subject to confirmation by empirical evidence. Even if the memory claims in the few supposed cases of rebirth are taken as authentic, these are far from sufficient to prove the theory. An overwhelming majority of people have no memories of a past life. Moreover, it may be possible to explain the apparent memory claims on the basis of some other psychic phenomena like clairvoyance, telepathy, etc. Those who affirm rebirth generally do not consider the claim of counter evidence and seem to treat the theory as unfalsifiable. It is clear that the various suppositions in the theory are neither verifiable nor falsifiable by empirical evidence and we do not find many attempts to justifiy these except some like the ones mentioned earlier. John Hick has used the idea of 'eschatological verification' to support the Christian belief in survival of the soul after death.[3] However, it is debatable whether that idea is applicable in the context of rebirth.

In my view the search for empirical evidence for rebirth is misplaced since the theory appears to be a metaphysical one rather than scientific. To discuss the question of empirical or scientific evidence in favour or against the theory is not a very fruitful exercise. However, despite its unverifiable and unfalsifiable metaphysical character, the theory is part and parcel of the karma theory and its significance in the context of this theory cannot be denied.

Rebirth in the Indian tradition is regarded as a result of ignorance and signifies bondage. The cycle of birth and death ceases only when a person attains liberation. As already mentioned, karmic causality is supposed to function across several lives of an individual; actions performed in one life may bring about their consequences in the next life or even later. Every individual is morally responsible and accountable for one's actions and must bear the consequences of those actions in this or later lives. It may be kept in mind that the Indian tradition accepts the possibility of an individual being born as an animal in the next life due to wrong actions and also the possibility of an animal being reborn as a human being as a result of good actions. For the sake of simplicity, the present discussion will not discuss the possibility of such movement from human to animal kind or vice versa. As already mentioned, the caste, length of life and the quality of experiences of a person after rebirth depend upon the consequences of that person's actions in the past lives. In this context a critical question is whether the quality of people's lives and experiences is totally determined by their past actions or individual effort also plays a significant role. This will be taken up in the next chapter.

The karma theory emphasizes that people continue to bear moral responsibility for their actions, not only in the present life but in successive lives. Moral responsibility presupposes personal identity and therefore, the question of personal identity acquires great importance in the context of the karma theory. A person can be held morally responsible for one's own actions, not for others' actions and similarly a person can be rewarded or punished for one's own actions alone, not for actions performed by others. The karma theory maintains that after rebirth a person morally deserves the consequences of actions performed in the previous birth. This implies that the person now is identical with the person who performed those actions in the previous birth, even though that person is someone who existed and died before this individual was even born. The consequences of actions that accrue to a person across several births can be said to be morally deserved by the person, only if, the person remains identical or numerically the same person across those births. The issue of personal identity, therefore, becomes much more complex in the context of the theory of rebirth than the issue of identity of an individual during one's life span.

When we ascribe personal identity to a person, it implies that the person at time t_2 is the same person as some person at time t_1. A person undergoes many changes over a period of time with respect to physical appearance, character traits, likes and dislikes and behaviour pattern, etc. Yet we regard the person as being identical despite such changes. A question of personal identity arises whenever we think of the continued existence of a person over a period of time and re-identify a person after a lapse of time to be the same as some earlier person. This implies that despite many changes, the person is numerically the same as the earlier one. Identity implies persistence, the uninterrupted existence of one and the same thing at two different times. Let us leave the question of rebirth aside for the time being and focus on a person's identity during life. We believe that a person remains identical from birth till death despite different kinds of change. What is the ground of this belief? This brings us to the question of the criterion of personal identity. By 'criterion' is meant necessary and sufficient condition of personal identity over time. The criterion determines which changes in a person do not amount to a loss of identity and which do. We generally do not find a very detailed and systematic discussion on the issue of personal identity within the Indian tradition when the issue of rebirth is discussed. This issue, however, is taken up in the context of Buddhist philosophy because of its denial of a permanent self. The very concept of rebirth presupposes personal identity and therefore it is essential to examine the grounds for ascription of personal identity across lives.

It would be pertinent at this point to briefly outline the debate on the issue of the criterion of personal identity in Western philosophy, especially within the analytic tradition. It will help us to understand the conceptual problems that arise when identity is ascribed across many lives. Philosophers have primarily mentioned three principles as criterion of personal identity, (a) identity of the soul, (b) continuity of memory and character traits and (c) bodily identity. The first takes the identity of the spiritual substance or the soul, the unitary conscious subject of all mental activities of a person, as the basis of personal identity. The second defines identity in terms of continuity of mental life, especially memories and the third takes bodily identity as necessary for personal identity. The latter two are called reductionist theories, since these analyse identity in terms of one or the other kind of continuity or some combination of those. Let me briefly outline these approaches.[4]

Those who subscribe to mind-body dualism maintain that personal identity consists in the identity of the soul of a person. (One exception is John Locke and his approach will be discussed later). For them a person is essentially a soul, a conscious substance distinct from the body and independent of it and as long as the soul is the same, the person is the same. According to dualism, a person's thoughts and experiences etc. change over a period of time but the soul to which these belong remains the same and, therefore, the person remains the same. It does not matter that a person's body and personality changes over a period of time or the person does not remember a large number of past experiences; so long as the soul remains the same, the person remains the same. This approach allows the possibility of change of body, disembodied existence of the soul and a person's survival after death.

It would be pertinent to mention the arguments given by Joseph Butler and Thomas Reid in favour of this kind of approach. Butler states that one knows one's identity immediately or intuitively when one compares the consciousness of the present self with the consciousness of the past self, whether of immediate past or distant past. One knows one's past self through memory,....."by reflecting upon that which is myself now, and that which was myself twenty years ago, I discern they are not two but one and the same self."[5] Reid argues that a person is indivisible; to talk of a part of a person is a 'manifest absurdity'. The identity of a person consists in the uninterrupted and continued existence of that indivisible thing, which he calls his self. A person is not only aware of one's own thoughts, feelings and emotions, etc., which keep changing, but also of the fact that these thoughts and feelings belong to one and the same substance, which one calls oneself or one's mind. "Every man has an immediate and irresistible conviction, not only of his present existence but of his continued existence and identity, as far back as he can remember."[6] Reid says that the identity of a person is revealed to him in a paradigmatic way through his memory. One does not require any proof for this conviction, nor can any proof be given for it. Both Butler and Reid agree that memory is evidence of personal identity but personal identity itself is logically prior to it. They also agree that personal identity is perfect and does not admit of degrees.

Butler and Reid's views are open to several difficulties. The empiricists raised serious questions about the very existence of the soul and challenged the supposition that the substance to which all our thoughts and feelings are supposed to belong is revealed in experience. David

Hume, an empiricist and a sceptic, denied the existence of a unitary, permanent soul as the subject of all mental states of a person on the ground that we do not observe it. He said that whenever we introspect we only come across some perception, of heat or cold, pleasure or pain, etc. but we never have experience of the subject to whom these experiences belong. According to him, the self is nothing but a bundle of distinct but related perceptions, which succeed each other with "an inconceivable rapidity and are in a perpetual flux and movement".[7] Hume further states that, strictly speaking, self can neither be regarded as simple, nor as identical over a period of time; it is a complex of distinct and independent perceptions and these perceptions appear and disappear in quick succession. Our belief in personal identity is a 'fiction of imagination' arising from a confusion between the perception of continued and uninterrupted existence of one object over a period of time and perception of a rapidly moving succession of related objects. Hume admits that our belief in a unitary and identical self is a natural belief and we cannot but entertain this belief, even though our experience cannot justify it. This kind of phenomenalistic and reductionist analysis of self was supported by several later empiricists like William James, Bertrand Russell, A.J. Ayer and G.P. Grice among others.

It may be noted that Hume's view of self as a series of constantly changing perceptions is close to the Buddhist conception of self as a series of causally connected impermanent elements. However, the serial view of self is extremely problematic and unable to explain the features of our mental life like recollection and recognition and above all our sense of our identity. These difficulties have been debated at length in the Western philosophical tradition and also in the Indian tradition, especially with regard to the Buddhist theory. The critics have argued that the denial of a permanent subject of a person's experiences seems paradoxical and counter-intuitive. Within the Western tradition the dualists and the double aspect theory of Strawson, discussed earlier in chapter two, are two major counter perspectives to the serial view of self. The dualistic perspective is widely supported in the Indian tradition also and is challenged by the materialists, apart from Buddhists.

Identity of the soul as the criterion of a person's identity over time is faced with serious difficulties. As aheadly mentioned, the Western empiricists challenged the very existence of the self. Many later philosophers have tried to show that the concept of a person cannot be reduced to a mere series of experiences and a unitary and permanent subject of experiences has to be accepted to make sense of one's mental life. However, the question of the nature of this subject and the criterion of its identity is a separate matter. Even if it is granted that each one of us has direct awareness of ourselves in every experience we have, such awareness is necessarily subjective and not available to other people. Everybody's access is restricted to one's own self. Even if we agree with the claim that we have direct immediate knowledge of ourselves, a person can have such knowledge of one's own self alone but not of the soul of another person. If soul-identity is the criterion of personal identity, a person can apply it only in one's own case. It follows that a different criterion of identity for persons other than oneself would be needed. Reid admits this and says that our judgements of the identity of others will be based on grounds of similarity, etc. Moreover, it remains questonable whether one always has an immediate awareness of one's identity and can be certain of it in every case. In case of amnesia or loss of memory, for example, a person would most probably be unsure or confused about her identity. If a person's certainty about her identity alone matters, then in cases where a person is not sure of who she is, no other ground will be available to judge a question of personal identity. Ascription of moral responsibility for actions and consequent entitlement of reward or punishment for those actions presupposes personal identity. It is, therefore, extremely problematic to base such ascription solely on one's subjective certainty about one's identity. Suppose there is a dispute about a person's identity, we would have to depend upon factors other than subjective certainty of the person about who he or she is.

One point that emerges from the discussion above is that a distinction can be made between a first person perspective of personal identity and a third person perspective of it. From the first person perspective, one may be said to have a direct awareness of one's identity as far back as one remembers. However, when a question of another person's identity is concerned, it becomes a third person perspective and the subjective certainty of a person about her identity would not be enough. Further, if a person has no recollection of certain past events from one's own life, then one would not be able to identify with those events. Thus intuitive awareness of one's self cannot be the basis of personal identity in all cases even in a first person perspective. It follows that bodily identity cannot be ignored as far as the third person perspective is concerned and may be relevant even in the first person perspective, since that provides a way to check the veracity of memory claims made by people. More will be said on this point later in the context of psychological continuity.

Contemporary discussions of the criterion of personal identity in the Western tradition have focussed on psychological or bodily continuity or some combination of these. Psychological continuity includes similarity of personality and character traits and memories of past experiences. A person changes substantially over a period of time but this change is generally gradual and the basic pattern of one's personality and character traits remains largely the same. However, a person's character and personality may change significantly over time but this does not imply that the person is now a numerically different one. Continuity of character and personality traits is thus an important additional consideration but not a necessary condition of identity by itself. Having memories of one's past experiences, however, is extremely important in this context. Memories provide the bond, which enables us to identify with our past experiences and provides a sense of identity over time. Memory as the sole criterion of personal identity implies that a person P_2 at time t_2 is identical with a person P_1 at t_1, if and only if, P_2 remembers at t_2 having the experiences that P_1 had and doing what P_1 did. This kind of memory is sometimes referred to as 'experience memory' or 'memory from the inside' to distinguish it from those cases of memory where a person remembers someone else's experiences or actions. For example, one may remember many people watching a car accident or one's father hitting one's brother at a certain point of time. However, if one remembers oneself being very angry with one's father because he hit the brother or remembers stealing a book belonging to someone else, this memory implies identity of oneself with the concerned person earlier.

John Locke, an empiricist, maintains that memory is the sole criterion of personal identity; it is both a necessary and a sufficient condition of personal identity. Locke distinguishes between the idea of a person and that of a man. The identity of a man, according to him, consists in participation in the same continued life while being united to the same body. The identity of a person, on the other hand, consists in the identity of consciousness, in other words having memories of one's past experiences. The identity of a person, Locke maintains, does not consist either in the identity of the soul, or in the identity of one's body, but in the identity of one's consciousness. Identity of the body constitutes identity of a man, not of a person. As regards the soul, though he accepts the existence of spiritual substance, he regards it as the mysterious and unknown substratum about which we do not really know anything and maintains that its identity is irrelevant for questions of personal identity.

> *"For since consciousness always accompanies thinking, and it is that makes everyone to be what he calls self, and thereby distinguishes himself from all other thinking things; in this alone consists personal identity, i.e. the sameness of a rational being. And as far as this consciousness can be extended backwards to any past action or thought, so far reaches the identity of that person: it is the same self now it was then, and it was by the same self with this present one that now reflects on it, that action was done."*[8]

Locke constructs many thought experiments or imaginary cases to clarify his view. Such thought experiments have been extensively used in contemporary discussions on the issue of personal identity. He admits the possibility that a person's identity may be preserved through a change of thinking or immaterial substance or through a succession of several thinking substances. Suppose two distinct and incommunicable consciousnesses are associated with one body, one during the day, other during the night. Locke asserts that the night and day persons are as distinct as Socrates and Plato.[9] Further suppose the same consciousness is associated with two distinct bodies at regular intervals, this for Locke means that there is one person having two bodies. Similarly, suppose the soul of a Prince, carrying with it the consciousness of his experiences and actions, enters the body of a cobbler, then the cobbler will be the same person as the Prince and will be accountable for prince's actions.[10] Locke maintains that personal identity can be asserted, if and only if, consciousness is the same irrespective of change of body and/or change of the soul. By 'sameness of consciousness' Locke essentiallly means "having memories of one's past experiences and actions." He is of the view that people are morally accountable only for those actions which they remember.

One major objection raised against Locke's theory is that it is circular. Butler argued that memory presupposes personal identity and therefore, personal identity cannot be said to consist in memory.[11] Reid raised a similar objection and said that Locke has confused personal identity with evidence for it, namely memory. This criticism appears valid. It is a logical truth that one can remember only one's own experiences, not someone else's experiences. Thus, one's having a memory of 'x' presupposes that one experienced 'x'. If we say that memory constitutes personal identity, then it amounts to saying that one is identical with the person who experienced 'x', if and only if, one remembers experiencing 'x', but one can remember 'x', only if one is identical with the person who experienced 'x'. Thus, the reasoning becomes circular.

The other major difficulty is that memory criterion leads to paradoxical conclusions. It implies identity where we would normally not ascribe it and denies it where we would normally assert it. If memory is a necessary condition of personal identity, then a person suffering from amnesia cannot be said to have remained identical. A sleepwalker who does not remember the experiences had or actions done while sleep walking would not be the same person after waking up. A drunkard who, after becoming sober, has no memory of his earlier actions would not be the same person as the drunkard. These conclusions are clearly contrary to our common beliefs. Moreover, the criterion destroys the transitivity of identity. An example given by Reid illustrates this clearly. Suppose an officer was flogged when at school for robbing an orchard. Later as a young officer he took a standard in his very first battle. At that time, he remembered being flogged. Later, he becomes a General and then he remembers his taking the standard but has no memory of being flogged. Now if memory is the criterion of personal identity, then it follows that the young officer is identical with the school boy and the General is identical with the young officer, but the General is not identical with the school boy. This is an absurd conclusion.[12]

Anthony Quinton introduces the idea of 'indirect continuity of memory' to solve the difficulty mentioned above. The General in the above mentioned example does not have direct memory continuity with the young boy but he has indirect continuity with him; he has direct memory continuity with the young officer, who has direct memory continuity with the boy. Therefore, the General is identical with the boy.[13] Some philosophers have introduced the idea of 'potential memory' to deal with the difficulties arising because of loss of memory. People may not actually remember all their past experiences and actions but they have potential memories of these and can remember them at some point of time, since these are their own experiences.[14] Others support a causal view of memory grounding it in brain-identity. David Wiggins is of the view that memory and continuity of character together with identity of the brain provides the criterion of personal identity.[15] However, all these proposals are beset with difficulties, which have been debated at length, and their plausibility remains open to question.

The importance of memory for questions of personal identity is evident. Our awareness of our identity is dependent on our memories. Even if the body is identical and our character remains more or less similar over time, we will not have a sense of our identity with our past self in the absence of memories. But we need a criterion to distinguish between genuine and false memory claims. Not every memory claim can be taken at its face value. Even an honest memory claim may not be veridical because one can be mistaken whether one really remembers an event or the apparent memory of it is based on reading a report about the event in question or being told about it. A memory claim would be veridical, if and only if, the event remembered did happen and one who makes the memory claim was a 'witness' to that event and one's belief about the event is based on one's own experience. Since personal identity is the basis of moral responsibility, one's subjective certainty about a memory claim is not enough. We must have objective ways of testing the veracity of a memory claim. It is clear that a person can genuinely remember only those experiences which one had in the past. Wiggins introduced the requirement of brain identity for this reason since science has shown that our brain is the seat of our memories. However, generally speaking we take some one's memory claim as reliable, if the bodily presence of the person can be established at the place and time of the concerned event. Thus bodily identity of the person who makes the memory claim becomes extremely important in this context.

It has been argued above that veracity of a memory claim needs to be established through independent criteria. This becomes important for another reason. Sometimes, a person may claim to remember an event, which apparently belongs to the life-history of another person. It is said that the English king George IV claimed in his old age that he remembered having fought valiantly at the battle of Waterloo. Reports about supposed cases of rebirth claim that people seem to remember events from the lives of persons long since dead. It is said that small children are sometimes able to give vivid and accurate details about events that occurred in the past in some real persons' lives. If these are honest memory claims, then should one conclude that the persons having those memories are actually identical with the dead persons in question? If not, then how to explain this phenomenon? The opinion is divided on this issue. Some thinkers will argue that an honest memory claim is ground for assertion of identity. Others argue that even if such memory claims appear to be honest, it is problematic to treat these as ground for asserting personal identity unless backed by bodily identity. While the significance of memories for questions of personal identity cannot be denied, as mentioned earlier, not every memory claim can be regarded as veridical and a criterion to judge the veracity of such claims is required. This leads us to the question how important bodily identity is for assertion of personal identity. If we allow that identity is preserved despite change of body, then bodily identity becomes irrelevant for questions of personal identity. The dualists, we have seen, allow this possibility on the ground of the identity of the soul and Locke and others on the ground of psychological continuity and memory.

Some philosophers, however, argue that bodily identity or spatio-temporal continuity of a person's body cannot be ignored in this context. A.J. Ayer and Terence Penelhum are among those who argue that bodily identity is the criterion of personal identity. Bernard Williams, however, maintains that bodily identity is a necessary condition of personal identity but not its sufficient condition and considerations of psychological continuity, especially memory, are important. This implies that personal identity cannot be asserted in the absence of bodily identity. Williams' argument is based on the premise that identity is a transitive relation and therefore, the concept of identity cannot admit the possibility of reduplication of a person. The criterion of psychological continuity does not ensure this but bodily identity as a necessary condition of personal identity guards against such a possibility.

Williams argues his case with the help of an example. Suppose a person Charles suddenly one day begins to exhibit character and personality traits of a dead person Guy Fawkes and claims to remember having experiences and performing actions belonging to the life history of Fawkes. He does not remember experiences and actions from his own life that he did remember earlier. On inquiry we find that the events and actions that he claims to remember did happen in Guy Fawkes' life. Can we say that Charles is Guy Fawkes? Suppose we say it is so. It is logically possible that two persons exhibit character and personality like those of Fawkes and make memory claims about events in his life. Thus, suppose Roberts also claims that he had experiences and performed actions that belong to the life-history of Fawkes. If so, following conclusions are possible in such a situation:

(a) Both Charles and Roberts are identical with Guy Fawkes.

(b) Only one of them, say Charles, is identical with Guy Fawkes.

(c) Neither Charles nor Roberts is identical with Guy Fawkes.

If both Charles and Roberts are identical with Fawkes, then they must be identical with each other. William's argues that this implies that the same person is in two different places at the same time and that is an absurd conclusion. We also cannot plausibly conclude that only one of them is identical with Fawkes while the other is only exactly similar to him. This in William's view would be a 'vacuous manoeuvre'. Since both the persons exhibit character traits similar to Fawkes and make memory claims suitable to Fawkes' life, there is no significant and relevant difference between them to give us a ground for drawing different conclusions about them. Therefore, Williams concludes that the correct conclusion in this case is (c). Both Charles and Roberts cannot be said to be identical with Fawkes. He further argues that if we deny identity in the case where two persons seem to make memory claims about experiences and actions of a dead person, then the same conclusion should be drawn in the case where only one person makes such claims. Though there is no reduplication in the earlier case, the relevant factors are the same in both the cases. Charles has the same relationship with Guy Fawkes in the first case as both Charles and Roberts have with him in the second. Williams concludes that Charles should be regarded as exactly similar to Guy Fawkes.

> "We can then say that Charles has the same character, and the same supposed past, as Fawkes, which is just the same as to say that they are in these respects exactly similar. This is not to say that they are identical at all. The only case in which identity and exact similarity could be distinguished, as we have just seen, is that of the body - "same body" and "exactly similar body" really do mark a difference. Thus I should claim that the omission of the body takes away all content from the idea of personal identity."[16]

One may, however, object that the presence of a competitor and consequent reduplication is a significant difference between the two cases. Therefore, it is not essential to draw the same conclusion in both instances. In the case where there is no reduplication, one can plausibly say that Charles is the same person as Guy Fawkes. However, Williams is of the view that this conclusion would be vacuous, because for such a case there would not be any grounds to justify a judgement of identity as opposed to a judgement of exact similarity.[17] Williams further adds that when the consequences of two judgements have significantly different consequences, it is important that the grounds for making those judgements should be different. A judgement of personal identity implies moral responsibility and entitlement for reward or punishment whereas a judgement of exact similarity between two persons does not. In the supposed case of Charles' psychological continuity with Guy Fawkes, it can be a ground for asserting exact similarity between the two but no further grounds are available to justify ascription of identity between the two. Two important points emerge from the above discussion. One, we cannot make a distinction between 'exact similarity' and 'identity' in the context of persons without referring to their bodies. Secondly, psychological continuity does not guard against the possibility of reduplication and is unable to preserve the transitivity of identity. According to Williams, these logical considerations show that psychological continuity cannot be the sole criterion of personal identity and bodily identity must be regarded as its necessary condition.

C.B. Martin does not agree with William's conclusion. He argues that spatio-temporal continuity of the body is also open to the possibility of reduplication.[18] An amoeba splits into two and becomes two amoebas. We cannot say that the two resultant amoeba are identical with the original one because then they would be identical with each other. They are obviously separate entities. We also cannot say that one of those is identical with the original one, since both have the same relation to the original amoeba. Both have a shared life history and were one at an earlier point of time. Suppose we were to extend this example to a human body and admit the possibility of it splitting in two. We face similar issues here as in case of amoeba. This shows that bodily identity criterion also suffers from the same weakness as does the psychological continuity criterion. Williams responds to Martin's criticism by pointing out that the spatio-temporal continuity criterion has the advantage that its application would necessarily reveal the reduplication. Therefore, bodily identity must be taken as a necessary condition of personal identity.

If bodily identity is regarded as a necessary condition of a person's identity, then change of body or survival after death becomes inadmissible. Mythological stories often talk of change of body of a person. Religions in general accept that a person continues to exist after the destruction of the body and continues to bear moral responsibility for actions performed during one's worldly existence. The idea of survival after death has been widely accepted by philosophers also. Most philosophers admit that the notion of such survival is not self-contradictory or logically impossible. Even Strawson who, as already mentioned, supports a double aspect theory of person, allows the possibility that an embodied being may continue to exist in a disembodied state after death. He, however, says that such a disembodied being can be called a person only in a logically secondary sense.[19] A materialist like Armstrong also admits that disembodied existence is a logical possibility, but denies that it is a factual or empirical possibility.[20] If bodily identity is a necessary condition of personal identity, then disembodied existence of a person or change of body is conceptually ruled out. Granted that the idea of a disembodied person does not appear obviously nonsensical, it is clear that this idea and its conceptual implications are not clear at all. The difficulties in this and other related ideas have been discussed in detail elsewhere.[21] It would suffice to say here that the conceptual dimensions of the idea of survival of a person in a disembodied state or in a new body are not clear and the evidence in favour of such survival is far from conclusive.

Philosophers have extensively discussed thought-experiments of brain transplant and duplication, fission and fusion of persons to bring out the difficulties in the proposed criteria of personal identity. A paradigm case of personal identity is where both bodily and psychological continuity is preserved. Both kinds of continuities are deeply embedded in our concept of personal identity. When these two types of continuities are seen to be in conflict as a result of supposed body-switch or brain transplant or some other factor, it becomes essential to decide which one is more fundamental. The decision is not easy and philosophers disagree on this issue. When our usual criteria do not give us a clear answer, should we conclude that the question of personal identity has become conceptually undecidable? Or should we say that it is possible to lay down the rules or the convention, which will determine an answer in such cases as we do in borderline cases of material things? Both the suggestions are deeply disturbing and unsatisfactory, keeping in mind that a question of personal identity has serious implications regarding one's moral responsibility and hopes for the future.

Richard Swinburne rejects the reductionist approach, which defines personal identity in terms of some kind of continuity.[22] He argues that the difficulties mentioned above arise because the approach itself is incorrect. According to him, we have to appreciate a vital difference between questions of identity of material objects and those of personal identity. In the case of material objects the logically necessary and sufficient conditions of identity coincide with the public evidence for it but in the case of personal identity logically necessary and sufficient conditions for it cannot be given. In his view continuities of character, memory and body constitute evidence of personal identity, which normally give clear decisions about a person's identity. However, personal identity is something ultimate and absolute; it is over and above such observable continuities and cannot be analysed into these. His standpoint is close to the views of Butler and Reid discussed earlier. Swinburne maintains that there is always a true answer to the question of a person's identity, though sometimes we may not be able to know this answer because of the insufficient or conflicting nature of the available evidence. B. A. Brody and R. Chisholm also support a similar non-empiricist, non-reductionist approach. For them personal identity is a 'further fact' and various kinds of continuities mentioned earlier are its evidence.[23] The further fact here is the identity of the soul or the self.

Swinburne makes following observations to clarify the logical gap between continuities and identity:

(a) Identity is a matter of all or nothing, 'x' is either identical with 'y' or not, but continuity is a matter of degree.

(b) Personal identity is always determinate but thought-experiments about fission and fusion of a person show that psychological and bodily continuity may not yield a determinate answer in every case.

(c) Since continuity is a matter of degree, the possibility of borderline cases in its case always remains. But personal identity does not admit the possibility of such cases.

Swinburne is right that identity is not a matter of degree and borderline cases cannot be ruled out in case of continuities. The distinction between the two contexts of ascription of identity was mentioned earlier. The first person context is where one has an awareness of one's own identity over time derived from experience memory of one's past. The resultant subjective certainty of one's identity is something very personal and available to oneself alone. However, one also ascribes identity to persons other than oneself and this is a third person context. This is done on the basis of various kinds of observable continuities, which in most cases do provide a clear answer. Still, it cannot be ruled out that in some cases we may not have a clear answer to the question of identity of a person. Dualists like Swinburne assume that in such cases also there is a true answer to the question of personal identity, though we may never know it. They seem to give primacy to the first person context and seem to assume that a person always has certain knowledge of one's own identity. But this assumption is open to question. A person who has amnesia or who suddenly discovers that her body is significantly different from what she remembers it to be, will be confused about one's own identity. Even if it is granted that each person has a unitary and permanent soul, it is not knowable by others and they can judge identity only on the basis of various continuities. If these continuities do not provide a clear answer, it is of no help to say that there is an unknowable true answer.

In the context of problems highlighted by thought experiments, Derek Parfit suggests a radically different approach; he recommends that we should use the concept of 'survival' instead of 'identity'.[24] He rejects the claim that identity is a further fact over and above continuities. He maintains that what matters is not identity but survival and it is psychological continuity, which is important for personal survival. When there is no reduplication of psychological continuity, we can speak of identity. However, in supposed cases of reduplication, fission or fusion of persons, it is more appropriate to use the concept of survival of a person since survival does not imply identity and admits of degrees. Therefore, we can meaningfully talk of one person surviving as two, or conversely, two persons surviving as one. Moreover, relations that matter for survival are a matter of degrees and, therefore, it is possible to talk of degrees of survival.

The concept of 'survival' presents a new perspective to explain the problematic thought-experiments discussed earlier. In a case of reduplication or fission of a person 'A', we would conclude that 'A' survives as both the resultant persons and in a case of fusion of two persons 'A' and 'B' into 'AB', we would say that both of them survive in 'AB'. Parfit thinks that memory and other psychological phenomena can be defined without presupposing personal identity. He argues that ascription of moral responsibility should be on the basis of survival. He does not regard personal identity as a necessary condition of moral responsibility and regards a person's moral responsibility for an action to be directly proportionate to that person's psychological continuity/connectedness with the agent of the concerned action. Parfit's theory is not free from difficulties but it definitely offers a radically different perspective on the issue of personal identity and moral responsibility.

Let us now reflect over the issue of rebirth and moral responsibility in the light of the above discussion on the concept of personal identity. What is the criterion of personal identity in supposed cases of rebirth? Obviously bodily identity is irrelevant here. Continuity of character and personality traits is also not very significant here. The theory of rebirth does not require that the person in a new birth should bear a similar character and personality as the one had in earlier life, nor is it required that the person in new birth must have memories of experiences and actions from the past life. Though having memories of experiences appropriate to the life of a dead person are sometimes cited as evidence in favour of the theory, such memories are not regarded as a necessary condition of personal identity in the theory of rebirth. According to the theory, each person has had a series of past lives, though the person may not have any memories of those lives. Thus, both bodily and psychological continuity become irrelevant in this context as far as the question of the criterion of a person's identity is concerned.

What then is the ground for an assertion of identity of the person now with some person long since dead and why is the person now accountable for actions done by the dead person? It may be noted that the theory does not tell us with whom a certain person now is identical; it just asserts that the person had a previous life and continues to be morally responsible for the actions performed in that life.

What connects a person with a past birth is the supposed association with the dead person's soul together with the karmic residue of actions performed in the previous life. The identity of the soul carrying the karmic residue from the past life constitutes the basis for assertion of identity in this context. The theory of rebirth thus must depend upon a non-reductionist theory of personal identity, which takes identity of the soul as the sole criterion of identity. The problems that such a theory faces were discussed earlier. There is an additional problem here. Philosophers like Butler, Reid and Swinburne, who take identity of the soul as the criterion of personal identity, explain one's intuitive knowledge of one's identity on the basis of memories of one's past experiences and actions. In the context of rebirth, however, memories of one's past life are not available in most cases. A person is believed to be identical with some unknown and unknowable dead person. It is evident that the person cannot have any present awareness or knowledge of his or her identity with the self in the previous birth. The claim of one's moral responsibility for actions performed in one's past life, therefore, becomes extremely problematic in this context. One does not know who one was and what one did in one's past life and why. Thus one is supposed to be morally accountable for actions of which one has no recollection, done by an agent whose identity one does not know and to whom one cannot relate in any way. The claim of a living person's identity with some unknown dead person and the assumption of moral responsibility of the living person for actions performed by the dead person both become hugely problematic and difficult to justify.

The theory of karma affirms that the karmic process bestows rewards or punishments on the appropriate person. One may object whether a person can be rewarded or punished for actions of someone unknown and for actions which one does not recollect. As mentioned earlier, Locke believed that memories of past actions are a necessary condition of moral accountability of a person for those actions. Ordinarily, in the absence of memories of concerned events, we may still hold a person responsible for past actions on the basis of the person's bodily identity with the agent. But that is ruled out in the context of rebirth. It is, therefore, difficult to understand the grounds that justify the claim that events in a person's present life are morally appropriate reward or punishment for actions performed by that person in a past life. Thus, the central thesis of the theory of karm*a*, that events in one's present life are to be understood as morally just consequences of one's past deeds, remains an assumption which is extremely problematic.

Unlike other philosophical schools, Buddhism, as mentioned earlier, explains rebirth without the supposition of a unitary and permanent soul. It regards a person as a series of different psycho-physical elements, which are causally linked. Strictly speaking, a person cannot be said to remain identical over time in this theory. There is nothing that remains unchanged in the aggregate of impermanent psycho-physical elements that constitute a self. Therefore, diachronic identity in a strict sense cannot be ascribed to a person. Scholars differ how the no-self theory of Buddhism is to be understood. Some view it as a 'reductionist theory of self', analysing self as a bundle or series of different elements. Some like Sue Hamilton and Keith Ward interpret it as a 'stream or process theory of self' the view that 'self' is a continuous flow of connected mental events.[25] Giles regards it as an 'eliminative theory', which eliminates unitary self and personal identity altogether.[26] He argues that our use of words, like 'I' or 'self' are merely grammatical devices. Buddhist scholars regard our common belief in personal identity either as expressing conventional reality of persons, which helps to achieve the objective of minimizing suffering, or as a pragmatic device to help us lead a self-less life.

It is clear that scholars disagree on the interpretation of ascription of personal identity to individuals and its implications. It is not clear what is taken to constitute personal identity in the absence of a permanent self since the link between the dead person and the new birth is simply the causal connection between the last member of the serial self and the first member of the fresh series in the next birth. To account for memory and recognition, etc., and also the passing on of karmic responsibility from one birth to another, Buddhists claim that every successive member in the aggregate that constitutes a self retains traces of the past members. William James comes close to this idea in his analysis of the self as a stream of connected experiences, as discussed earlier. The bundle theory of self in Buddhism leads to the denial of personal identity in a strict sense and reduces it to a conventional truth. This, however, remains a very problematic issue in the Buddhist theory.[27]

A serial view of self leads to the conclusion that self can neither be regarded as simple, nor can we ascribe identity to it over a period of time. Yet all of us believe in our identity throughout our lives and this belief is hard to give up. We find that Buddhism, on the one hand, implies that our common sense belief in personal identity does not represent reality but, on the other, rehabilitates this belief on the basis of conventional or pragmatic considerations. Personal identity is a necessary condition of moral responsibility and it is not clear how to account for a person's continued moral responsibility over several rebirths in the face of denial of identity. Does it imply that, strictly speaking, moral responsibility for past actions cannot be ascribed to individuals? It is problematic to ground moral responsibility in an erroneous belief or a pragmatic or conventional device. This, therefore, remains a very difficult issue in Buddhist philosophy.

As mentioned earlier, Parfit gives a radical proposal to replace our discourse of personal identity with that of survival and use the idea of personal survival as the basis of ascription of moral responsibility to people for their actions. However, it is debatable whether Parfit's suggestion can be applicable in the context of Buddhist theory because the latter does not emphasize psychological continuity between the past self and the self after rebirth. According to Buddhism, 'rebirth' means that one aggregate, before going out of existence, causally gives rise to another. The new aggregate is neither totally different from the earlier one nor the same. The doctrine of dependent co-origination provides the middle path between the two extremes by linking the two through a causal chain.[28] If we grant for the sake of the argument that the potentiality of actions to produce certain results is passed on from one member to another, it may provide a basis to connect the person in one birth to the person in another. However, it is open to question whether persistence of karmic potentiality by itself provides a satisfactory ground for continued moral responsibility for past actions. Clearly Buddhist philosophy gives rise to difficult questions for both the theory of rebirth and the karma theory.

From the discussion above, it is clear that the issue of the criterion of personal identity in the context of rebirth is a really problematic one. Psychological and bodily continuities are not relevant here. Except in Buddhism, sameness of the soul provides the criterion of personal identity in case of rebirth. However, both the dualistic theory of person and the non-reductionist theory of personal identity face serious difficulties. It is also open to question whether identity of the soul can be regarded as a justified ground for ascription of moral responsibility in the absence of bodily and psychological continuity. Both kinds of continuities are deeply embedded in our ordinary concept of personal identity. In a paradigm case of personal identity both kinds of continuities go hand in hand. However, when the two are supposed to pull in different directions or one of them or both are absent, we do not have a clear answer to the question of a person's identity. Some of the answers that have been provided in contemporary Western philosophy are unable to clear our perplexity but it also does not seem acceptable to lay down new conventions to decide questions of personal identity. These issues have been discussed at some length elsewhere.[29] It would suffice to say here that the theory of karma and rebirth fails to provide a satisfactory criterion of personal identity.

The claim of complete karmic justice of actions and their just consequences across several births of individuals cannot be justified without providing a plausible criterion of personal identity. However, this issue has not received the attention it deserves in discussions of the theory.

Notes and References

1. Karl H. Potter, 'Karma and Rebirth: Traditional Indian arguments', Rama Rao Pappu, ed., *The Dimensions of Karma,* Chanakya Publications, Delhi, 1987, p.139
2. Ibid, p. 155
3. John Hick has used the concept of 'eschatological verification' to support the idea of survival after death. He argues that certain kind of experiences after death can verify the belief in the survival of the soul after death. However, this concept involves Christian religious assumptions and ideas and is problematic. It is open to question whether it gives us a notion of verification as commonly

understood. See John Hick, *Faith and Knowledge,* Collins, Fontana Books, Glasgow, 1966, and *Philosophy of Religion,* second edition, Prentice Hall of India, New Delhi, 1978, pp.90-92

4. For a detailed and critical discussion of various theories see Vibha Chaturvedi, *The Problem of Personal Identity,* Ajanta Publications, Delhi, India,1988
5. Joseph Butler, "Of Personal identity', W.E. Gladstone, (ed.) *The Analogy of Religion,* OUP, Oxford,1896, p.345
6. Thomas Reid, *Essays on the Intellectual Powers of Man,* Baruch A Brody (ed.) M.I.T. Press, England 1969, p.35
7. David Hume, *A Treatise of Human Nature,* A.D. Lindsay, (ed.), J. M. Dent & Sons Ltd., London 1911, vol.1, p.238
8. John Locke, *An Essay Concerning Human Understanding,* A. C. Fraser (ed), Clarendon Press, Oxford, 1984, vol. 1, Book II, ch. XXVII, 10, p.451
9. Ibid, p.464
10. Ibid, p.457
11. Butler, *The Analogy of Religion,* p.346
12. Reid, *Essays on the Intellectual Powers of Man,* pp.213-14
13. Anthony Quinton, 'The Soul', B. A. Brody, (ed.) *Readings in the Philosophy of Religion,* Prentice Hall, New Jersey, 1974, p.645
14. For a detailed critical account of memory- criterion see Mrinal Miri, 'Memory and Personal Identity', *Mind,* vol. LXXXII, No. 325, Jan. 1973, p.4
15. David Wiggins, *Identity and Spatio-Temporal Continuity,* Basil Blackwell, Oxford, 1967
16. Bernard Williams, 'Personal identity and Individuation', *Problems of the Self,* Cambridge University Press,Cambridge, 1973, p.10
17. Ibid, p.20
18. C.B. Martin, 'Identity and Exact Similarity', *Analysis,* vol. 18, No.4, 1957-58, pp.83-88
19. Strawson, *Individuals,* Methuen, London, 1959, p.115
20. D. M. Armstrong, *A Materialist Theory of Mind,* Routeledge &Kegan

Paul, London, 1968, p.19

21. Vibha Chaturvedi, *The Problem of Personal Identity,* pp.104-112
22. Richard Swinburne, 'Personal Identity', *Proceedings of the Aristotelian Society,* new series, vol. LXXIV, 1973-74. Also 'Persons and Personal identity', in H.D. Lewis, (ed.) *Contemporary British Philosophy,* George Allen &Unwin, London,1961, Fourth series,1976
23. Baruch A. Brody, *Identity And Essence,* Princeton University Press, 1980, pp. 52, 56 and R.M. Chisholm, Person And Object, Allen and Unwin, London, 1976, p.112
24. Derek Parfit, 'Personal Identity', Jonathan Glover, (ed.), *The Philosophy of Mind,* Oxford University Press, Oxford, 1976 and, *Reasons And Persons,* Clarendon Press, Oxford, 1984
25. Sue Hamilton, *Indian Philosophy: A Very Short Introduction,* Oxford University Press, oxford, 2001 and Keith Ward, Religion and Human Nature, Oxford University Press, Oxford, 1998
26. James Giles, The No-Self Theory: Hume, Buddhism, and Personal Identity', *Philosophy East and West,* vol.43, No.2, (Apr. 1993), pp175-200.
27. Anthony Rudd, 'No Self? Some Reflections on Buddhist Theories of Personal Identity', *Philosophy East and West,* vol.65, No.3, (July2015). Rudd discusses different interpretations of the Buddhist theory and their difficulties pp. 869-891.
28. For a discussion on the issue of self in various schools of Buddhism, see James P. McDermott, 'Karma And Rebirth in Early Buddhism', Wendy Doniger O'Flaherty, (ed), *Karma And Rebirth In Classical Indian Traditions,* Motilal Banarsidass, Delhi, 1983.
29. Vibha Chaturvedi, *The Problem of Personal Identity,* ch.6

Chapter 5

Free Will And Fatalism

Let us briefly recapitulate the important points that emerge from the discussions in the preceding chapters. With the exception of materialists, all orthodox and heterodox schools of classical Indian philosophy accept the theory of karma. There is broad agreement among philosophers that the theory is aimed at explaining inequities at birth and suffering of innocent and good people. The Indian tradition takes cognizance of the fact that this feature of our lived reality is problematic and attempts to explain it in terms of morally appropriate consequences of human actions. This approach is different from the way the general problem of evil is discussed in Western philosophy. The theory claims that there is perfect retributive justice in the world, since everybody has to bear the consequences of their actions in accordance with the moral quality of those actions. The strict, law-like version of the theory supported by modern Indian scholars has wide acceptance and has come to be seen as the standard version of the theory. It is important to note, however, that a look at various discussions on the karma theory within the tradition, makes it clear that some versions differ from the strict version on one or more points. Various schools of philosophy differ on questions like the nature of the karmic residue, the modalities of the karmic process, inescapability of karmic consequences and other related issues. We also find differences among various schools on notions of self and agency. Yet we can find some common threads among these varying views. They accept rebirth and transmigration of residue of an individual's actions to the next birth and maintain that the circumstances at birth and the quality of life of an individual, specially happiness and suffering experienced in one's life, is determined by this residue. There is general agreement on the point that the relation between actions and their consequences is causal and the karmic process unfailingly ensures that everybody bears the consequences of one's actions, most of the time after a time-gap and in the next birth. We also find a broad agreement on the point that an individual bears the consequences of one's own actions alone, not of actions performed by another. The strict theory claims that all the happiness and suffering that individuals experience in life are deserved consequences of their own past actions, though some formulations refer to other causes also in this context. In short, despite inner complexity and diversity of views on the issue of actions and their consequences, we can find broad agreement within the tradition on key issues and central claims of the theory and the formulations of the theory by modern Indian philosophers try to capture these elements.

The theory of rebirth is an essential corollary of the karma theory in the Indian tradition and is accepted by all philosophical schools, except the materialists. However, we do not find many attempts to support the belief with arguments in philosophical discussions. Potter observes that the tradition for the most part accepts this theory and does not feel the need to justify it by arguments. Commenting on the cases of people apparently exhibiting memories of their previous lives, Potter says, "Indian philosophy does not characteristically argue for rebirth and thus hardly mentions, much less explores, these explicit recollective experiences, accepting their possibility and validity without much question."[1] It seems that the tradition has an implicit faith in the theories of rebirth and karma as received wisdom. The idea of a previous birth explains the circumstances at birth and the quality of experiences of an individual in the present life and the idea of future births provides a ground for assertion of perfect justice of rewards and punishments for an individual's actions. The belief in rebirth is neither verifiable nor falsifiable through empirical evidence and the evidence from apparent memories of past life cited in its favour is inadequate and admits of alternative interpretations. The karma theory incorporates several other elements besides the idea of rebirth, which are not verifiable or falsifiable. A question arises: what is the logical status of the theory?

We find a wide divergence in the views of philosophers on this issue. Karl Potter is of the view that the classical Indian tradition takes the theories of karma and rebirth in the spirit of scientific theories.[2] Rama Rao Pappu regards the law of karma as a 'naturalistic principle,' which is both "descriptive and prescriptive, naturalistic and normative."[3] Puligandla regards it as a synthetic apriori principle, which is necessary for the possibility of a rational, systematic knowledge of the world. He takes it to be at par with fundamental scientific theories.[4] Mohapatra maintains that the law of karma ".. is proffered as a transcendental argument that claims to make intelligible some very important facts of life which would otherwise remain unexplained."[5] I have argued that the karma theory cannot be compared with a fundamental scientific theory because of its unverifiable and unfalsifiable character. Puligandla and Mohapatra seem to draw inspiration from Immanuel Kant' theory of knowledge and use the ideas of synthetic apriori and transcendental principles respectively.However, this comparison does not seem valid. Kant's concept of 'trancendental principles' referred to those synthetic apriori principles, which provide necessary conditions of the possibility of our knowledge of objects and refer to our conceptual framework. The karma theory is not put forward as an essential element of the epistemological apparatus of human beings; it does not constitute a principle, which is necessary for making knowledge of objects possible. It is supposed to explain an aspect of reality or certain phenomena, which we find morally problematic.

Sometimes the law of karma is regarded as an ethical or moral law but this view is also untenable. The theory is not an ethical one, though it has an ethical dimension. Its subject matter does not relate to issues of normative ethics. It posits the moral ideal of perfect retributive justice in the world and makes the ontological claim that this ideal is realized in the real world through the operation of karmic processes. The karma theory ignores the categorial distinction between 'what is the case' and 'what ought to be the case.' The law of karma is regarded as an extension or application of the law of causation, which functions within the world quite like a natural law. The theory has an explanatory objective and uses several unverifiable elements to fulfil that objective and it relates actions with their just rewards and punishments and, therefore, has a moral dimension. Perhaps it is this multi-dimensional character of the karma theory which gives rise to diverse and conflicting views on its logical status. Sometimes the theory is considered to be a dogma and that makes it a matter of faith rather than critical reflection. I think the theory of karma is a metaphysical one and attempts to explain certain features of the real world that we find morally problematic.

The conception of the karmic process posits the idea of residue of actions and asserts that these transmigrate with the self and generate their consequences after maturation in future or in the next birth of individuals. Most of the philosophical schools seem to support a dualistic conception of a person and define 'person' essentially as a unitary, permanent soul. An action is performed by an embodied being. However, it is not tenable to identify the agent with the embodied being in a straight forward manner because the body is destroyed at death but the individual exists in a new body and continues to bear the moral responsibility for actions in one's future births. It follows that agency cannot be ascribed either to the body of an individual or to the combination of the body and self that constitutes an individual but only to the self. The notion of the agent becomes even more complex as a result of the metaphysical standpoints of different schools on the fundamental nature of the self. As mentioned earlier, some systems maintain that the self in its true or essential nature cannot be ascribed agency. However, the issue of the essential nature of the self does not seem relevant while discussing the question of agency since the idea of action and its consequences is applicable only to embodied individuals at the empirical level, who are yet to attain liberation. And from the empirical point of view it seems that agency can be ascribed to the conscious self. Since Buddhism denies a permanent soul, agency in this context has to be ascribed to the series that constitutes a person. Both the dualistic conception of a person and the no-soul theory are faced with several serious difficulties, which have been outlined briefly in earlier chapters. It has been argued that a dual aspect theory of person, which gives due weightage to both the bodily and psychological aspects of human beings appears more plausible. However, it becomes difficult to account for ideas of survival after death and rebirth on this theory.

Different terms are used in the tradition to refer to the residue of actions. There is, however, a broad agreement on the issue of consequences of past actions. The form of life (animal or human), caste, circumstances at birth, length of life and quality of experiences of an individual are widely accepted as consequences of past actions. The theory claims that good actions lead to happiness and bad ones to suffering and loss but does not outline specific consequences of specific kinds of action. The idea of maturation of residue of actions suggests that there has to be a gap between performance of actions and occurrence of their consequences but the duration of that gap and conditions of maturation remain unclear. Consequences are regarded as constituting morally appropriate and just rewards or punishments for actions. It is claimed that the consequences of the residue, which has matured, are inescapable for individuals. As clarified earlier, the notion of consequences in the karma theory is different from our ordinary understanding of the term 'consequence' and is problematic. It seems that the karma theory presents a very complicated and unclear picture of the relation between our actions and their consequences such that we neither know which past actions are responsible for our present condition, nor what will be the consequences of our present actions and when will these materialize. The theory also does not tell us about the interplay of the impact of our present actions and past ones.

Views can be found in the tradition, which differ from the strict law-like formulation of the theory. Some regard the Supreme Divine Being to be essential for the unfolding and proper functioning of the karmic process. The possibility of avoiding consequences of actions through repentance, expiation, meditation and devotion, etc., is accepted by some, as is the possibility that performance of rituals or sacrifices and devotion to God can bring gains and success in our ventures and avoid loss. We also find the idea of transfer of merit from one person to another and the idea that a boon or curse by a seer can bring consequences for a person. Thus, the possibility of one person bearing the consequences of another person's action is admitted. Sometimes multiple agencies are held to be responsible for the quality of human life. It is important to remember that the tradition presents a wide variety of ideas on karma. However, the strict version, which maintains that the law of karma operates on its own and ensures that nobody escapes the just rewards or punishments for past actions, remains the dominant interpretation of the theory.

The karma theory posits a causal connection between an individual's actions and their consequences and its non-theistic formulation maintains that the karmic process works on its own and ensures that people experience appropriate consequences of their actions. This conception of the karmic process is problematic and seems untenable. A causal connection is a uniform and universal relation of regular sequence between two kinds of events. In the *varṇāśrama dharma* scheme, the moral value of an action, its rightness or wrongness, is relative to the agent who performs that action because prescribed duties for different castes and stages of life are not the same. The notion of causality does not incorporate this kind of agent-relativity. Moreover happiness is relative to subjective considerations and therefore, happiness as a consequence cannot be subjected to mechanical causal processes. Since a consequence is regarded as a morally appropriate reward or punishment for an action, therefore, the karmic process must include some mechanism for moral evaluation of actions and their appropriate rewards or punishments. The conception of the karmic process on the lines of a mechanically functioning causal process is thus not tenable. The capability to make moral evaluation can neither be ascribed to Nature, nor to the karmic process itself. The theistic versions of the theory ascribe the moral evaluation to a divine being. However, such theories are open to other difficulties and the dominant view of the law of karma believes it to work independently. The karma theory posits the idea of a moral order in the universe which implements karmic justice. This idea can be challenged on many counts.

One of the major problems with the karma theory relates to the issue of the criterion of personal identity. The theory asserts that an individual continues to bear moral responsibility for one's actions across successive rebirths. Personal identity is a necessary condition of moral responsibility. One can be held accountable for and deserves reward or punishment for one's own actions alone. We do not find detailed discussions on the issue of the criterion of personal identity in the classical Indian tradition. Discussions in contemporary Western philosophy on the issue mention three factors, identity of the soul, psychological continuity including memories of past experiences and actions and bodily identity. Bodily identity is ruled out in the context of rebirth and continuity of memory is also not regarded as essential. An overwhelming majority of people actually have no memories of their past life. Therefore, only sameness of the soul can be said to provide the criterion of identity. There are serious problems with this criterion, which need to be addressed. The identity of the soul by its very nature is not subject to observation and it is debatable whether a person can be held morally responsible for actions of a dead person, which one does not even remember. The Buddhist view of self denies that a self remains identical and yet accepts rebirth and karmic responsibility. The issue of personal identity and rebirth in Buddhism is therefore extremely problematic and its plausibility remains open to question. The karma theory fails to provide a cogent and tenable criterion of personal identity, which may justify its claim of perfect karmic justice.

Form the above discussion it is clear that the theory has several problematic dimentions. Let us now consider some major objections frequently raised against the karma theory in philosophical discussions.

KARMA AND FREE WILL

One major objection against the theory is that it leaves no room for freedom of the will. Freedom, along with personal identity, is also a necessary presupposition of moral responsibility. A person can be said to be morally responsible only for those actions, which the person has freely chosen to perform; where the person was not forced or coerced to do something. It is not, however, easy to clarify what this freedom implies over and above absence of physical coercion. We do not find a systematic or detailed discussion of the notion of 'free will' in the Indian philosophical tradition. Much of the discussion on individual freedom focuses on the issue of liberation and freedom from the cycle of birth, death and rebirth. The issue of free will is also sometimes side-lined by the argument that the real self is always free.

As mentioned earlier, *Sāṁkya*, for example, denies that the real self is an agent and Shankar argues that the individual self is ultimately identical with the one supreme reality and plurality of empirical selves and their actions belong to the realm of empirical reality. The distinction between the ultimate and phenomenal reality seems to pave the way for the argument that the real self or pure spirit is always free and the question of karmic consequences has no significance in this context. This view finds an echo in some modern Indian thinkers also. Radhakrishnan, for example, asserts that the law of karma has no relevance for the 'real man'. In a similar vein, Chattopadhyaya asserts that the self is not an agent and, therefore, does not participate in the karmic process.[6] However, karmic considerations govern the empirical life of individuals who have not achieved liberation. Actions of a liberated individual do not accrue residue and do not bind that individual. Therefore, as far as the empirical life of embodied beings is concerned, the issue of freedom as a presupposition of moral responsibility remains important. It pertains to the question whether the actions people perform are free or predetermined by karmic causality. In other words, the issue is whether the choices people make in life are free or determined by their past actions.

The issue of free will has been debated at length in the Western philosophy. In theological contexts, one of the questions it centres on is the apparent incompatibility between divine omnipotence and omniscience on the one hand, and human freedom on the other. If human beings have free will, then God cannot control what they do, nor can God have foreknowledge of their actions. Conversely, if God has foreknowledge of human actions and has control over these, human beings are not free and not morally responsible for their actions. A similar conclusion follows in case it is argued that destiny predetermines people's choices and actions. The theory of karma is often criticized for leading to fatalism and this objection would be valid, if the consequences of past actions of an individual determine what that individual does in the present life.

The metaphysical debate on free will is focused on the issue whether the choices people make are determined by prior causes, such that a person is bound to choose or do what one does, or people have control over their actions. Human beings are part of Nature, which is governed by the Law of Causation; every event that occurs must have a cause. Does the law govern our will also? Hard determinism argues that human actions have prior causes and are not free. People could not have done otherwise than what they actually do at any point of time. The desires and intentions of human beings are determined by factors like their physical and mental make-up, their upbringing and social environment, etc., factors which are not under their control. Determinism implies that the choices people make could not have been otherwise and therefore, strictly speaking, people are not morally responsible for their actions. This position is obviously problematic and most philosophers do not accept it. Belief in free will implies that people have the capacity to choose their actions and have control over their actions. They could have acted differently had they chosen to do so.

People decide in accordance with their desires, aspirations and motivations, etc., and act accordingly. This capacity to choose and control our actions is integral to our existence as humans and is the basis of our moral responsibility. One deserves to get reward or punishment for some action, only when that action is free. We live in a social environment and our interactions are based on the belief that people are morally responsible for their actions.

Many philosophers arugue that free will is compatible with causal determinism.[7] So long as our actions are not constrained or forced by external factors, we act freely. Our actions have their causes in our desires, motivations and preferences and even if these are shaped by our upbringing and environment, etc., our actions are free since these causes are internal to us. Our actions are free so long as we do what we choose or prefer to do and could have done otherwise, if we chose to do so. The fact that people have second order desires is important in this context. Though generally our actions are directed towards fulfilling our desires, it is also possible that we may choose not to fulfil a desire and that reflects a second order desire. For example, a person who is very fond of sweets may decide not to have any because of a desire to lose weight. Thus, so long our actions depend upon our choices and are not coerced by external factors, we act freely. However, it is not easy to clarify the relevant capacity to choose and the relevant kind of control over actions that define free will. Philosophers have different views regarding these. It is not necessary for us to discuss these debates and we can in general say that a person is morally responsible for those actions, which are based on her free choices.

It is a well-known fact that our desires and preferences are greatly influenced by our upbringing, family values and social institutions. Human beings live and act in a social environment and have to engage with social structures while acting. Sociologists' opinions differ on the question whether individuals or social structures have primacy in the context of human agency. Some give more importance to social institutions and point out that social structures like class, gender, religion, ethnicity, sub-culture and caste impact our choices and limit individual freedom significantly. Social structures also influence the opportunities available to individuals to choose and pursue their goals. However, others argue that individuals have the capacity to modify and reconstruct their social environment and therefore, individuals should be given primacy in this context. Some sociologists acknowledge the influence of both social structures and individual agency and take these as complimentary forces, which influence each other. It is undeniable that individuals' choices and decisions are impacted by their family and social environment and yet it cannot be denied that the individuals also influence these. Feminists have pointed out how patriarchal structures influence women's socialization, which leads to internalization of patriarchal values, and consequently women often choose to follow the patriarchal social norms and behaviour patterns even to their own detriment. This is referred to as "failure of autonomy."[8] Similarly, freedom of choice and availability of opportunities gets severely restricted in case of people belonging to economically weaker and socially oppressed groups and often leads to failure of autonomy. Even though theoretically every individual has free will, the capacity to exercise this freedom is impacted significantly in real life by the social environment in which people perform actions. An individual's power is directly proportionate to her ability to choose her actions. While the impact of social structures on an individuals' capacity to exercise freedom is undeniable, it remains true that individuals have the capacity to rise above their circumstances and defy social influences. We find that two persons placed in similar social conditions may chart out the course of their lives in very different ways and have very different achievements. Human enterprise is a very important factor in shaping individual achievements.

Does the karma theory impose constraints on the free choice of an individual? Hiriyanna offers a kind of compatibilist account and argues that an individual's actions are preordained by past actions but the karma theory does not deny individual freedom. According to him, freedom does not mean 'total absence of determination or mere caprice' but 'being determined by oneself' and the karma theory affirms self-determination. The causes that determine an individual's actions lie in the individual's own past actions and their consequences and this does not imply determination by external factors. Therefore, human freedom is compatible with the supposition that "everything that happens in the moral realm is preordained."[9] One wonders whether this is a case of self-determination or denial of freedom. Can the actions of a past life be treated as internal to an individual in the present life like one's desires etc.? It would be pertinent here to mention a view that tries to explain how our past actions impact our present choices. It is claimed that an action leaves a tendency (*vāsanā*) in the agent to repeat it. It follows that good actions would give rise to a tendency to repeat good actions and would thus make us good persons. Similarly, bad actions would result in making us bad persons inclined to perform bad actions. It seems that a person who performs good actions in one life will be naturally inclined to perform good ones in the next birth and is highly likely to perform such actions. The same would apply to bad actions of an individual, which would leave tendencies to repeat bad actions in subsequent lives. Suppose we accept that an individual's desires and choices are influenced by tendencies generated by his past actions, does this imply a denial of free will?

Kaufman argues that if past actions are taken to causally determine an individual's character or dispositions in the future life, then it implies denial of human freedom. An individual who performs wrong actions will not only get lowly circumstances in the next birth but also wicked and malevolent dispositions. Similarly, one who has performed good actions in previous life will get good circumstances and also good dispositions in the next birth. "Now even one's character and moral choice are influenced, even determined by, one's past lives; this threatens to do away with free moral choice altogether."[10] He adds that it would be impossible for an individual, who inherits wicked dispositions in the present life, to improve the moral quality of her actions. In other words, the wicked actions of one life will result in an individual being doomed forever. On the other hand, good deeds would equip an individual with good dispositions and pave the way for future improvement.

Kaufman's conclusion does not seem valid. Even if an individual's dispositions or tendencies are determined by one's past actions, it does not follow that the individual has no freedom to choose. First of all, on compatibilist accounts of free will mentioned above, acting on one's own tendencies and consequent desires, etc., would constitute acting freely, since the causes lie within the agent and do not represent outside force. Thus individual freedom can be reconciled with the supposition that our tendencies or nature are shaped by our past actions. Secondly and more importantly, human beings have the capacity to curb their tendencies. They have 'second order desires' and these are a significant dimension of their freedom. An individual may have a natural inclination to do something or have a strong desire to do something but the individual may also have a second order desire to suppress or ignore that inclination or desire and may act accordingly. Therefore, it remains within the power of a human being to choose to perform good actions despite being pulled in the opposite direction by bad tendencies. *The Bhagvad Gītā* teaches us that inborn tendencies are very powerful but it is possible for people to control these and people should endeavour to do so. Taking a similar approach, T.M.P. Mahadevan argues that though an individual acquires certain tendencies and dispositions from past actions and these influence how the individual acts in the present life, yet the individual is free to change these and shape the future as one wishes.[11] N. A. Nikam also asserts that the law of karma ".. does not state an unalterable necessity but a modal possibility or a conditional relativity."[12] Thus, even if past actions are believed to determine the present tendencies of a person, it remains possible for the person to overcome those tendencies and choose to follow the right path. It is true that acting morally would be easier for a person having a good character and inclinations, whereas it would be much more difficult for a person who has to struggle against her natural tendencies to follow the right path. In a sense everybody has an opportunity to improve one's future but some will face greater hurdles in this endeavour than some others.

The karma theory, on the one hand, talks of determination of the quality of our lives by our past actions but it also, on the other hand, emphasizes that everyone has the opportunity to improve future life by performing good actions in the present life. As mentioned earlier, a person is bound to bear the consequences of ripened residue of one's actions, but one can impact the consequences of rest of the accumulated residue through self-effort. A person can improve the future life by performing good deeds in the present life. The message is that one should make serious efforts to rise above one's bad tendencies and perform right actions and thus improve one's future life. The karma theory, therefore, does not deny individual freedom and does not undermine individual effort. Though it does put constraints on the start one gets in life and the conditions in which one has to function, it does not imply that our decisions are predetermined by past actions.

As mentioned earlier, the conception of the soul varies in different schools of Indian philosophy and these differences have implications for their conception of human freedom. However, many philosophical standpoints have explicitly affirmed freedom of the individual. Shankar, as mentioned earlier, regards plurality of individual selves as ultimately unreal and the question of individual agency and freedom is valid in his philosophy only at the level of the phenomenal reality. Clooney points out that Shankar admits that we can attribute moral responsibility to human beings, only if they are free agents and he accepts human freedom on the authority of the scripture. According to him, the scripture tells us both that "*Brahman* alone is the cause of everything" and that "human beings are free." Clooney adds that the *vedantins* like Badarayan and Shankar acknowledge the apparent conflict between the supposition that '*Brahman* is the ultimate omnipotent and intelligent source of the universe and cause of all action' and the assertion that 'human beings have free-will', and try to reconcile the two.[13] It seems that Shankar tries to address it by an appeal to the scriptural authority, though the conflict is not really resolved. Timalsina states that Shankar accepts free will at the conventional level of reality. Individuals are free to choose their actions but they do not have control over the consequences of actions. However, this acceptance of agency and free will at the conventional or empirical level does not conflict with the meta-level discourse about *Brahman* alone being real and the unreality of agency at the ultimate level of reality. In Shankar's philosophy the concept of agency is a result of ignorance since at the ultimate level of reality there is no agent and no action and thus the issue of free will becomes irrelevant.[14]

Ramanuj has a different view. He regards individual selves as part of the ultimate reality and hence real. He also supports the idea that individuals' decisions to do something are their own and the Supreme Self does not interfere with these. The Supreme Self takes note of their decisions and the actions that flow from those, and appropriately rewards or punishes them.[15] Ganeri points out that though the supreme Self is the cause of all other things in Ramanuj's philosophy, he regards each finite self as an agent who freely chooses actions. The Supreme self does not determine the actions of individual selves. It brings about things 'as a form of consent (*anumati*)' to what individuals freely choose to do. In other words, the Supreme Self makes the realization of individuals' choices possible.[16] Ganeri comments that Ramanuj ascribes real and free agency to the individual selves. But he also "emphasizes that the finite self's fulfilment comes from the recognition of its dependency on and service to the Supreme Self." Ramanuj's account thus expresses "a form of compatibilism".[17] It is, however, open to question whether Ramanuj really succeeds in showing that the agency of the Supreme Self and of the individual selves can operate without conflict.

Jainism also accepts that every individual has control over one's life and has to face the consequences of one's actions. An individual can choose to increase the defiling effect of actions on the soul or move towards freedom from rebirth by purifying the impact of one's actions by following the prescribed ethical rules. Individuals have freedom to choose their actions and, therefore, are morally responsible for their actions and must face the consequences of these actions. Jainism does not accept the possibility that an individual can mitigate or avoid the consequences of one's actions with the help of a deity or higher beings. Jainism thus asserts that the accumulation of karmas in the soul or expelling of these from the soul is dependent upon an individual's free choices alone. Chappel comments that Jainism presents a sharp contrast to grace oriented philosophies.

> "Jainism stands starkly at the existential edge, proclaiming that each individual carries ultimate control over his or her own life. Karma determines all things, and each soul faces, moment to moment, the decision to continue in patterns of behaviour that densify karma and hence obscure the soul or to take up the steady path to purification."[18]

Buddhism provides a perspective on human freedom, which is different from the ones mentioned above. As discussed earlier, Buddhism denies that actions have their origin in an agent, since there is no self over and above the elements that constitute it. It does not have a notion of free will, which is equivalent to the one found in the Western philosophy. Given its principle of dependent origination, Buddhism cannot accept that something exists without a cause. Some philosophers, therefore, think that Buddhism implies determinism. Meyers, however, does not agree with this view. He observes that the Buddhist ideal of liberation requires that individuals should have some control over their mental states and, therefore, it has to accept some kind of free will. Buddhism maintains that freedom is ascribed to individuals in a conventional sense. It recognizes that individuals enjoy empirical freedoms to choose and control their actions and accepts that the freedom to choose is real from a conventional perspective.[19] From the ultimate perspective, freedom is not real since there is no self to enjoy it. However, from the conventional perspective, individuals have the freedom to choose to cultivate their mental attitudes and control their actions in a way which would lead them to liberation. According to Meyers, "..the logic of liberation not only presumes the empirical freedoms of choice and control recognized by libertarians and compatibilists alike, but involves the cultivation of *greater* freedom and self-control through the recognition of non-self."[20] However it is debatable whether this view provides a plausible explanation of ascription of agency and freedom to persons. Moreover, it becomes difficult to explain the idea of individuals' moral responsibility for their actions because of the denial of personal identity. Buddhism accommodates the ideas of personal identity and freedom as conventional truths. Whether this move succeeds in providing a satisfactory account of human agency and freedom remains controversial.

From the above discussion it follows that the Indian philosophical tradition broadly agrees that individuals have freedom to choose their actions, though the idea of free will does not always fit in smoothly in the metaphysical perspectives of many schools. The issue has not received the attention it deserves and is often overshadowed by the emphasis on liberation as freedom from the cycle of rebirths. The karma theory states clearly that individuals remain morally responsible for their actions across several births and must bear the consequences of those actions. Thus, past actions do put a constraint on individuals in so far as they cannot avoid the impact of the consequences of their past actions on their lives. At the same time, the theory provides individuals the option to improve their future life through performance of good actions. At the empirical level, however, the karma theory does impose constraints on the range of choices and opportunities available to an individual, since past actions are said to determine the caste and circumstances at birth of a person. As mentioned earlier, Hindu ethics lays a lot of emphasis on everyone following one's own caste duties (*svadharma*). The circumstances at birth determine the start an individual gets in life and the opportunities available for self- advancement. Clearly factors like lower caste, low economic status of the natal family, poor health and low intelligence of the newborn, etc., put serious constraints on the opportunities and options available to an individual for growth and development. These may seriously diminish their ability to exercise free choices. Both caste and gender considerably affect the power of an individual to make free decisions. Thus even if the karma theory does not deny free will, it implies that consequences of past actions do significantly affect individuals' capacity to exercise free choice.

The social environment of an individual may facilitate and strengthen her freedom or put constraints over it. Severely constraining external conditions like slavery, debilitating poverty and extreme social oppression may almost negate or substantially reduce the actual power of an individual to make free choices. However, it remains possible that an individual may overcome such constraints to some degree and be able to develop oneself. Therefore, the theory of karma does not imply that past actions completely determine our present life, though it clearly implies a significant impact of past actions on the conditions in our present life. S. Radhakrishnan provides an interesting analogy to explain the interplay of individual freedom and the impact of past actions. He compares life to a card game, namely Bridge. The players are dealt a hand each and then what they make of that hand depends on how well they play with those cards in accordance with the rules of the game. A good player would be able to see possibilities and use them to score well, whereas a bad player would not be able to do so. Thus past karma determines the circumstances in which an individual begins life but it is in the hands of the individual to utilize these well or not.[21] Summing up the modern Indian approaches on the issue of individual freedom, Creel observes,

> "The basic question that is posed is whether the doctrine of karma admits freedom: if we are the sum of our yesterdays, how can we affect our tomorrow? Hindu thinkers generally reply that our karma places us where we are but does not determine how we shall react to, or act in the situations in which we find ourselves. For Radhakrishnan and many others, karma sets conditions but does not impose rigid limits."[22]

KARMA AND FATALISM

The karma theory is often criticised on the ground that it leads to fatalism and implies that whatever happens in one's present life is predetermined by past actions and is bound to happen. Human effort cannot change what is predetermined to happen. It would be pertinent to mention a few points regarding the notion of deferred consequences here. The theory maintains that the consequences of past actions are actualized only after maturation of their residue and occur after a lapse of time, mostly in future births. This creates an impression that the consequence of an action cannot follow immediately after the action. It may be noted that this idea of 'consequence' is different from its ordinary notion, which allows both that the consequence may follow an action immediately or may be delayed. The supposition that the consequences of our actions can occur only after a time-gap seems to make the connection between actions and consequences very complicated and opaque. The karma theory does claim that the consequences of our actions may be delayed and occur after a considerable lapse of time but it does not seem to categorically assert that it would be so in every case. However, the idea of maturation does suggest that there would be a time-gap between the performance of an action and actualization of its consequences, though no time line is given for maturation and actualization of the consequences. The theory does not posit clear and definite links between an individual's actions and the quality of her experiences. Moreover, the theory does not clarify the interplay between the consequences of past actions and the impact of present actions of an individual in shaping her life.

An important issue in this context is whether one's actions and efforts (*puruṣakāra)* in the present life can make a difference to one's present conditions or the present life is solely determined by one's past actions. We find that this question is debated in the tradition. As mentioned earlier, some formulations of the karma theory mention fate or destiny among the multiple causes of the quality of human life and the fate is often identified with accumlated karma. A question then arises whether one's life is predetermined by fate or destiny or one can shape it through self-effort. Three answers are possible here:

(a) Destiny is all powerful and self- effort is ineffective against it.

(b) Self-effort is all important and can overcome the destiny.

(c) Both destiny and self-effort are important for success and happiness in life.

All these views are reflected in the debates on the relative influence of destiny and self-effort in determining the quality of one's life. Flaherty mentions examples, which show that this issue figures in *Purāṇas.* Fate and karma are often said to work together, sometimes these are even regarded as identical. For instance, the *Bhāgvat Purāṇa* says, "By karma impelled by fate" a being is born with a body. Similarly, a sage tries to dissuade Parashar from killing all the demons as revenge for his father's murder by arguing that it was his father's fate that brought about the murder. In another instance, a sage tries to persuade Dhruva not to kill yakṣas by arguing that the cause of birth and death is fate.[23] Flaherty points out further that the question whether gods are subject to karma and fate is also debated. She observes, "In the light of these two beliefs-that god controls fate, and that the gods are controlled by it-many texts argue that man himself can do nothing to battle these inexorable forces. Yet this argument is challenged as often as it is stated without challenge."[24] As mentioned earlier, the *Mahābhārata* mentions several causative factors responsible for human condition including fate and scholars differ whether these are separate from the impact of past actions or identical with it. Bruce Long observes that the term 'fate' in the Epic is identified with a variety of factors like divine providence, past actions, time etc. However, despite the fact that the specific meaning of the term differs in various contexts, "... the term fate consistently indicates certain external forces over which the individual exercises no control, either in actualizing or deactualizing any particular state of affairs."[25] Long mentions in his discussion several examples from the Epic, where characters debate the impact of destiny on one's life and also sometimes blame other factors like gods and Time for what happens with them.[26] He mentions Yudhishthir's comment from the 'Sabha Parva' where he blames fate for his inability to say no to the second invitation for gambling from Duryodhana, despite knowing about the bad results of the game with the cunning Shakuni as his opponent. He mentions other observations in the Epic, which suggest that fate controls decisions and actions of people. As mentioned earlier, Long believes that the reference to different agencies as causes of events by the characters shows that they accept multiple causes of human condition. However, many others have a different opinion on this issue. Yuvraj Krishan, for instance, maintains that the conflict between *daiva* or fate and man's effort is resolved in the Epic by establishing a close link between the two. The *Mahābhārata* claims that fate cannot give results unless aided by effort and effort can modify fate. At another place it is said that fate follows karma.[27] The Epic, as discussed earlier in chapter two, also provides examples where multiple causative agencies are either identified with or made subservient to the impact of past actions.

It is clear that the tradition presents diverse opinions on the role of destiny or fate and self-effort in shaping human life. Earlier three possibilities about their relation had been mentioned. The possibility that sometimes fate can compel a person to act against his better judgement is accepted but so is the possibility of fate being assisted and modified by effort. The dominant view seems to reject multiple causes of human condition and accepts the impact of one's past actions as the sole cause. This view, however, does not imply that an individual's efforts are of no value. As mentioned earlier, the theory allows free will and, therefore, it is possible for an individual to overcome the circumstances and tendencies determined by past actions. One can improve one's future life through efforts in the right direction and can also vastly damage one's future by one's wrong actions. It is also sometimes accepted that the residue of evil actions, which has not yet matured, can be reduced or cancelled through performance of right actions. The tradition puts great emphasis on following one's duties and performing right actions. Thus, the theory does not imply that an individual's efforts in the present life bear no fruit and everything is predetermined by past actions. However, individuals have to live under the constraint that they cannot avoid the consequences of matured residue of their past actions. To that extent certain things are predetermined to happen, irrespective of the moral quality of one's actions in the present life. The impact of past actions may also influence the success one gets in one's efforts. One factor, which is definitely beyond human control, is the occurrence of the consequences of past actions. The theory does not clarify, however, when and how these consequences occur. The overall emphasis of the theory is to encourage individuals to accept their moral responsibility for their present lot and suffering and try to ensure a better future life through their efforts in the right direction. Above all the Indian tradition advises individuals to work towards the ultimate aim of liberation and get out of the cycle of birth and death.

It is thus clear that the karma theory neither denies free will nor implies fatalism totally. However, it does set conditions under which free will is exercised and self effort bears fruits.

Notes and References

1. Karl H. Potter, 'Karma and Rebirth: Traditional Indian Arguments', Rama Rao Pappu, (ed.) *The Dimensions of Karma*, Chankya Publications, Delhi, 1987, p. 155
2. Ibid, p. 139
3. Rama Rao Pappu, (ed.) *The Dimensions of Karma*, 'Introduction', p.3
4. R. Pulingandla, 'Karma, Operational Definitions And Freedom', Rama Rao Pappu, (ed.) *The Dimensions of Karma*, pp.121-138
5. P.K. Mohapatra, 'Karma, Freedom and Responsibility', *Sandhan*, Journal of Centre for Studies in Civilizations, vol. XV, Number 1&2, Jan-Dec. 2015, p.80
6. Austin B. Creel, 'Contemporary Philosophical Treatments of Karma and Rebirth', in Ronald W. Neufeldt, (ed.) *Karma And Rebirth: Post Classical Developments*, State Univ. of New York Press, Albany,1968, pp.4-5
7. 'Free Will', *Stanford Encyclopaedia of Philosophy*, first published Jan 7, 2002, revised Aug 21 2018. The article discusses the various attempted definitions of free will and their implications and difficulties. Also see 'Compatibilism', by M Mckenna, April 2004. Both accessed on April 12, 2019
8. 'Feminist Perspectives on Autonomy', *Stanford Encyclopaedia of Philosophy*, first published on May 2, 2013, Revised Dec. 11, 2018, accessed on April 12, 2019
9. M. Hiriyanna, *Essentials of Indian Philosophy*, George Allen &Unwin Publishers, Great Britain, 1949, Unwin Paperbacks, London, 1978, pp. 46-47
10. Whitley Kaufman, 'Karma, Rebirth and the Problem of Evil', *Philosophy East and West*, vol.55, No.1, Jan2005, (15-32), p. 26

11. T.M.P. Mahadevan, 'Indian Ethics and Social Practice', Charles A. Moore (ed.), *Philosophy and Culture East and West: East-West Philosophy in Practical Perspective,* Honolulu, University of Hawaii Press,1962, p.483 quoted by Austin Creel, 'Contemporary Philosophical Treatments of Karma and Rebirth', Ronald W. Neufeldt (ed.), *Karma And Rebirth: Post Classical Developments,* p. 4

12. N.A. Nikam, *Some Concepts of Indian Culture: A Philosophical Interpretation,* Indian institute of Advanced Study, Simla, 1967, p. 29, quoted by Creel, p.4

13. Francis, X. Clooney, 'Evil, Divine Omnipotence and Human Freedom: Vedānta's Theology of Karma', *The Journal of Religion,* vol.69, No.4, Oct. (1989), pp. 530-548

14. Sihaneshwar Timalsina, 'Self, Causation and Agency in the Advait of Śankara, Matthew R. Dasti and Edwin F. Bryant, (eds), *Free Will, Agency and Selfhood in Indian Philosophy,* OUP, Oxford, New York, 2014, p.197

15. Elisa Freschi, The Indian Philosophy Blog, https://indian philosophy-blog.org/2015/01/21 free-will-in-Ramanuja/ posted on 21st Jan. 2015, accessed on 14th Jan. 2019 at 12:45 PM

16. Martin Ganeri, 'Free will, Agency, and Selfhood in Ramānuja', Dasti and Bryant (eds), op. cit., p. 243

17. Ibid, p. 253

18. Christopher Key Chappel, 'Free Will and Voluntarism in Jainism', Dasti and Bryant (eds), op cit., p. 84.

19. Karin Meyers, 'Free Persons, Empty Selves', Dasti and Bryant, (eds.) op. cit., pp.50, 64

20. Ibid, p. 51

21. Sarvapalli Radhakrishnan, 'Karma and Free will', *Modern Review,* 3, (May 1908), 424-428 as quoted by Autin B. Creel, op cit, pp.3-4

22. Creel, 'Contemporary Philosophical Treatments of Karma and Rebirth', op cit, p. 3

23. Wendy Doniger O' Flaherty, 'Karma and Rebirth in the Vedas and Purāṇas, Flaherty, (ed.) *Karma and Rebirth in Classical Indian Traditions,* pp.23-24.

24. Ibid p. 25

25. Bruce Long, 'Human Action and Rebirth in the Mahābhārata', O' Flaherty (ed.) *Karma and Rebirth in Classical Indian Traditions,* p. 45

26. Ibid, pp.45-47

27. MBH 13.6.22 and MBH 13.6.47 as quoted by Yuvraj Krishan, *The Doctrine of Karma,* ch. 21, section VIII, pp. 258-259

Chapter 6

DIFFCULTIES AND LIMITATIONS

Some problematic dimentions of the theory of karma have been discussed in earlier chapter. However, there are certain other issues, which pose a serious challenge to the theory. This chapter outlines some of these.

KARMA AND THE PROBLEM OF EVIL

The karma theory is sometimes regarded as offering a solution to the problem of evil and suffering in the world. The problem of evil in Western philosophy is posed as a challenge to the belief in an omnipotent and benevolent God as the creator of the world. It is a logical problem of apparent incompatibility between three claims made by theists, (a) God is omnipotent, (b) God is benevolent and (c) evil exists in the world. If God is benevolent, He would wish to eradicate evil and suffering from the world, if He is omnipotent, He would do so. Therefore, there would be no evil in the world. But evil exists, therefore, either God is not omnipotent or He is not benevolent. However, Christianity believes that God, the creator of the world, is omnipotent, omniscient and benevolent and the argument from evil attempts to show that the theistic position is not tenable. Theists have tried to provide different solutions to this problem. They argue that the existence of physical evil like disease, poisonous animals, plants and natural calamities, etc., are compatible with the notion of a benevolent creator because God allows these for a good reason. With regard to the existence of moral evil or man's wrongdoing, theists argue that human beings are free and are responsible for their wrong actions, therefore they themselves, and not God, is responsible for the existence of moral evil in the world. The difficulties in the suggested solutions have been widely discussed in philosophical writings and none of these suggested solutions seems fully satisfactory.

Philosophers differ on the question whether the karma theory provides a solution to the problem of evil or not. Flaherty thinks that the Indian philosophical tradition does not seem to recognize the problem of evil and may be said to not even have the concept of evil, but Indian mythology does.[1] Arthur Herman, on the other hand, maintains that the karma theory offers a satisfactory solution to the problem of evil.[2] It may be noted that the theory of karma is not primarily aimed at solving the problem of the existence of evil in the world, but it does address the issue why the quality of experiences of people differs and why good people suffer. Kaufman observes that the karma theory can be seen as addressing the 'existential problem of evil,' namely, why there is suffering and death in the world.[3] It is important to recognize that the theory attempts to explain human suffering in the wider context of explaining the inequities at birth and the differences in the quality of life of individuals. It implies that all the suffering of individuals constitutes deserved consequences or punishment of their own past actions. Wherever natural events seem to cause suffering to individuals, these are viewed as means of actualization of the consequences of past actions of those individuals and become part of the unfolding of karmic causality. However, all natural evil is not explicitly ascribed to past actions of individuals. Moral evil or evil intentions and actions of people are ascribed to their free-will. The strict version of the karma theory implies that all human suffering, whatever be its source, is deserved punishment for wrong past actions whose moral responsibility rests on the suffering individuals themselves. It follows that all suffering is morally justified punishment for wrong actions freely chosen by people.

However, this explanation has several problematic dimensions. Some difficulties in the idea of karmic causality as an instrument of retributive justice were discussed earlier in chapter three. It was argued that moral evaluation of actions and their just rewards and punishments is integral to the idea of karmic justice but the karma theory is unable to account for it in a cogent manner. Moreover, the issue of the criterion of personal identity becomes highly problematic in the context of multiple rebirths and it is questionable whether a person can be said to have remained identical in the absence of relevant physical and psychological continuities. Kaufman in his critique of the theory mentions two reasons why an individual's suffering cannot be regarded as just punishment for his own past wrong-doing.[4] He argues that justice demands that the person being punished should know the misdeed for which punishment is being given. However, in case of rebirth the suffering individual has no idea why he is being punished. This criticism seems valid since the theory does not enable an individual to relate instances of present suffering to specific past actions. In some mythological stories a seer or a saint is brought in to identify the past wrong deed, which is the cause of the present suffering of an individual. However, the individual has no memory of the actions of the past life to be able to understand which wrong action of his is the cause of his present suffering. Can the suffering then be regarded as just punishment? Kaufman answers in the negative. He endorses the view of Christmas Humphreys, who maintains that an individual's suffering for the actions of a person about whom the individual remembers nothing, would be unjust.[5]

As mentioned earlier, the theory of rebirth does not claim that an individual must remember in the present life one's experiences or actions performed in previous life. Since the theory does not mention causal connections between specific actions and specific consequences most of the time, people cannot know which past actions have caused their present suffering. If the punishment were to follow immediately after the wrong action, an individual would probably be able to establish a connection between the two. However, the punishment for wrong actions may occur after a long gap in time or in the next birth. Thus the theory does not clarify how an individual would be able to know why he/she was being punished. An individual has no means to understand the nature and the circumstances of the wrongdoing and therefore not able to get any lessons for future improvement in conduct. Kaufman comments that, "... given the apparently random and arbitrary pattern of rewards and punishments," the theory of karma would not be useful for moral education or moral progress. He adds that absence of memories of actions of past life makes the karma theory "more of a revenge theory than a retributive one-and hence morally unacceptable."[6] Kaufman's use of the terms 'random' and 'arbitrary' here can be challenged because the focal point of the theory is that all the suffering and all the happiness an individual gets in life constitute morally appropriate consequences of individual's own actions. Perhaps Kaufman simply wishes to point out that there is no understandable pattern to occurrence of these rewards and punishments, since we do not know when they would occur and why.

Chadha and Trakakis do not agree with Kaufman's line of reasoning.[7] They argue that it is not necessary that the person who is punished be aware of the specificities of the crime for which punishment is being given. They support a weaker interpretation of the expression 'being aware of one's crime,' which only requires that a person has some understanding of why one is being punished. They argue that since the karma theory explains every case of suffering as a necessary consequence of a person's own past misdeeds, the person in a general way would understand why he is being punished.[8] However, it appears that the punished person's lack of memory of past misdeeds poses a serious problem. Given that one accepts the karma theory, all that one can acknowledge is that one must have done something wrong at some point of time in some past life and the present suffering is a punishment for that. But if one does not know specific details like what wrong one did, under what conditions one did it and whether and how it caused harm to others, etc., it is impossible for anyone to judge whether the punishment is justified. It is to be noted that a judgement of morally appropriate punishment, as we ordinarily understand it, is based on such specificities of the wrong deed. If the connections between particular type of actions and particular type of consequences are not stated and the specific details of the wrong action and its impact are not known, it is not possible to judge whether a certain punisment is just or not . Moreover, we find that even with full knowledge of the specific details about a crime, two judges may differ regarding the appropriate punishment for it. Chadha and Trakakis seem to assume rather than justify the claim that every case of present individual suffering is a necessary consequence and just punishment of a past wrong action of the individual. What is said here about suffering would also apply to happiness as reward for past good actions. In the absence of memory of past good actions and specific causal connections between good actions and good results, an individual cannot relate the present happiness to specific past actions. This point is not relevant to the problem of evil, but to the broader claim that karmic causality delivers perfect justice.

Kaufman's second objection is based on the requirement of proportionality of the punishment to the crime in question. In other words, the degree or severity of suffering must be appropriately proportionate to the evilness of the wrong deed. Kaufman argues that the magnitude and variety of suffering we see in the world make it difficult to understand what kind of wrong doings deserve such terribly harsh punishments like people slowly starving to death in a famine, being subjected to terrible torture, being burnt alive in a fire, young children being crippled in an accident and people dying a painful death due to some terminal disease like cancer. "It is difficult to believe that every bit of this kind of suffering was genuinely earned."[9] He adds that even the idea of the 'pool of karmic residues' fails to justify such severe suffering. It is debateable that a huge collection of past wrongs can justify "a single, horrible punishment" and it is morally more appropriate than "smaller punishments over a longer period."[10] Chadha and Trakakis rightly point out against Kaufman that we do find horribly cruel, brutal and malevolent actions in the history of human civilization and these are equally hard to understand.[11] It seems that it may sometimes be possible to justify a case of terrible punishment to an individual by linking it to a horrible wrong deed. The difficulty, however, is much deeper. The karma theory does not tell us how to connect kinds of suffering to kinds of wrong-doing. We, therefore, get no road map to connect wrong actions to appropriate suffering and right actions to appropriate happiness, apart from the general contention that happiness and suffering of individuals in the present life are appropriate rewards or punishments of their past actions.

Kaufman argues that the karma theory does not really offer an explanation of human suffering. It explains the circumstances and quality of the present life through an individual's actions in a previous life, and the quality of that previous life is explained on the basis of one's actions in the life prior to that one and so on ad infinitum. It, therefore, just 'pushes the problem back' instead of solving it.[12] Flaherty observes in a similar vein, "Karma "solves" the problem of the origin of evil by saying that there is no origin...But this ignores rather than solves the problem."[13] The Indian tradition does regard the world and karma to be devoid of a beginning (*anādi*). Shankar says that this is a truth derived from the Scripture. Hiriyanna, regards the question 'when an individual first incurred the responsibility for one's wrong action' itself as inadmissible. The theory of karma posits a series of births of an individual having no beginning, which comes to an end once the individual attains liberation. Roy Perret offers a different jusification. He argues that the idea of a beginning-less series of births is not problematic. He is of the view that the karma theory provides a satisfactory explanation of every particular instance of human suffering and that is enough. It is unreasonable to demand an 'ultimate explanation' of the origin of human suffering.[14] Though the Indian tradition widely endorses the view that the karma is devoid of a beginning, we find a difference of opinion among philosophers on the issue whether the idea of an infinite series of previous lives provides a satisfactory explanation of the origin of suffering or we require an additional ultimate explanation in terms of the first cause of suffering.

From the above discussion it becomes clear that even if it is accepted that the question of the ultimate origin of suffering is not valid, the claim that individuals' present suffering is a just and deserved punishment for their own past wrong actions remains deeply problematic. The theory cannot be said to provide an adequate explanation of human suffering.

KARMA AND THE SOCIAL DIMENSION OF ACTIONS

A major weakness of the theory of karma is its inability to explain satisfactorily the suffering or happiness of an individual that is caused by the actions of another person. As mentioned earlier, the theory claims that all the suffering and all the happiness a person gets in present life is a consequence of the person's own actions. But our experience shows that actions of other people have an impact on our lives and our actions impact the lives of others. Suppose a person 'A' burns the house of another person 'B' leading to serious hardships for 'B' and his family. Suppose further that 'A' is jailed for this crime and he himself and his family also suffer as a result. In this case the action of 'A' is ostensibly responsible for the suffering of 'B', his family members and also of his own family members. As we ordinarily understand the idea of moral responsibility, only 'A' is morally responsible for the crime in question and deserves to be punished for it. However, the theory of karma says that all the suffering of 'B' is because of his own actions. Following positions can be taken regarding this example:

(a) 'A' is responsible for the loss and suffering of 'B.'

(b) 'B' himself is responsible for his loss and suffering.

(c) Both 'A' and 'B' are responsible for the loss and suffering of 'B.'

(d) Neither 'A,' nor 'B', are responsible for the loss and suffering of 'B.'

We can rule out (d) here. Ordinarily we will accept (a) as the correct description of the situation. According to the theory of karma, however, all the suffering of an individual is a consequence of her own actions, therefore, (b) is the correct description. A is morally responsible for his wrong action and will have to face its appropriate punishment at some point of time. But the loss and suffering of 'B' is to be ultimately attributed to his own past actions. Thus, strictly speaking, 'A' is not morally responsible for the suffering experienced by 'B.' It is to be noted that not only the suffering of 'B' will have to be traced to his own past actions but the suffering of every other affected person in the example will have to be traced to his or her own past actions. This is obviously problematic. How to explain this simple event in a way such that it is consistent with the claim that every individual has to face the consequences of one's own actions alone and that all the suffering an individual experiences is just punishment of one's own actions?

One solution offered is through the idea of instrumentality of implementing karmic consequences. Just as natural events are treated as means or instrumentalities of actualizing the karmic consequences of individuals, persons may also be regarded as instrumentalities in a similar way.

Parameswara, for example, takes this route. He admits that people seem to suffer due to the actions of other persons who belong to his group. But according to him, "... what falls to the lot of a person as a result (to all appearance)of other people's karma is neither more nor less than the fruit of that person's own unexpended karma reaching him through the implementing instrumentality of those other people."[15] This approach, however, raises several difficult questions. Suppose we accept that the suffering of 'B' is due to his own past actions, then how do we explain the role and responsibility of 'A' here? If we say that 'A' is simply an instrumentality of implementing karmic consequences of past actions of 'B,' then the implication is that karmic causality predetermined the present action of 'A' and it also predetermined the set of people who would be affected adversely by it, since they deserve it. This implies that the action of 'A' is not free and, strictly speaking, he is not morally responsible for it. This conclusion is definitely not acceptable. Obviously 'A' is morally responsible for his wrong action and deserves punishment for his action. If we say that the action of 'A' is not predetermined by karmic causality, then it remains unexplained how this action of 'A' becomes the means to fructify a consequence of some action of 'B;' rather a means of realizing the consequences of past actions of all those who suffer due to the action of 'A.' In other words, we cannot assume that people who suffer because of the wrong action of 'A' deserve their suffering due to their own past actions and are not innocent. In trying to explain one person's action causing suffering to another person, we either end up denying human freedom or the claim that all suffering is deserved punishment for people's own wrongdoing. Same issues would arise when we consider examples where one individual's action brings a gain and happiness to others.

Kaufman also raises this issue in his critique of the karma theory. He says that suppose a terrorist is planning to detonate a bomb. If the karmic process functions in a determinate and mechanical way, then the terrorist's action is predetermined and he is bound to act in a certain way. Moreover, the people who suffer due to his action are those who deserve suffering due to their past actions. Alternatively, if the terrorist's action is free then he inflicts suffering on innocent people and this is against the claim that all the suffering of an individual is deserved punishment for one's own actions.[16] Chadha and Trakakis's in their response to this objection argue that the karmic process is impersonal and inherent in the world and it distributes appropriate rewards and punishments to people. The terrorist is not supposed to punish people for their wrong actions so he is doing something which he is not authorized to do. On this approach the terrorist is morally responsible only for performing an unauthorized action.[17] However, this response appears strange and fails to provide an adequate answer to the difficulty mentioned above. The question is whether the terrorist's action is predetermined by the karmic process or not and secondly, whether people's suffering because of his action is deserved by them or not. If it is predetermined, then the terrorist's action is not free and suffering of people is deserved. If it is not predetermined, then the action is free and people's suffering does not constitute deserved punishment. We cannot assume that only deserving people suffer because of such acts. In fact, the terrorist's action is morally reprehensible precisely because it causes suffering to innocent people. The attempt to explain the impact of one person's action on others through the idea of instrumentality of realizing the deserved consequences of the concerned person's actions is not plausible and gives rise to further problems of a serious nature. Reichenbach suggests that karma theory should only be taken to explain natural evil and not suffering that is caused by wrong actions of people.[18] However, this cannot be regarded as a satisfactory answer to the difficulty mentioned above because it restricts the scope of karmic causality and leaves such instances unexplained. In short the theory of karma cannot plausibly explain our common experience that one person's actions can cause suffering or joy to another. If we try to accommodate such instances within the framework of the theory, it leads to internal incoherence and raises further problems.

The claim that an individual's suffering is always a just punishment for the individual's own wrong actions, becomes extremely problematic in examples of natural disasters in which large number of people in a certain area get adversely affected. The implication in such cases is that the karmic consequences of people are implemented through the instrumentality of a natural event. The idea that natural causality is subordinate to karmic causality is, as pointed out earlier, far from plausible. In case of a natural disaster, which adversely affects a large number of people, the conclusion that all those who suffer as a result of it deserve to suffer due to their own past evil deeds, seems to violate our moral sensibility. Moreover, it is evident that human depravity also causes a lot of human suffering. Human history has several examples of wars, loot and plunder, mass murders and genocides where powerful people inflict tremendous cruelty, mass destruction and suffering upon large sections of population. It seems pernicious to hold in such cases that the victims deserved what happened to them.

Daya Krishna suggests an interpretation of the claim that all the suffering or happiness an individual gets is a consequence of the individual's own actions. He tries to explain this claim by making a distinction between moral and non-moral consequences of actions. According to him, 'moral action' necessarily presupposes and involves 'causality' in the natural realm. An action belongs to the natural realm and has consequences for both human beings and the natural world. An action also has consequences for the individual who is the agent. Daya Krishna argues that the theory of karma makes a radical distinction between the two kinds of consequences mentioned above. 'Consequences for others' cannot have any moral component since 'moral intelligibility' demands that one person cannot bear the consequences of another person's action. Therefore, only those consequences of an action, which are for the agent alone, have a moral dimension.

> "It is only the moral consequences of my action which have to be suffered by me, according to the theory, and not any and every consequence of my action. I can and do suffer the non-moral consequences of others' actions, just as they can and do suffer the non-moral consequences of my action."[19]

On this interpretation the theory requires a criterion to distinguish between moral and non-moral consequences of an action. Daya Krishna suggests that the theory entails that moral 'consequences' of an action are those, which may belong to the agent alone and to nobody else. An experience belongs only to the person who undergoes it (*bhoktā*), not to others who may observe the person (*draṣṭā*). "..it is the *bhoga* aspect of the *karma-phala* or the fruit of action which cannot but be undergone by the agent alone."[20] In the example mentioned earlier, burning of B's house will be a non-moral consequence of the action of 'A'. It seems that Daya Krishna on the one hand, admits that our actions can have consequences for other people and on the other hand, excludes these from the ambit of the karma theory by calling them non-moral consequences. It is also not clear how the experience of suffering by 'B' and other affected persons is to be characterized. Are we to say that suffering caused by non-moral consequences of an action would not have relevance for the karma theory?

Daya Krishna's interpretation fails to show a cogent way to explain the impact of one person's actions on others in conformity with the karma theory. Firstly, it implies that the use of 'consequence' excludes all the natural consequences of an action. But the theory mentions caste, longevity, family circumstances, etc., also as consequences of actions, and these cannot be reduced to experience of suffering or happiness of the concerned person. Secondly, while it is true that the experience of suffering belongs to the suffering person alone, yet the suffering person cannot be regarded as morally responsible for it when it appears to be due to an action by somebody else. Thirdly, an experience of happiness or suffering in a person does not normally arise in a vacuum; there are circumstances, natural events, own actions or others' actions, which trigger these. It seems arbitrary and unacceptable to exclude all the natural consequences of an action from the class of 'consequences' of an action and Daya Krishna's explanation appears to be stretched and artificial.

Daya Krishna believes that the supposition that no one suffers the consequences of the actions of others is important because it is regarded as a demand of moral intelligibility of the universe. The theory of karma in the traditional Hindu thought reflects "..this basic presupposition that it would be an immoral world indeed if one were to reap the fruits of someone else's actions."[21] He is of the view that this presupposition is based on a perspective, which views an individual in isolation or as essentially apart from relations with others. Clearly this perspective is difficult to reconcile with our ordinary understanding of human interaction and their social and moral life. Human beings are socially embedded. They live and act in social contexts and our experience shows that our actions affect others. Many values in our moral system acknowledge this fact and laud the spirit of altruism and declare actions that harm others to be wrong. Daya Krishna admits that the notion of moral intelligibility, which denies the impact of one individual's actions on others, makes moral action in the sense of action aimed at the good of others, rather than oneself, impossible. The difficulty therefore, is that the two central suppositions of the theory, namely that 'a perfectly just moral order exists in the world, where everybody must get the morally appropriate consequences of one's own actions alone' and that 'all happiness and suffering of a person is the just reward or punishment of her own actions' are in conflict in this context. Justice demands that nobody should be rewarded or punished for someone else's actions, from which it follows that one person's happiness or sorrow cannot be due to the action of another person. However, given our common experiences in life, the impact of an individual's actions on others cannot be denied and the theory does not explain how the above mentioned conflict is to be resolved.

COLLECTIVE ACTION AND SOCIAL RESPONSIBILITY

The theory of karma in the classical Indian tradition focuses on the impact of an individual's actions on her life and experiences alone. It denies that one person's actions can have consequences for others. It was mentioned earlier that natural events that cause happiness or sorrow to people are viewed in the karma theory as instrumentalities of actualizing consequences of their own actions. However, the theory fails to provide a satisfactory account of natural disasters. It would be pertinent to mention here Mahatma Gandhi's comments on the massive destruction and casualties due to earthquake in Bihar in 1934, which refer to a certain kind of actions by a collective of people and the impact of such actions. Gandhi said that this earthquake was 'divine chastisement' for the sin of untouchability practiced by Hindus. Rabindranath Tagore criticized him for this comment and called his view unscientific and observed that "physical catastrophes have their inevitable and exclusive origin in certain combination of physical facts." He added further that "... our own sins and errors, however enormous, have not enough force to drag down the structure of creation to ruins."[22] Gandhi reiterated and defended his approach in his reply to Tagore. He argued that he believed that physical phenomena produce both physical and spiritual results and the spiritual phenomena also produce physical results. He did not regard the earthquake either as caprice of God or a result of mere blind forces and added that events like droughts, floods and earthquakes may seem like purely natural events, having physical origins, but he believed that these were connected with man's morals. He admitted his inability to prove the connection between the Bihar earthquake and the practice of untouchability, but tried to justify his claim by saying that he instinctively felt that such a connection exists and declared that the connection between "cosmic phenomena and human behaviour" was for him "a living faith."[23]

Gandhi's comments make some interesting points. He endorses the view that natural calamities are a punishment for human wrongdoing and believes that consequences of human conduct can cause natural events. He views the Bihar earthquake as a consequence of a social practice of Hindus prevalent for centuries, which he regards as morally undesirable. However, he is referring to similar actions of a multitude of people performed at different times and in different locations. This may be called 'group' or 'collective karma' as opposed to an individual action. Unlike the classical theory of karma, which draws a connection between one individual's actions and their consequences for that individual, Gandhi draws a connection between a collective of wrong actions performed by many people and a natural disaster as their common consequence. Moreover, the people who suffer because of the earthquake are not claimed to be the same as those who performed the wrong action. In other words, the set of people who perform a certain kind of wrong actions in question is not identical with the set of people who suffer as a result of the natural disaster caused by their wrong actions. According to Gandhi, the suffering of the people affected by the earthquake is a result of the actions of all those who practice untouchability, which includes people other than those who are affected by the earthquake and also allows the possibility that some of those who suffer may not be practicing untouchability and hence innocent. Gandhi is clearly admitting that people's actions have consequences for others and can cause suffering to the innocent. This goes against the claim of the karma theory that everybody bears the deserved consequences of one's own actions alone and not those of others' actions.

Ramchandra Gandhi describes Gandhi's remark as "a theological earthquake," whose significance and implications have not been recognised fully.[24] He interprets Gandhi's view as implying that:

> ".. continuing great or small moral wrongdoing on our part deeply roots sinfulness in human reality and by reason of a reciprocity more mysterious than causality, which could be called karma, make others, quite arbitrary others, suffer greatly or modestly in physical intensity, but embarrassingly faith-undermining and existentially, not for specific sins of specific human beings (although these could be cited) but for the sinfulness of humanity."[25]

Ramchandra Gandhi regards the notion of a causal connection between an individual's actions and his suffering posited by the theory of karma as 'crude' and says that the right understanding of karmic connections is "a way of taking upon oneself the sins of others."[26] It is not important for me here to evaluate the adequacy of Ram Chandra Gandhi's interpretation of the karma theory or Mahatma Gandhi's comments. It is clear, however, that his interpretation implies that collective human wrong doing can have disastrous consequences for large sections of humanity, including innocents. Both Mahatma Gandhi and Ramchandra Gandhi are rejecting the framework provided by the karma theory.

The traditional theory of karma does not seem to incorporate the idea of 'group or collective karma'. The dominant view, for example endorsed by *Upaniṣads, Sāṁkhya-Yoga, Advaita Vedānta* and *Jainism* among others, believes that karma is individual, non-transferable and inexorable. Rama Rao Pappu, however, maintains that "... methodological collectivism has dominated Indian social thought" and, therefore, group karma has an important place there, though philosophers have not paid adequate attention to it. He defines the term 'collective karma' very widely such that it not only includes a collective of actions performed by a group of people but also transference of karma, divine grace and forgiveness. As pointed out earlier, these reflect the variety of views on karma found in the tradition. Rama Rao argues that an individual cannot enjoy or suffer his karmic consequences without a group, which he affects and is affected by it. He explains the idea of group karma with the help of caste groups which, according to him, cannot be reduced to aggregates of individuals constituting them and have a life of their own. Such groups have rights, duties and privileges and carry with them a certain 'moral credit,' presumably because of the supposition that those who perform good actions are born in higher castes in their next life. He admits that karma is invoked to explain why certain castes have greater rights etc. than others, however, every member of a caste group may not exhibit the qualities associated with the group. According to Rama Rao, groups become important in discussion of karma because groups with differing social environments are a necessary condition for persons to enjoy or suffer their karmic deeds.[27] A person is born in a social group in accordance with the consequences of one's past actions and participates in the activities of that group and enjoys the rights and privileges of that group. These make it possible for a person born, for example, in a high caste to enjoy the fruits of his good deeds. Conversely, a person born in a low caste as a result of past bad deeds would experience the disadvantages, the restrictions, limited opportunities and social exclusion associated with that caste, which are necessary for experiencing the bad results of his deeds. Rao's idea of group karma, thus, refers to the advantages or disadvantages that an individual has because of belonging to a certain caste group, and which provide the conditions for experiencing the good or bad consequences of one's past actions. The karma theory maintains that good past deeds lead to birth in a higher caste and good family and bad past deeds lead to birth in a lower caste and bad circumstances. An individual participates in the activities of the social group one belongs to and is influenced by the activities of that group. Rama Rao thus emphasizes the social environment, which provides the backdrop to a person's actions and points out the advantages or disadvantages that the membership of a caste group brings in and how these contribute to an individual's enjoying or suffering the consequences of one's past actions.

Modern Indian writers seem to realize that the interpersonal impact of people's actions cannot be denied and have, therefore, tried to address the issue in different ways. Surama Dasgupta, for example, acknowledges that individuals have social ties and are related to others. According to her, every individual is not only responsible for his own actions but also shares the collective responsibility for the good of society and the law of karma emphasizes the collective responsibility. "It is not merely the subjective changes of one's own or those of others that are caused by our actions, but changes in objective nature around us can also be effected by them ...We suffer or enjoy also in consequence of other people's actions, and this is found to be very true in political and social spheres."[28] Dasgupta refers not only to the impact of an individual's actions on others but also on our natural environment, which in its turn has consequences for human beings. Pratima Bowes draws our attention to another important point while explaining the impact of our actions on others. She argues that the environment in which one is born due to one's past actions is itself a product of the actions of several human beings and their interactions and its constraints and limitations cause suffering to an individual. This suffering cannot be said to be the result of the individual's own actions alone. She observes, "... this social dimension of the law of karma has not received any attention in the Hindu tradition because it could make one critical of the caste system."[29] Bowes is right; both the natural and the social environment are affected by the actions of people and these may cause suffering to individuals. The responsibility for the limitations of the environment, in which an individual is placed, belongs to a collective of persons and, therefore, the suffering caused by it cannot be ascribed to the suffering individual alone. We find that thinkers like Rama Rao, Dasgupta and Bowes wish to draw our attention to the social context in which people act and also to the fact that both the natural and the social environment affect people in many ways and are affected by our actions. It was mentioned earlier that the constraints imposed by one's social environment and status often adversely affect an individual's capacity to exercise free choice for one's development. This aspect of interaction of individual agency and social institutions needs to be given adequate attention in discussions of human agency and human suffering. The theory of karma focuses on an individual's own actions but does not take into account the impact of social embeddedness of individuals on their actions and quality of life. However, an acknowledgement of this impact implies limiting the role of an individual's own actions in explaining human suffering or flourishing.

One of the objections raised against the karma theory is that it leads to social apathy. In his critique of the karma theory, Swami Ishwarananda observes that the theory focuses only on an individual's own actions in explaining his quality of life and ignores two other important factors, the impact of natural processes and of actions of others. He thinks that this misplaced emphasis is harmful for social good because it strengthens an attitude of callousness towards the needs of others. People are encouraged to accept their lot in life and try to improve their future life by their own effort and right conduct. He adds that the theory gives the rich and the powerful "an engine of oppression and exploitation of the unfortunate millions" and an excuse not to be obliged to do anything to better their lot.[30] The supposition that one's quality of life and suffering is a just and necessary consequence solely of one's own actions may be taken to imply that efforts by others to improve an individual's situation or reduce his suffering cannot be effective. Such efforts may also appear to be morally undesirable because these would amount to interfering with the karmic process of delivering just punishment to an individual. S.K. Sen shares this apprehension and observes that the karma theory may justify callousness in the face of human suffering.[31.]

It was argued earlier that it is necessary to consider the impact of natural processes and others' actions on us while explaining human condition and efforts to reduce these two factors to consequences of individuals' own actions lead to unacceptable conclusions. But is it correct to say that the karma theory leads to callousness or social apathy? It does not seem so. Even if a person's own actions are responsible for the suffering faced by that person, moral values like sympathy, charity, non-violence and benevolence etc. teach us to cultivate an attitude of helping people facing adversity and alleviate suffering. Altruism is admired and emphasized in the moral codes of all religions and cultures, including Indian religions. The very idea of right conduct incorporates values like charity and compassion, and thereby the karma theory in its highlights on right conduct emphasizes the need to be sensitive to others' plight and help them. Arvind Sharma points out how the concern for the well-being of others is expressed in many ways in the Indian tradition. It is regarded as a duty of the king to look after his people and their welfare and social welfare is defined as a major concern of the state and the king. Benevolence is supposed to produce virtue and malevolence is regarded as a sin, therefore people are encouraged to be benevolent. Buddhism and Jainism emphasize humanitarian concerns through their ideas of compassion and non-violence (*ahiṃsā*).[32] The emphasis on right conduct though is based more on an individual's concern for improving one's own life rather than a commitment to social equality and human dignity. Thus, the karma theory does not seem to explicitly encourage social apathy among individuals. However, it does seem to encourage an attitude of resignation towards social inequality of various kinds and may make people more tolerant of social exploitation and subjugation of people because of the belief that their suffering is justified punishment for their own past actions.

KARMA, CASTE AND GENDER

Classical discussions of the karma theory in the orthodox schools of philosophy, as mentioned earlier, regard caste of an individual as a consequence of past actions. Buddhism and Jainism, however, accept the theory of karma and rebirth but do not support the caste system. This linkage of the theory with the caste system (*varṇa vyavasthā)* is seriously problematic. It was mentioned earlier that the form of life (animal, plant, human) and the caste (varṇa) of a person are widely considered to be consequences of an individual's past actions. It is maintained that good actions lead to rebirth in higher castes and bad deeds to rebirth in lower castes. The karma theory thus can be seen as the basis of caste distinctions. Yuvraj Krishan points out that the *Chāndogya Upaniṣad* states clearly that good actions enable one to be born in high castes like *brāhmaṇa* and *kṣatriya* but bad deeds bring about an evil birth in a low caste, even as a *cāṇḍāla*. Manu regards mental sins as cause of birth in a low caste and the *Mahābhārata* also sometimes traces a low birth of an individual to past evil actions. Krishan maintains that the karma theory 'justified and sanctified' the caste system based on birth and as resulting from past actions and this idea 'made for social stability and social stagnation.'[33] The opinion of modern Indian thinkers, however, is divided on the linkage between the karma theory and the caste system.

Arvind Sharma discusses the connection between the two at some length. He is of the view that the *varṇa* system historically precedes the karma theory as shown by the observations in the *Chāndogya Upaniṣad* and the theory gives a post-facto rationalization of the system. According to him, the law books specially emphasize the connection between actions and caste in three ways: an individual is said to be born in a high or low caste due to past actions, one's duty consists in performing one's caste duties and non-performance of caste duties is said to lead to very evil consequences.[34] The performance of caste duties thus acquires an ethical dimension in the law books. Sharma points out that we find views in the tradition, which regard the linkage between past actions and caste problematic and a question is raised whether one's caste should be based on one's present actions or on past actions, on birth or qualities of individuals. "The traditional resolution of the issue, in theory, seems to be in favour of birth plus conduct, e.g., a *brāhmaṇa* should be such by birth as well as conduct or learning. In practice, however, birth seems to have sufficed."[35] This difference of opinion is reflected in the views of the modern writers on the Indian tradition, especially in their interpretations of the *Gītā*. Some thinkers interpret it as saying that the caste system is based on birth. However, others like P.V. Kane, K.M. Sen and K.M. Pannikkar, etc., argue that the text takes the caste to be based on character and actions and not on birth. However, we find that caste continues to be based on birth as far as popular belief and common practices of Hindus are concerned.

Sharma also mentions that the gender of a person is also sometimes linked to the karma theory in the Hindu tradition, though that is not always explicitly stated. For example, birth as a high caste male was supposed to be superior to birth as a female and the practice of *'satī'* was sometimes justified on the basis of the karma theory.[36] Sharma mentions that it was believed that the wife who commits *'satī'* could secure good fortune for her husband, could purify the grave sins of her husband, could save him from hell and enjoy long periods of togetherness with him in heaven. Even if the wife had led an immoral life or her self-immolation was not voluntary, she would ensure that both her husband and she get a place in heaven. According to Altekar, the karma theory was modified to justify the practice of *'satī.'* The case of a *'satī'* is seen as an exception; "... the merit of her self-sacrifice was more than sufficient to annihilate her husband's sins and raise him to heaven to live in eternal union with his wife."[37] As mentioned earlier, the karma theory states that everybody gets appropriate consequences of one's own actions. If the moral values of actions of the husband and wife are different, their consequences would be different.

Therefore, strictly speaking, the consequences of the wife's actions cannot be experienced by the husband. It seems that the belief in transfer of karma is a vital aspect of the belief in the efficacy of the merit of '*satī*.' However, the strict theory denies any possibility of transfer of merit.

It has been discussed earlier how social institutions, including caste impact opportunities available to individuals and their power to exercise their free well. The linkage between cast and the moral value of past actions of individuals reflect a seriously problematic dimention of the theory.

CONCLUDING REMARKS

Eminent scholars of Indian philosophy like S. Radhakrishnan, S.N. Dasgupta, M. Hiriyanna and others regard the theory of karma as the most basic postulate of classical Indian thought.[38] The theory has evoked a lot of interest among philosophers both in India and abroad. It offers a perspective on evil and human suffering, which is quite different from those offered by religions like Christianity and Islam. Several thinkers have singled it out for high praise. Kaufman, though a critic of the karma theory, points out the ingenuity of the solution it provides. He remarks that it combines the idea of retributive justice with multiple births of individuals in which they bear the consequences of their past actions and tries to provide a "complete and consistent retributive explanation of evil" in which "all suffering can be explained by the wrongdoing of the sufferer himself."[39]

Arthur Herman was very impressed by the theory initially and commented that the theory of karma and rebirth is superior to Western theodicies of evil and is able to answer objections that they cannot. He, however, revised his opinion later on.[40] Rama Rao Pappu regards it as "the principle of justice," which enables us to explain social inequalities and also hereditary differences.[41] Yuvraj Krishan thinks that the karma theory provides the most rational explanation of human inequality and suffering.[42] Karl Potter endorses the view that the theory offers a world view, which fits experience more closely and is preferable to any alternative account.[43]

The karma theory attempts to explain inequities at birth and seemingly undeserved suffering of good people in the world. Various aspects of this explanation have been analyzed in preceding pages and an attempt has been made to clarify their implications and difficulties. The widely accepted and dominant formulation of the theory asserts that the law of karma operates on its own and represents a moral order in the world. However, the Indian tradition presents other versions also, which do not support some of the basic claims of the strict law-like version. The theory makes four major claims: (a) every individual must face the consequences of one's intentional actions, in the present or future lives. (b) the quality of an individual's present life reflects consequences of that individual's past actions (c) good actions lead to good consequences and happiness, bad ones lead to loss and suffering and (d) the consequences of one's actions are deserved rewards or punishments of those actions. The difficulties relating to these claims have been outlined earlier. The theory makes use of several concepts that are neither verifiable, nor falsifiable by empirical evidence. The plausibility of the theory is to be judged on the basis of its capacity to provide a coherent and satisfactory explanation of the facts of life sought to be explained by it. The claims mentioned above are related and the theory explains these by positing residue of actions, which actualize when mature and bring the deserved consequences to an individual in the present or future life. The discussion in preceding pages, tries to show that various aspects of the theory have several problematic dimensions, which have not been resolved. The idea of subjecting actions and their morally appropriate consequences to causal processes is flawed because it fails to account for moral evaluation of actions and their consequences or rewards and punishments in a satisfactory manner. Linking the idea of karmic justice to rebirth has its own difficulties because of lack of adequate evidence to support the phenomenon of rebirth and because of the failure to provide a satisfactory criterion of personal identity. The supposition that the karmic moral order pervades in the world is difficult to accept because the theory fails to clarify the interplay of natural and karmic causality and, moreover, the idea is not supported by our experience and empirical evidence. Many things remain unclear in the explanation offered by the theory, for example, modalities of karmic causality, specific connections between kinds of actions and kinds of consequences and the time frame of maturation of residue and actualization of consequences of actions. Modern scientific theories help us to understand facts related to birth, disease, longevity, etc., in a more verifiable and intelligible manner than the idea of karmic justice.

The very fact that the theory addresses the perplexing question of perceived inequities at birth and suffering of good people adds to its appeal. It attempts to explain certain aspects of our life that are morally disturbing for us, even though it is unable to give a perfectly cogent and tenable explanation of these. The explanation offered by it is very complex and raises a wide variety of problematic issues, which are not addressed satisfactorily within the theory. There is an attempt to reduce the multiple causative factors, that appear to affect the quality of our life in our common experience, to a single factor, namely our own past actions. The theory does acknowledge the impact of natural processes on human beings but attempts to explain these in terms of their past actions by taking these to be the instrumentality of implementing the consequences of those past actions. However, the explanation is far from plausible. One major weakness of the theory is its failure to account for the impact of actions of other persons on an individual's quality of life. An attempt to reduce such impact to an individual's own past actions leads to serious problems about individuals' freedom to act and our understanding of human interaction. The theory emphasizes people's own actions alone to explain their situation and experiences in life but ignores two other major factors in this context, natural forces and actions of other people. Modern critics of the theory have discussed this at some length and have rightly pointed out that the impact of those two factors in shaping human lives can neither be ignored nor undervalued. I have argued that it is important to acknowledge that people act in a social environment and their interpersonal dealings have great significance for our understanding of morality and society. The Indian tradition seems to mention sometimes multiple causes of our lot in life but the dominant view tries to explain the human condition only in terms of our own past actions and their consequences. This explanation may have the advantage of simplicity and parsimony but the advantage comes at the cost of plausibility.

Some social implications of the theory are really worrisome and questionable. Linking of an individual's caste (*varṇa*) to one's past actions is significant here. As mentioned before, many formulations of the theory assert that birth in a high caste is a consequence of past good actions while birth in lower castes is a consequence of past bad actions. This reaffirms the hierarchy implicit in the four-fold classification of caste. The caste system justifies a high social status, privileges and greater opportunities for higher castes as opposed to lower castes, which as a result face several disadvantages. In this respect the karma theory seems to provide a rationale for the undesirable stratification and power structure inherent in the caste system and the consequent exploitation, oppression and subjugation of lower castes. The claim that our suffering is always a just punishment for our wrong actions in the past shifts the focus away from social injustices. As mentioned earlier, the gender is also sometimes linked to past actions and this may imply a justification of the inferior status of women. Modern scholars have widely critiqued this aspect of the theory and rejected the supposition that individual ability and social role of an individual is to be defined by birth.

Critics of the theory argue that it tends to encourage an attitude of passive acceptance among people towards poverty, deprivation and social exploitation. The role of social institutions in generating or perpetuating social inequality and injustice is not given adequate attention. Moreover, some critics believe that the theory may promote or justify a callous social attitude and discourages people from alleviating the suffering of others.[44] It seems that the emphasis on right conduct incorporates in a way the idea of doing one's duty and helping those in distress. It is not therefore, fair to say that the theory promotes callousness towards others, though it remains true that the theory shifts the focus away from the injustices inherent in social institutions and the necessity of collective action to remedy the situation. The point is that the karma theory's claim that all the suffering of an individual is just punishment for her own actions has the potential of being used as an apology for suffering caused by exploitative and unjust practices of people or society. Human history has been a witness to massive suffering at the hands of cruel and unethical people in power and we cannot explain away all the suffering inflicted by such people on others as just consequences of the wrong actions of the victims themselves. Surely the victims of genocides and holocaust cannot be held morally responsible for their plight. The importance of acknowledging the impact of social structures and practices on people's quality of life cannot be neglected or underrated. It appears that the theory of karma does not adequately emphasize our modern ideas of equality, social justice and social responsibility.

The theory attempts to provide a rational explanation of the inequities at birth and undeserved suffering of innocents. The explanation has several problematic dimensions and raises more questions than answers them. It seems that the theory is not really able to provide a cogent explanation of the suffering of innocent and good people. But it may help people in finding solace in the face of apparently undeserved suffering, which is difficult to comprehend rationally and morally. It is natural to be confused and bewildered by the suffering of an innocent child or a good person or success and prosperity of a bad and immoral person. The karma theory provides us a rationalization of sorts of such events. It may also provide some comfort to a person when faced with a severe loss, disease or bereavement despite good conduct. Those who believe in God, when faced by something similar, draw solace from an admission that what has happened is ultimately God's will and they must accept it. Similarly, a reference to one's past actions may succeed in giving solace to a person who finds one's present condition morally incomprehensible. Generally speaking, we tend to refer to past actions to explain some loss or suffering only when we are unable to explain it on other grounds. In a way it is a way of admitting that our present condition is due to factors, which are mysterious and beyond our control.

The theory of karma is an expression of our moral

ideal that good people should get happiness and bad ones should suffer and it tries to incorporate this ideal through the supposition of a moral order in the world. However, our experience tells us that the natural order does not express a moral order. Life is not always fair. We have to come to terms with that realization and must continue to strive to do the right thing with courage and persistence and work towards building more equitable social structures and just social institutions, in short a better society. Such a society improves the chances of people being appropriately rewarded or punished for their actions. The quality of life of a person at any point of time is not solely determined by the person's own actions. It is a result of a complex interplay of one's own actions, circumstances, natural processes and actions of others in a social context. Our life is shaped not by our own actions alone but other forces also which are beyond our control. In today's world it is extremely important to acknowledge how our actions impact our natural environment and work towards environment protection. We also owe a responsibility to people around us and the society in which we live and it is our moral duty to work for a better society. We have a responsibility not only to make our own lives better but also to create an environment conducive to human flourishing.

Let me now say a few words about some of the psychological advantages ascribed to the theory by its supporters. It is often argued that the theory is emotionally satisfying and has great motivational force in encouraging people to follow the right path in life. It may also be said to act as a deterrent for evil actions. The belief that one cannot avoid the evil consequences of one's wrong actions may have a positive impact on people and discourage them from following the wrong path. In the absence of cogent evidence it is difficult to say whether it actually does so. It is also debatable whether karma theory has a great motivational force for people to perform right actions. The theory does warn people against the inescapable evil consequences of immoral actions, but it does not clearly establish connections between specific kind of actions and specific kind of consequences. The punishment for wrong actions is not immediate but deferred to an unknown date and time in future. Thus, the theory provides only a general guidance to individuals to avoid wrong actions and do the right thing for the sake of improving their next birth and securing their own happiness in the long run, but it does not tell them what the specific consequences of their good actions would be or when these would occur. One wonders whether the theory can then really be a powerful deterrent against evil actions or an effective motivator for performing good actions. It is also claimed some times by supporters of the theory that it has a great psychological advantage; it enables people to cope with their suffering and losses with resignation and fortitude and teaches them not to blame others for these. As against this, critics of the theory argue that it encourages an attitude of fatalism and passivity. Clearly the theory implies that there is much in our lives, which is an impact of our past actions and cannot be changed or avoided, so it may be the best pragmatic policy to bear that with patience. However, the theory also allows the possibility to make our future better by self-effort. Ultimately only sociologists and psychologists can throw light on the claimed psychological advantages or otherwise of the theory.

In an important sense the principle enshrined in the theory of karma that good actions lead to good results is true. Good actions have a salutary and morally elevating effect on the agent. Good conduct helps us to become good persons and this in itself is a reward. The karma theory tells us that our right actions will always bring us good fortune and happiness and our experience does not corroborate that supposition. However, as moral and social beings it is important that we focus upon following the right path not so much for the benefits it would bring us in this or future lives, but in our endeavour to become better persons.

The theory of karma, despite its several problematic dimensions, remains important because of its unique and innovative metaphysical perspective on innocent suffering and a perfect moral order in the world.

Notes and References

1. Wendy Doniger O' Flaherty, *The Origins of Evil in Hindu Mythology,* University of California Press, Berkeley, 1976, p.4
2. Arthur Herman, *The Problem of Evil and Indian Thought,* Motilal Banarsidass, Delhi, 1976, p. 288
3. Whitley, R. P. Kaufman, 'Karma Rebirth and The Problem of Evil', *Philosophy East and West,* vol.55, No.1, January 2005, (15-32), pp. 16-17. Kaufman in his detailed critique of the theory raises five major objections against it.
4. Ibid, p. 19
5. Humphreys, Christmas, *Karma and Rebirth,* London, Curzon Press, 1983, p.84
6. Kaufman, 'Karma Rebirth and the Problem of Evil', p. 20
7. Monima Chadha and Nick Trakakis, 'Karma and the Problem of Evil: A Response to Kaufman', *Philosophy East and West,* vol.57, No. 4, Oct. 2007, (533-556)
8. Ibid, p. 535
9. Kaufman, 'Karma Rebirth and the Problem of Evil', p. 21
10. Ibid, pp.21-22
11. Chadha and Trakakis, 'Karma and the Problem of Evil', pp. 538-39
12. Kaufman, Karma Rebirth and the Problem of Evil', p.22
13. Flaherty, *The Origins of Evil in Hindu Mythology,* p. 17, Kaufman, Karma Rebirth and the Problem of Evil, p.22
14. Roy Perrett, 'Karma and the Problem of Suffering', *Sophia,* 24, (4-10), p. 7, Kaufman, 'Karma Rebirth and the Problem of Evil', p. 2
15. P. Parameswara, *Soul, Karma and Rebirth,* The Author, Bangalore, 1973, p.172, Creel, Contemporary Treatments of Karma and Rebirth'., R. W. Neufeldt, (ed) *Karma and Rebirth: Post Classical Developments,* State university of New York Press, Albany 1968, p.6
16. Whitley Kaufman, 'Karma Rebirth and the Problem of Evil', pp. 25-

26

17. Monima Chadha and Nick Trakakis; Karma and the Problem of Evil', p. 546
18. Kaufman, 'Karma Rebirth and the Problem of Evil', p.25
19. Daya Krishna, *Indian Philosophy-A Counter Perspective,* Sri Satguru Publications, Delhi, 2006, p.240
20. Ibid, p.240
21. Daya Krishna, *Social Philosophy, Past and Future,* Indian Institute of Advanced Study, Shimla, 1968, p.14, Creel, op cit, p. 6
22. Rabindranath Tagore's letter published in *Harijan* on 16th February, 1934, Sabyasachi Bhattacharya, (ed.), *The Mahatma And The Poet,* National Book Trust, India, 1997, pp. 158-159
23. Gandhi's reply to Tagore published in *Harijan* in February 1934, *The Mahatma And The Poet*, pp. 159-161
24. Ramchandra Gandhi, 'Earthquake in Bihar: the Transfiguration of Karma', a lecture, R. C. Gandhi, (ed.) *Language, Tradition and Modern Civilization, Indian Philosophical Quarterly,* No. 5, Poona 1983, pp. 125-26
25. Ramchandra Gandhi, 'Earthquake in Bihar: the Transfiguration of Karma', pp. 125-26
26. Ibid, p. 134
27. Rama Rao Pappu, 'Karma Individual and Collective', Rama Rao Pappu (ed.) *The Dimensions of Karma,* pp.308-312
28. Surama Dasgupta, *Development of Moral Philosophy in India,* Orient Longman, Bombay, 1961, p.211, quoted by Creel, 'Contemporary Treatments of Karma and rebirth', pp.5-6
29. Pratima Bowes, *The Hindu Religious Tradition,* Routledge and Kegan Paul, London /Boston, 1977, p. 72, as quoted by Creel, 'Contemporary Treatments of Karma and Rebirth', pp.5-6
30. Swami Ishwarananda, *Does the Soul Reincarnate?,* Sri Ramakrishna Ashrama, Trichur, 1964, pp. 44-51, Creel, 'Contemporary Treatments of Karma and Rebirth', p. 8
31. Sanat Kumar Sen, 'Indian Philosophy and Social Ethics', *Journal of*

the Indian Academy of Philosophy, 6, No.1, 1967, pp.67-68

32. Arvind Sharma, 'The Social Implications of Karma', Rama Rao Pappu (ed.) *The Dimensions of Karma,* pp. 282-84
33. Yuvraj Krishan, *The Doctrine of Karma,* p. 455
34. Arvind Sharma, 'The Social Implications of Karma', Rama Rao Pappu (ed.), *The Dimensions of Karma,* p.270
35. Ibid, p. 272
36. Ibid, p 279
37. A.S. Altekar, *The Position of Women in Hindu Civilization,* Motilal Banarsidass, Banaras,1956, p.122, Sharma, 'The Social implications of Karma', p. 280
38. Rajendra Prasad, *Karma, Causation and Retributive Morality,* p. 210
39. Whitley Kaufman, 'Karma Rebirth and the Problem of Evil', p.15
40. Arthur Herman, *The Problem of Evil and Indian Thought,* p.287, Kaufman, op cit, p.15
41. Rama Rao Pappu, *The Dimensions of Karma,* p. 4.
42. Yuvraj Krishan, *The Doctrine of Karma,* Preface, p. xi
43. Karl. H. Potter, 'Karma and Rebirth: Traditional Indian Arguments', Rama Rao Pappu,(ed.), *The Dimensions of Karma,* p. 161
44. Creel, 'Contemporary Treatments of Karma and Rebirth', pp.8-9

Select Bibliography

Books:

Altekar, A. S., (1956), *The Position of Women in Hindu Civilization*, Motilal Banarsidass, Benaras

Barrett, Cyril, (ed.), (1966), *Ludwig Wittgenstein, Lectures and Conversations on Aesthetics, Psychology and Religious Belief*, Basil Blackwell, Oxford

Bowes, Pratima, (1977), *The Hindu Religious Tradition*, Routledge and Kegan Paul, London

Chakraborty, Aparna, (1988), *Karma, Freedom and Responsibility*, Kaveri Books, New Delhi, India

Chatterjee, S. C. & Datta, D. M., (1939), *An Introduction to Indian Philosophy*, University of Calcutta, Calcutta

Chaturvedi, Vibha, (1988), *The Problem of Personal Identity*, Ajanta Publications, Delhi, India

Dasgupta, S.N., (1922), *A History of Indian Philosophy*, Cambridge University Press, Cambridge

Dasgupta, Surama, (1961), *Development of Moral Philosophy in India*, Orient Longman, Bombay,

Dasti, Matthew R. and Bryant, Edwin S., (eds.), (2004), *Free Will, Agency and Selfhood in Indian Philosophy*, Oxford University Press, USA

Datta, D.M., (1971), *Philosophical Perspectives: A Selection of Essays*, Bharati Bhawan, Patna

Descartes, René, (1911), *Meditations on First Philosophy*, E. S. Haldane and G. T. Ross, (ed.), *The Philosophical Works of Descartes*, Cambridge University Press, Cambridge

Deutsch, Eliott, (1969), *Advaita Vedānta : A Philosophical Reconstruction*, East West Press, Honolulu,

Gray, Tim, (1991), *Freedom*, Macmillan Education Ltd., Houndsmill,

Basingstoke, Hampshire and London

Hamilton, Sue, (2001), *Indian Philosophy: A Very Short Introduction*, Oxford University Press, Oxford

Herman, Arthur, (1976), *The Problem of Evil and Indian Thought*, Motilal Banarsidass, Delhi

Hiriyanna, M., (1949), *Essentials of Indian Philosophy,* George Allen and Unwin, Great Britain, Unwin Paperbacks, 1978

Hume, David, (1956), *A Treatise of Human Nature*, A. D. Lindsay, (ed.), J.E.M. Dent and Sons Ltd., London

Humphreys, Christmas, (1983), *Karma and Rebirth*, Curzon Press, London

Ishwaranand, Swami, (1964), *Does the Soul Reincarnate*? Sri Ramakrishna Ashrama, Trichur

Jauhari, Manorama,(1968), *Politics and Ethics in Ancient India*, Bhartiya Vidya Prakashan, Varanasi, India

Jhingran, Saral, (1989), *Aspects of Hindu Morality*, Motilal Banarsidass, Delhi

Kant, Immanuel, (1978), *Critique of Pure Reason*, Norman Kemp Smith, (tr.), The Macmillan Press Ltd., London and Basingstoke

Kant Immanuel, (1997), *Critique of Practical Reason,* Mary J. Gregory, (ed.), Cambridge University Press, Cambridge

Keyes, Charles F. and Daniel, E. Valentine (eds.), (1983), *Karma, An Anthropological Inquiry*, University of California Press, Berkeley, Los Angeles, London

Kopf, Gereon, (2001), *Beyond Personal Identity, Dogen, Nishida, and a Phenomenology of No-Self,* Curzon Press, Richmond Surrey, U.K.

Krishan, Yuvraj, (1997), *The Doctrine of Karma*, Motilal Banarsidass Publishers, Delhi

Krishna, Daya, (1968), *Social philosophy, Past and Future,* Indian Institute of Advanced Study, Shimla

Krishna, Daya, (2006), *Indian Philosophy, A Counter Perspective*, Sri Satguru Publications, Delhi

Locke, John, (1984), *An Essay Concerning Human Understanding,* A.C.

Fraser (ed.), Clarendon Press, Oxford

Mackenzie, John, (1922, 1971), *Hindu Ethics*, Oxford University Press, London

Madan, T. N., (ed.),(2012), *Religion in India*, Oxford University Press, New Delhi, India

Magill, Kevin, (1997), *Freedom and Experience, Self-Determination without Illusions*, Macmillan Press Ltd, Houndmills, Basingstoke, Hampshire and London,

Neufeldt, Ronald W., (1968) *Karma and Rebirth: Post Classical Developments*, State University of New York Press, Albany, USA

Nikam, N. A., (1967), *Some Concepts of Indian Culture: A Philosophical Interpretation*, Indian Institute of Advanced Study, Shimla

O' Flaherty, Wendy Doniger, (1983), *Karma and Rebirth in Classical Indian Traditions,* California University Press, 1980, Motilal Banarsidass, Delhi, 1983

Pappu, S.S. Rama Rao, (ed.), (1987), *The Dimensions of Karma*, Chanakya Publications, Delhi

Parameswara, P., (1973), *Soul, Karma and Rebirth,* The Author, Bangalore

Parfit, Derek, (1984), *Reasons and Persons*, Clarendon Press, Oxford

Prasad, Rajendra, (1989), *Karma Causation and Retributive Morality*, Indian Council of Philosophical Research, New Delhi, in association with Munshiram Manoharlal Publishers Pvt. Ltd., New Delhi,

Radhakrishnan, S., (1929), *Indian Philosophy*, H. D. Lewis, (ed.), Muirhead Library of Philosophy, George Allen and Unwin Publications, vol.1 and 2

Siderits, Mark, (2003), *Personal Identity and Buddhism*, Ashgate Publishing Company, Burlington, USA

Strawson, P. F., (1959), *Individuals*, Methuen, London

Swinburne, R. and Shoemaker S.S., (1984), *Personal Identity*, Basil Blackwell, England

Ward, Keith, (1998), *Religion and Human Nature*, Oxford University Press, Oxford

Williams, Bernard, (1973), *Problems of the Self*, Cambridge University Press, Cambridge

ARTICLES IN ANTHOLOGIES AND ACADEMIC JOURNALS

Arya, Usharbudh, (1972), 'Hindu Contradictions of the Doctrine of Karma', *East and West*, vol.22, No.1/2, March to June, pp.93-100

Bhattacharya, Kalidas, (1964), 'The Status of the Individual in Indian Philosophy', *Philosophy East and West,* vol. 14, pp. 131-144. Reprinted in C.A. Moore, (ed.), *The Indian Mind*, East West Centre Press, Honolulu, 1967

Bryant, Edwin F., (2014), 'Agency in *Sāṃkhya* and *Yoga*- The Unchangeability of the Eternal', Matther R. Dasti and Edwin F. Bryant, (eds), *Free Will, Agency and Selfhood in Indian Philosophy*, Oxford University Press, Oxford, New York, 2014

Chadha, Monima and Trakakis, Nick, (2007), Karma and the Problem of Evil: A Response to Kaufman', *Philosophy East and West*, vol.57, No.4, Oct., pp.533-556

Chappel, Christopher Key, (2014), 'Free Will and Voluntarism in Jainism', M.R. Dasti and E.F. Bryant, (eds), *Free Will, Agency and Selfhood in Indian Philosophy*, OUP, Oxford, New York, 2014

Chaturvedi Vibha, (1992), Indeterminateness of the Concept of a Person', *Indian Philosophical Quarterly*, vol. XIX, No.2, April, pp.115-124

Chaturvedi, Vibha, (2001), 'Causality of Karmic Justice', *Journal of Indian Council of Philosophical Research*, (JICPR), vol XVIII, Number 3, July- Sept. pp. 129-156

Chaturvedi, Vibha, (2004), 'The Idea of a Morally Ordered Universe', D. P. Chattopadhyaya, in association with A. K. Sen Gupta (ed.), *Self, Society and Science: Theoretical and Historical Perspectives, History of science, Philosophy and Culture in Indian Civilization*, vol XI, Part 2, Centre for Studies in Civilization

Chennakesavan, Sarasvati and Reddy, K. Vasudeva, (1997) 'Morals and Society In Indian Philosophy', Brian Carr and Indira Mahalingam, (ed.),

Companion Encyclopedia of Asian Philosophy, Routledge, London, 1997

Clooney, Francis X, (1989), 'Evil, Divine Omnipotence, and human Freedom: *Vedānta*'s Theology of Karma', *The Journal of Religion*, vol.69, No.4, Oct., pp.530-548

Creel, Austin B., (1968), 'Contemporary Philosophical Treatments of Karma and Rebirth', Ronald W. Neufeldt, (ed.), *Karma and Rebirth: Post Classical Developments*, State University of New York Press, Albany, 1968

Dasti, Matthew R., (2014), 'Nyāya's Self as Agent and Knower', M.R. Dasti and E.R Bryant, (eds), *Free Will, Agency and Selfhood in Indian Philosophy,* OUP, Oxford, New York, 2014

Deutsch, Eliot S., (1965), 'Karma as a "Convenient Fiction" in the *Advaita Vedānta*', *Philosophy East and West*, vol.15, No.1, Jan, pp.3-12

Flaherty, Wendy Doniger O', (1983), 'Karma and Rebirth in the Vedas and *Purāṇās*', *Flaherty*, (ed.), *Karma and Rebirth in Classical Indian Traditions,* Motilal Banarsidass, Delhi, 1983

Flew, Antony, (1971), 'Can a Man Witness his Own Funeral'? W. T. Blackstone, (ed.), *Meaning and Existence*, Holt, Rinehart and Winston, New York, 1971

Flew, Antony, Hare, R.M., and Mitchell, Basil, (1971), 'Theology and Falsification' B. Mitchell, (ed.), *The Philosophy of Religion*, Oxford University Press, Oxford, 1971

Freschi, Elisa, (2014), 'Freedom Because of Duty', M.R. Dasti and E.F. Bryant, (eds), *Free Will, Agency and Selfhood in Indian Philosophy*', OUP. Oxford, New York, 2014

Freschi, Elisa, (2014), 'The Indian philosophy Blog', https://indianphilosophyblog.org/2015/01/21free-will-in-ramanuja/ posted on 21st January, 2015, accessed on 14th Jan. 2019, at 12:45 P.M.

Gaeffke, Peter, (1985), 'Karma in North Indian Bhakti Traditions', *Journal of the American Oriental Society*, vol.105, No.2, (April-June), pp. 265-275

Gandhi, Ramchandra, (1983), 'Earthquake in Bihar: The Transfiguration of Karma', a lecture, R. C. Gandhi, (ed.), *Language, Tradition and Modern Civilization, Indian Philosophical Quarterly*, No.5, Poona, pp.125-135

Ganeri, Martin, (2014), 'Free Will, Agency and Selfhood in *Ramānuja*', M.R.Dasti and E.F. Bryant, (eds), *Free Will Agency and Selfhood in Indian Philosophy*, OUP, Oxford, New York, 2014

Giles, James, (1993), 'The No-Self Theory, Hume, Buddhism and Personal Identity', *Philosophy East and West*, vol.43, No.2, pp.175-200

Halbfass, Wilhelm, (1983), 'Karma, *Apūrva* and Natural Causes', Flaherty, (ed.), *Karma and Rebirth in Classical Indian Traditions*, Motilal Banarsidass, Delhi,1983

Herman, A. L., (1987), 'Karmadicy: Karma and Evil in Indian Thought', Rama Rao Pappu (ed.), *The Dimensions of Karma*, Chanakya Publications, Delhi, 1987

Kalghatgi, T. G., (1965), 'The Doctrine of Karma in Jain Philosophy', *Philosophy East and West*, vol.15, No.3/4, (July-October), pp.229-242

Kalghattgi, T. G., (1987), 'Karma in Jain Thought', Rama Rao Pappu, (ed.), *The Dimensions of Karma*, Chanakya Publications, Delhi, 1987

Kaufman, Whitley, R. P., (2005), 'Karma, Rebirth and the Problem of Evil', *Philosophy East and West*, vol.55, No.1, Jan. pp.15-32

Kaufman, Whitley, (2007), 'Karma, Rebirth and the Problem of Evil: A Reply to Critics', *Philosophy East and West*, vol. 57, No.4, Oct., pp.556-560

Keown, Damien, (1996), 'Karma, Character and Consequentialism', *The Journal of Religious Ethics*, vol.24, No.2, fall, pp.329-350

Kolenda, Pauline Mahar, (1964), 'Religious Anxiety and Hindu Fate', *The Journal of Asian Studies*, vol.23, Aspects of Religion in South Asia, Jun., pp.71-81

Long, J. Bruce, (1983), 'The Concepts of Human Action and Rebirth in the *Mahābhārata*', O' Flaherty, (ed.), *Karma and Rebirth in Classical Indian Traditions*, Motilal Banarsidass, Delhi, 1983

Mahadevan, T. M. P., (1962) 'Indian Ethics and Social practice', Charles A. Moore, (ed.), *Philosophy and Culture East and West: East West Philosophy in Practical Perspective*, University of Hawaii Press, Honolulu, 1962

Malkani, G.R., (1965), The Rationale of the Law of Karma', *Philosophical Quarterly*, vol. 37, January 1965, pp.146-153

McDermott, P., (1983), 'Karma and Rebirth in Early Buddhism', O' Flaherty, (ed.), *Karma and Rebirth in Classical Indian Traditions*, Motilal Banarsidass, Delhi,1983

Meyers, Karin, (2014) 'Free Persons, Empty Selves', Matthew R. Dasti and Edwin F. Bryant (eds), *Free Will, Agency, and Selfhood in Indian Philosophy*, Oxford University Press, Oxford, New York, 2014

Mohapatra, P. K., (2015), 'Karma Freedom and Responsibility', *Sandhān*, Journal of Centre for Studies in Civilizations, vol XV, No. 1&2, Jan-Dec., pp. 73-88, Special Issue on *Responsibility and Freedom*, Guest editor, Rajendra Prasad

Morgan, K. W., (1953), 'The Nature and History of Hinduism', Morgan, (ed.), *The Religion of Hindus*, Ronald Press, New York, 1953

Pappu, Rama Rao, (1987), "Karma, Individual and Collective', Rama Rao Pappu, (ed.), *The Dimensions of Karma*, Chanakya Publications, Delhi, 1987

Parfit, Derek, (1976), 'Personal Identity', Jonathan Glover (ed.), *The Philosophy of Mind*, Oxford University Press, Oxford

Perret, Roy, (1985), 'Karma and the Problem of Suffering', *Sophia*, vol. 24, pp 4-10

Potter, Karl H., (1983), 'The Karma Theory and its Interpretation in some Indian Philosophical Systems', Wendy Doniger O' Flaherty, (ed.), *Karma and Rebirth in Classical Indian Traditions*, Indian Edition by Motilal Banarsidass, Delhi, Patna, Varanasi, 1983

Potter, Karl H., (1987) 'Karma and Rebirth: Traditional Indian Arguments', Rama Rao Pappu, (ed.), *The Dimensions of Karma*, Chanakya Publications

Potter, Karl H., (2001), 'How Many Karma Theories are there?' *Journal of Indian Philosophy*, vol.29, pp.231-239

Puligandla, R., (1987), 'Karma, Operational Definitions and Freedom', S.S. Rama Rao Pappu (ed.), *The Dimensions of Karma*, Chanakya Publications, Delhi

Radhakrishnan, Sarvapalli, (1908), 'Karma and free Will', *Modern Review*, 3, May, pp.424-428

Reichenbach, Bruce, (1988), 'The Law of Karma and the Principle of Causation', *Philosophy East and West*, vol.38, No.4, pp. 399-410

Rocher, Ludo, (1983), 'Karma and Rebirth in *Dharmaśāstras*', Wendy Doniger O' Flaherty, (ed.), *Karma and Rebirth in Classical Indian Traditions*, Motilal Banarsidass, Delhi

Rudd, Anthony, (2015), 'No Self? Some Reflections on Buddhist Theories of Personal Identity', *Philosophy East and West*, vol.65, No.3, pp. 869-891

Sharma, Arvind, (1987), 'The Social Implications of Karma', Rama Rao Pappu, (ed.), *The Dimensions of Karma*, Chanakya Publications, Delhi

Sharma, Ursula, (1973), 'Theodicy and the Doctrine of Karma', *Man*, New Series, vol.8, No.3, Sept., pp.347-364

Siderits, Mark, (1987), 'Beyond Compatibilism: A Buddhist Approach to Freedom and Determinism', *American Philosophical Quarterly*, vol.24, pp.149-159

Steinkraus, Warren E., (1965), 'Some Problems in Karma', *Philosophical Quarterly*, vol. 38, October 1965, pp. 145-153

Swinburne, Richard, ((1976), 'Persons and Personal Identity', H.D. Lewis, (ed.), *Contemporary British Philosophy*, George Allen and Unwin, London

Timalsina, Sihaneshwar, (2014), 'Self, Causation and Agency in the *Advaita* of *Śankara*', M.R. Dasti and E.F.Bryant, (eds), *Free Will, Agency and Selfhood in Indian Philosophy*, OUP, Oxford, New York, 2014

Upadhyaya, K. N. (1987), 'Karma in Hindu Thought -II: The *Bhagvad Gītā*', Rama Rao Pappu (ed.), *The Dimensions of Karma*, Chanakya Publications, Delhi, 1987

Wadia, A. R., (1965), 'Philosophical Implications of the Doctrine of Karma', *Philosophy East and West*, vol.15, pp.145-152

INDEX